My Name Is Ten

COLLEEN MACMAHON

Published by Sleeping Genie

ISBN: 9798815180505

DEDICATION

For my parents, Jean and Harry, who would be proud no matter what I did.

For Kevin, who never doubted me.

And for you, my reader, because the future is in your hands and I urge you to treat it with care.

MY NAME IS TEN

CONTENTS

MY NAME IS TEN

ACKNOWLEDGMENTS

My heartfelt thanks to Rufus Purdy whose early editorial advice was invaluable; to my lovely Beta readers Cara MacMahon, Wendy Edmond, Paul Marriner and Charlotte Drew; to Mel and Midge and all the dear friends and family who have encouraged me every step of the way.

Thank you to Yasmin Kane, my agent, whose belief in My Name Is Ten has almost exceeded my own.

To Laura Clayton, thank you for seeing my vision and recreating it in your fabulous book design.

And finally, there would simply be no book without Kevin.

Ye are bought with a price; be not ye the servants of men.

1 Corinthians 7:23

1 THE GIRL

I begin my story at the end, where I'm alone in the freezing darkness wondering how I will die. There is no clue in the silence that follows the closing of the thick, steel door at the end of the passage. We count the minutes until it opens again and the Guards emerge, wiping their sweaty hands on grubby cloths hanging from their belts. Then, when the Guardians come out, one of them extinguishes the tiny candle in the wall sconce as a mark of respect, before going off to do the paperwork.

All we are told is that it will be quick, and when The Kennels are quiet at night I spend too much time imagining the rest. And I wonder too what Mamma would say if she knew I'd ended up here, after all her hard work. I'm afraid she would be very angry indeed.

*****

'You are my jewel, Akara,' my mother told me as she prepared me for sale on my fourteenth birthday, 'the best and most beautiful of all my children. And that's a good thing for both of us because somebody's going to pay me a lot of money for you and when people pay a lot of money for something they tend to take care of it.'

She looked me over one last time, squinting to focus on every detail before stepping back to admire me.

'Thank you, Mamma,' I said, because I knew she expected me to and it was true that she had fed, educated and clothed me to the best of her ability, asking very little of me in return except obedience. But I stood trembling beside her, and what mother takes a frightened child to auction with no words of comfort, only a reminder of how grateful that child should be?

'Between us, your father and I gave you fine bones, good health and excellent skin,' Mamma had told me countless times, 'They are your greatest assets and must be looked after. No one will want you if you are ugly.' Beautiful though she was, Mamma's own complexion was very sensitive and prone to disfiguring allergies, so my perfect skin must have been thanks to my pappa, though I never knew him. Mamma would have chosen every one of our fathers with great care, so it must have been devastating when two of her other children were such disappointments after all her efforts.

Beetle, the youngest of my half siblings, was born prematurely with a misshapen leg; Ashley was older but never grew a single hair on his body as far as I know, and anyway was far too pale for Mamma's liking. Mamma was so ashamed of them that she never got them registered and barely acknowledged their existence unless it suited her to. Ashley, she said, was likely to be sickly and sterile and therefore worth nothing to anybody, whilst Beetle was simply not pleasing to look at and would probably be equally worthless. She called them aberrations, claiming they were throwbacks in spite of each having healthy fathers, and that she must have eaten something bad when she was carrying them. Being young I believed her at the time but, as I discovered later, Mamma didn't always tell the truth and I didn't always recognise it when she did.

It didn't matter to me what my brothers looked like, in those early years of our childhood I had no proper understanding of the disadvantages they had been born with and how physically blessed I was in comparison. That our mother didn't love them didn't seem to me like such a terrible thing for them to have to bear. For all my apparent perfection she didn't love me either.

*****

According to the Guardians, this is my third day in Block Six of an Adoption Centre. The collection wagon found me lying half dead somewhere in the bush, but I don't know how long that was after my leaving Malakai's. My Due Death Date is therefore less than six weeks away, at which point – unless I have been claimed or adopted – I will be taken down to the chamber at the end of the passageway and will find out what lies behind the big steel door. Today I started playing word games in my head to see which sounds the longest: six weeks...one and a half months...forty two days... And I search my memory for the words in French because I know I learned them once, but I can't find them. There are whole blocks of things I can't remember and that scares me almost as much as anything. Every part of my body is in pain and fear makes my hand shake, wasting precious paper with meaningless scribbles. I try to calm myself by breathing deeply, though it hurts my ribs, and rocking backwards and forwards to steady the rhythm of my heart. My vision is poor, one eye is still swollen and closed, but I can see enough to be aware of the hundreds of scratches on the walls around me. Some are legible names, some are just marks, made by the souls who occupied this stall before me who may, or may not, have got out alive.

'Our policy,' the physician had explained to me bluntly when they brought me in, 'is to euthanise after six weeks if you have not been reclaimed by an existing Patron, or adopted by a new one. Since you have no brand, no registration tattoo and no documentation I doubt anyone will claim you, so we must just hope for adoption.'

'What is euthanise?' I asked, because Mamma had never told me about Adoption Centres, having not expected me to end up in one.

'It means we will exterminate you in a quick and painless manner. It is considered much the kindest outcome for those who have no other prospects.' His voice softened a little, 'But you're young and seem healthy, aside from your current injuries. Now we've cleaned you up we'll hold you back for a few days, so you have some time for things to settle down and your condition to improve before Visitors see you. Who knows, someone may choose you, so you must not lose heart.' But he sounded weary and defeated, as if he had said the same thing before to too many skinny, half blind girls who had come in with no paperwork.

I knew I must look bad. Even so I wasn't prepared for what I saw today. The last time I looked in a mirror I had been in my dressing room, waiting to attend Malakai in my finest clothes. My hair had been long, thick and braided with strands of silver and gold thread; now my hair is so closely cropped you can see patches of scalp. My eyes had been bright, my skin clear and my mouth full and perfectly symmetrical; now my face is bruised and cut, my lips distended and my right eye bloodshot. When I lifted the dressing over my left eye, carefully unwinding the muslin bandage wrapped around my head, I was sickened by the sight of the bloody mess underneath.

If I disgust even myself what chance do I have of anyone else wanting me? An impeccable pedigree is no use if it can't be traced, and Mamma and Malakai were insistent that I should not have a registration tattoo marring my perfect skin. The certificates and records that they both took such care to maintain were the only proof I ever had of my provenance so without them I am nobody. My profile folder, which the Guardians will show to any Visitors who ask about me, contains a single sheet – clearly written by some lower caste illiterate - with the words: 'Stall Ten: juvenil female for adoption; details unnown.'

'Give it to me and I'll write it down properly for you,' I said. My voice was hoarse but I believed I could still speak with authority and a tall, morose looking man said, 'Can you actually write?'

'I keep telling you I can. Let me show you.'

Then the Guardian produced some scraps of paper and a pencil and handed them to me, 'Very well, but you must be aware that, without paperwork, it still proves nothing except that you can read and write. However, scribes are always in demand so it may be useful.' The Guardian's companions turned to one another and laughed; 'Sourface,' one of them said, 'you're an idiot. Look at the state of her - I doubt she's ever even seen a book, let alone read one,' and he looked me up and down with open disgust.

'Take care how you speak to me,' I said, 'My mother was Fiuri d'Ursoola and my Patron was Malakai d'Montagne so I can assure you I have read entire libraries of books - more than *you* have ever seen or could even dream of.' This seemed to stun them into respectful silence for a moment, then they all laughed again and I was shocked to realise that actually the names meant nothing to them.

*****

But my mamma had been as thorough with my education as she was about everything else, sometimes ripping her delicate hands to shreds scrabbling in piles of rubble and dirt to find old papers, books and magazines. She would trade and barter to acquire anything she considered important to expand my knowledge and, even when the nights were bitter and other fuel scarce, she never burned a single scrap of precious paper. Then when I went to Malakai I had access to more books than I could realistically have read in a lifetime, row upon row of them safely stored in the coolest part of the cellar to protect them from the desiccating daytime heat. The entire basement was reinforced with struts and pillars to survive quakes, and the shelves were raised well above the ground in case the rains, which were torrential when they came, managed to seep in. There was nothing, Malakai said, which could defend against more solar flares if they came and the building collapsed, but in that event he hoped to die with his beloved books. Even I, favoured though I was, was never permitted to take anything from the room; I did all my reading there and, looking back, I know I was at my happiest when I was lost in the worlds they took me to. The books were my escape as well as the source of so much knowledge, though nothing I read in any of them prepared me for this.

*****

The day the people from The Kennels found me I was parched and delirious. I couldn't tell them where I was from, or how I had got to where I was, but I remember insisting that Malakai was dead and asking someone to find my documents. I don't know how long the journey took but I came round fully as they lifted me out of the cart, carried me into one of the stone outbuildings, and laid me on a pallet in a room that smelled of sweat and vomit and stale incense. They removed what clothing I still had on and burned it in a huge, smoking incinerator at the far end of the room; then they hacked off my matted hair and burned that too. Two of them managed to hoist me up and took me into a flag-stoned room where there was a rigging of overhead buckets, ropes and levers and a big iron pump. Under this they washed me as thoroughly as they could whilst I dangled from their arms like a dead weight, mesmerised by the bloody water gurgling down the drain. The sounds, the smells, the pain – everything was nauseating and my stomach heaved, even though it was empty. A hand gently wiped away the dribble on my chin and a woman's kindly voice said, 'Don't worry, you gonna be okay. We'll look after you and you gonna be okay.'

They wrapped me up in some towelling, patted me dry and took me back into the infirmary, where they did their best to clean up my injuries and soothe them with a thin smear of ointment. The familiar smell of coconut and aloe reminded me of one of Beetle's liniments and I felt the pang of an old homesickness, still painful after three years. They helped me raise my arms and eased me into a cotton shift so old that it was bare in places where even the darns had worn away, but it was long and cool against my tender skin and I began to feel a little better. I believe I slept then for a while, until someone came back with water, which I drank, and some tasteless mash which I managed to eat because I was famished. Afterwards I felt strong enough to sit up on the pallet and ask where I was, though my voice was cracked and my throat still hurt.

'You're in an Adoption Centre, cariad,' replied the physician who was examining me, inspecting my injuries and prodding and poking at my stomach for signs of internal damage. He wasn't rough but very brisk, as if he had no time to waste on manners, and his dialect was unfamiliar enough that I struggled to understand it. Then when he'd explained the Adoption Centre Policy he concluded with, 'Yes, cariad, someone may choose you; we can but hope.'

'My name's not Cariad,' I protested, thinking he had me confused with someone else. Perhaps it was all just a terrible mistake and someone soon would discover it, hand me my documents and arrange for my return to the estate. The physician looked puzzled for a second, then gave a sort of half smile, 'Cariad's not a name, it just means child.' He looked to one of the Guardians and said, 'She's not local then,' before turning back to me to examine my face.

'Where am I?' I repeated, beginning to panic. If not local, how far could I have come since leaving Malakai's estate?

'The Borderlands, Eastern region,' he replied and when I opened my mouth to ask more he was suddenly stern, 'No more questions, cariad. You're not the only one needing to be taken care of. Save your talking till later and let me get on with my job.'

He was inspecting my left eye as he said it, so his face was very close and his breath was hot and garlicy, but not unpleasant. He had a mottled skin, pockmarked and coarse, and around his ears and at the corners of his mouth were the tell tale signs of the White Disease: uneven blotches where the pigmentation had died, or never been present at all. In seventeen years I've seen many such, and he is by no means the worst afflicted, but for the first time in my entire life I began to understand how it must feel to be considered inferior. No one beneath my own status had ever dared speak to me as he had just done; as the Protégé of someone as powerful as Malakai I have always been treated with respect. But now, damaged and disenfranchised, I am no longer elite and, as far as the physician was concerned, I was not even his equal.

I felt tears burn my eyes and the man gestured impatiently to one of the women to come and deal with me whilst he moved on to the person on the next pallet. The woman - a short, pale creature swathed in a bright, hooded djellaba and wearing an enormous turban-like arrangement on her head – dabbed at my damp cheeks and made soothing noises as she began to dress and bandage my swollen eye, 'There now, gonna feel better soon, my poor pet. Be brave girl and we'll have you fit and well again, no time.' She looked up at a chalk board on the wall and called across to someone, 'Has stall number ten been cleaned out yet? It don't show as free but Inki d'Allana was taken this morning, so it should be marked I think.' The response satisfied her and as soon as she had finished wrapping the muslin round my head the woman eased me slowly off the pallet and guided me out of the infirmary.

We emerged into a stone passage, took twenty or so paces down past a couple of heavy wooden doors and turned right into another passage which was long, roofless and flanked on either side by small, individual pens. Our progress was slow and painful and I had to lean heavily on the Guardian, my eyes flicking left and right and observing that every stall appeared to be occupied, until we reached the last but one on the right which was empty. The number 10 was painted crudely in black on the stonework above a wire mesh door and, hanging from a nail to the side of the door, was a board with the word INKI chalked on it in yellow letters. The woman, supporting me as well as she could with one arm, used her free hand to wipe the board clean and then ushered me into the pen. She guided me to a low pallet bed against the wall to my left and I sank down onto it, exhausted and overcome with the heat. The straw mattress and lumpy pillow had lost most of their stuffing and the bed covers were simply large, coarse sacks which had been roughly sewn together; they were not the soft skins and angora blankets I was used to and would be of little comfort during the bitterly cold nights, but for now it was a relief to be out of the stifling heat of the open aired passage. The stalls are afforded some shade by high roofs constructed from an untidy patchwork of rusty metal and corrugated plastic. The stone walls, though in poor repair, are thick and were designed to insulate against the heat when the building was originally erected, which was many years before the solar flares of '25 tested them to their limits.

As I leaned back onto the pillows, my head throbbing and my skin shredding with every movement, the woman fussed around me, chattering incessantly. I winced at the sound of her scraping something large and heavy over the floor, closed my eyes and told her to go away, but she kept on talking.

'Here's your slop bucket, cariad, I've pulled the screen around it so you get plenty privacy. Bucket you empty twice in the day, around same time they bring you breakfast and supper. You get fresh water as often as possible but not so much now after such a long dry season.' She had a soft, sing-songy voice which would have been soothing and pleasant to listen to if I had not wanted so desperately to be left alone. She, like the physician, had an accent I could not place – a jumble of dialects and an unfamiliar rhythm which made me feel disoriented and alien. It made me realise, with a sickening shock, how little of the world I knew beyond one small region in a country where I was now entirely friendless, unprotected and vulnerable. I felt the sting in my eyes threatening tears again and turned my throbbing head to the wall.

The woman came towards me, fabric rustling and a sigh on her lips, 'I can see you tired, poor thing, so I let you rest. It's already dark so you not gonna be disturbed again. Not by Guardians anyways. I just write you details on the board and leave you alone.' She touched me softly on the forehead then and I opened my eyes to see her smiling sadly at me, 'We'll do our very best for you, I promise.

You just concentrate on gettin' well.'

She left, closing the heavy mesh door behind her and padlocking it firmly. Then she paused outside, took a piece of chalk from a pocket hidden in the swathes of her robe and raised it to the board. 'What name you used to go by, cariad?' she asked me, peering through the wires; I sat up and spoke imperiously, 'My name is Akara - Akara d'Fiuri and I am not a child. I am seventeen years old and I do not belong here.'

'Don't be gettin' upset child, I only mean to be kind. I gonna put you name on the board but you gonna be called Ten while you here. You got no papers, no tattoo, nothin' at all.' She made some marks on the board and I demanded to know how she had spelled my name. With a heavy sigh she turned to look at me directly and shook her head, 'It's not gonna matter how I spell it; hardly anybody got readin' in here so you gonna be Ten and that's that. I'm sorry,' she said again, before shuffling off down the passage.

'What's your name?' I called out after her, but she'd gone.

'Mariam Arranah,' someone shouted out from one of the other stalls, 'We call her Sweet Mariam,' added another.

'Oh,' I said, 'My name is Akara. Akara d'Fiuri.'

But no one answered.

2 THE BOY

The first thing I did every morning was to check the night traps and release anything Uneatable or Forbidden that was still alive. Then I'd spend an hour or two sorting through the rest, separating them into different pans for roasting, frying or grinding down. It was time consuming and fiddly, picking creatures out of the fine meshed nets and stripping the legs and wings off tiny flies and beetles and so forth. It could be dangerous too - scorpions don't take kindly to being messed with but they're generally worth the effort if they're cooked right.

Usually Surrana, my new mother, would come and join me. She taught me what was good to eat raw, what best to dry in the sun first and what was totally inedible - which wasn't much. Most everything can be eaten if you're desperate enough and you know how to prepare it. Sometimes there was a bat or a bird tangled up in the net; if they were dead then it was acceptable by regional law to eat them; if they were alive then we freed them and that was always a good feeling. Rats in that region were still so plentiful that they were permitted if you could get one, but the scrubland rats were skinny, fast and usually too canny for us to catch. They get fatter and slower the closer you get to the towns but are more likely to be diseased, especially the ones that overrun the unregistered charnels in the shanties, which are not well regulated. Any man or beast desperate enough to go foraging in those places is likely to be dead themselves within a week.

One day I was pleased to see something much bigger than usual flailing about in one of the traps, but as I approached I realised that it wasn't a huge rat but a tiny, mangy black cat. It had got itself tangled up, probably looking for an easy meal in the netting, and the more frantically it struggled the more entangled it got. Half its tail was missing and one of its eyes was glued up with pus but it carried on fighting and, after ten minutes of being bitten and scratched trying to release it, I gave up. 'Stay there then, you stupid creature,' I told it, exasperated, and off I went to find someone to put it out of its misery.

Jiggs Munro was a giant even at the age of thirteen. He stood two or three heads taller than me and had the biggest dick I'd ever seen. We used to have competitions down at Gordie's Creek - chucking chips of gravel and taking it in turns to see who could hit them with a well aimed stream of piss. As the targets got further away it was always just me and Jiggs battling it out at the end. I was still small in those days, but deadly accurate; Jiggs was enormous, but clumsy with it, and couldn't control the flow once the target was more than three paces away. The more we laughed at him the madder he got and the wilder his aim, with spray going all over the place until his bladder was finally empty.

'Yer all just jealous,' Jiggs would say, 'Some day I'm goin' ta make bonnie babies with this beastie and you lads'll be sorry!'

'You'll have to learn where to put it first, you idiot!' I'd remind him, shouting from a safe distance so I had a head start on him.

'At least I can see mine, you wee, dickless baldie,' he'd

roar back at me, giving chase and tackling me to the ground. I wouldn't have stood a chance if he'd really meant business - Jiggs could crush the breath clear out of your lungs just by lying on top you – but he knew how to control his power even at that age.

So we'd scuffle in the dust for a bit, showing off for the girls and the other boys even when our throats were parched and we couldn't see for the grit in our eyes. The creek had been dry for years, so we washed our faces with our own spit and licked condensed water from the plastic sheeting I'd set up over the cactuses; it was one of the tricks I'd brought to the camp from my old, feral life. We didn't dare use the the camp's only watering hole to clean ourselves up; the muddy water was not, the older ones reminded us, to be wasted on cooling off stupid boys who hadn't the sense to stay out of the sun. Even my new mother, who was usually so lenient, lectured me sternly about that.

'I'm glad you have friends and are enjoying the freedom of your new life' Surrana said, taking me by the shoulders and looking earnestly into my face, 'but there is no doubt now that this region is getting hotter and drier, so the water you waste today could be the difference between life and death tomorrow. Do you understand?'

'Yes,' I said.

'I'm so sorry, this is not the childhood I would have wished for you, my son.'

'It's alright, Surrana,' I assured her, and it was true. With all its hardships and restrictions my life, there in the camp, was better than it ever had been before. Besides, once we learned that the tanners in the shanty towns would pay for it to cure their animal skins, we stopped wasting even our piss and collected it instead, trudging through the heat with as many steaming pots as we could carry and getting paid in stale bread or corn husks. It was worth the effort, even if we'd spilled it all on the way and earned

nothing, because time spent with Jiggs Munro was always good and I never laughed as much with anyone as I did with him.

I first met Jiggs the morning after I'd arrived at the camp, still feeling confused and shaken. My new mother had woken me with a weak brew of chai and some flatbread and I was sitting under the tattered awning outside her tent eating it when a huge shadow fell over me. I looked up into the face of a boy about my age, I guessed, but twice my size in height and breadth.

'What're you starin' at?' the boy growled at me in a thick, northern region accent.

'I'm not staring. You stopped right in front of me, I couldn't help looking.' I turned back to concentrate on my food. I didn't want a fight, especially not one I was certain to lose, but I wasn't a coward and after a few moments, when he hadn't shifted, I sighed and said, 'Could you move? You're blocking my view.'

'You ought ta be glad of the shade you wee, pasty thing!' he said, laughing. 'Ah, fukk you,' I muttered and made a lunge for the giant's ankles, hoping to topple him over. But his legs were thicker than tree trunks and stayed rooted to the ground. When I began pummelling at him with my fists he just laughed more and reached down to grab my wrists, leaving me to kick and scuff at the ground like a crazy wild animal until I'd knackered myself.

'Well,' he said, letting go of me at last, 'that was stupid. You'll never win any fights goin' about it that way.' Then he sat down, picked up the flatbread that had fallen in the dirt and began to stuff it into his mouth.

'That's mine!' I said, ready to fight again.

'Not any more, baldie. And if we're goin' ta be friends you're goin' ta have ta learn ta share.'

I dropped down next to him, rubbing at my bruises and trying, if I'm honest, not to cry. Was my life going to carry on being one long battle even here, just when my new mother had told me I would be safe at last? 'So what are you going to share with me then?' I asked as I watched my flatbread disappearing into his mouth. Up close I could see that, although he was young, he was already sprouting soft, dark hair on his chin and above his upper lip. His thighs were dark with a forest of thick, coarse curls snaking down from his groin, and his frayed cotton shorts were grubby and far too small, leaving his huge dick and balls straining to escape. I'd never seen anything like him. Even fully grown men were never as well favoured as he was already and most boys were like me, blessed with nothing better than a thimble to piss with and a couple of useless sacs between their legs. Jiggs was a splendid and remarkable specimen.

'Starin' again? I don't blame you. You'll not see many better around here, that's for sure.' And with that he leaped up, grabbing my arm as he did so and dragging me up beside him. 'Come on. I'll show you round the camp, baldie and we'll see if we can find ourselves somethin' else to eat.'

So that was how I became the best of friends with Jiggs Munro, and we must have been a comical sight, being so ill matched in looks and size. Jiggs became hairier with every passing month, whilst I was fourteen or fifteen before the first, blonde wisps appeared on my head and around my groin. His voice was already deep as a man's, whilst I sounded – according to him – like a 'wee, girlie bairn'. He had no kin in the camp, having wandered in alone some years before, covered in scratches and cuts and with no explanation for them. He told me he thought his family had been attacked and killed by wildcats or wolves out in the scrub whilst they were searching for shelter, but he really couldn't remember and didn't particularly want to. Every single one of us in the camp had a sorry tale to tell and just wanted a chance to build as good a new life for ourselves as we could. Surrana, my newfound mother, had shared her story with me the night she'd brought me there and, extraordinary as it was, it was no stranger than most.

For all his taunts about my pallid skin and puny, hairless body, Jiggs loved me like a brother and he soon abandoned his own shelter and moved in with us. He put his strength to good use by securing and enlarging our modest shack, and hauling back the treasures we found on our scavenging trips. We made a good team, he and I. Jiggs always said I was the clever one and, though he definitely wasn't stupid, it was true that I was good at certain things. I had an instinct for finding useful objects and devising the best ways to use them and my skill with traps meant we were rarely as hungry as many of our neighbours, and if we had a surplus of anything then we would always share with whoever needed it most. I even found some reasonable scraps of fabric at one of the better rubbish sites and Surrana washed them and cleverly stitched them together to cover Jiggs with some decent clothes, but he still always managed to make everything look too small for him and they very soon got filthy again.

Even beyond the camp Jiggs quickly got a reputation for his size and strength, and we soon attracted crowds when we had our mock fights at Gordie's creek. 'You should go to the pits, Jiggs,' people said, 'and fight properly, for real. You could make a lot of money.'

'Nah,' said Jiggs, 'I'm happy here. Besides, I only fight wi' people I like. I don't want ta fight properly, for real. One day, one of the girls here will begin her bleeds, we'll get bonded and have healthy big babies. That's all I want ta do. That and find a bit of decent land maybe, where we can raise the bairns and a few animals.' For all his muscles and big, deep voice, Jiggs was a kind and gentle soul and it was him I went to when I found the mangy cat stuck in my netting.

'You need to kill it, Jiggs. I can't,' I said as we walked back towards the pitiful sound of mewling.

'Kill it? Why?'

'Because it's suffering, you eejit. Look at it! It'll never survive, even if we can get it untangled.'

The cat was completely exhausted; it had stopped struggling and was just lying in my web hissing and crying whilst the flies and skeetos attacked the open wounds in its skin. Jiggs swatted them away and rested his hands on his knees to bend down and take a closer look. 'Poor wee thing,' he said, 'No worries, we'll have ye out of there in no time.' With great delicacy he managed to unhook teeth and claws from the mesh and release the cat's legs one by one. Instead of scratching and biting, as it had when I'd tried to help it, the creature just gave in, letting itself be twisted and turned in Jiggs' huge hands until it was completely free and cradled in my friend's arms like a baby. We walked back to Surrana's tent with it, where Jiggs gently bathed it in the water we were saving for our mid day chai, and my mother offered it the bowl of warm coconut milk I was expecting for my breakfast.

If that cat had been a human I might have been jealous of it, because Jiggs took it everywhere with him from then on. Usually the cat was perched on Jiggs' hairy shoulder, or would sit watching whatever he was doing, including taking a crap.

'You have to give it a name,' I said.

'Why?' Jiggs asked me.

'Well, so it knows to come when you call it.'

'It does that already. I just tell it ta come and it comes.'

'Well, so it knows to come when I call it then.'

Jiggs laughed, 'It hates you! It wouldn't come ta you if you were the last person on the scorched earth. Still, I'll give it a name if you like.'

Surrana was trying to teach Jiggs to read and write at

the time and, though he found it a struggle, he idolised my mother and persevered — driving me half crazy by constantly asking me to spell things out so he could copy the letters down in his slow, clumsy way. He looked around the tent and saw the basket of items we'd collected on our latest scavenging trip: a collection of mostly bent or broken scraps of this and that which one day might be useful, or worth trading.

'What's this?' he said, picking up a chipped and grubby plastic tube from the pile.

'It says... Chapstick. I think it must be the lid to something else we didn't find. Why?'

'What does it mean?'

'I don't know. Why?'

'That'll do then. I'll call the cat Chapstick.'

And so it was that the three of us - Jiggs, Chapstick and me - became quite famous far beyond the camp. Me for my skills as a finder, Jiggs for his size, and Chapstick because very few people - especially low castes - had ever seen a cat except in pictures. A lot of people offered Jiggs a lot of money for his cat but he wouldn't have parted with it for all the chai in Scardland. And a few people from the shanties tried to persuade him to go with them to the pits to become a champion fighter, but he turned them down too. He liked our humble little home, he liked being friends with me and learning to read and write with Surrana. He also liked one of the girls from a neighbouring camp and, from the way she looked at him, she liked Jiggs too. Her name was Myrah and she was two or three years older than us, with healthy skin and bright, almond shaped eyes. She had glossy brown hair — short but thick, with little tufts of it under her arms too — that she was very proud of, and Jiggs was certain he'd heard rumours that she'd begun her bleeds. She was what the older ones called 'promising'.

'I think she's the one,' Jiggs said to me, and I felt a sudden, sharp pain in my chest because I was afraid for *him, setting his sights on the daughter of a higher caste man who was known to be ambitious. 'She's good enough to sell, Jiggs,' I said, 'especially if she's fertile. Her father was talking about taking her to Maidentown and getting a Patron for her.'*

'I don't care. I'll have her, if she'll have me. Don't you worry, ma wee friend, I'll convince him somehow.'

From then on Jiggs concentrated on becoming the man he felt Myrah deserved and that her family would approve of, and it seemed to be working because the father began to take a keen interest in my friend's activities. Jiggs stopped play-fighting in the dirt of Gordie's Creek with me and started taking on local challengers, beating them all within minutes and attracting large crowds. Soon there were opponents - professional fighters - being brought in from further and further away and I hated what came with them: the jeering, shouting and baying for blood; the scuffling and arguments as bets were made and lost; and the parading of the challengers – all of them older and more experienced than Jiggs who was always apologetic when he'd knocked them flat and taken his winnings, assuring me afterwards that he would stop fighting the minute he was securely bonded to Myrah. 'I hate ta do it,' he said, 'but I will if that's what it takes. You wait till you find someone you want badly enough, ma friend. Though who'd look at you more than once I canna imagine!' We had one of our old style tussles then, calling each other every name under the sun and inventing insults as we lay back on the hot earth, panting. All the time, the cat sat on a rock and watched us through half closed eyes until Jiggs heaved himself up and she leaped onto his shoulder, making that funny growling noise she made in her throat that Jiggs said was a sign she was happy.

We had supper together as usual and sat for a long while by the main fire as the coolness of the evening set in. Jiggs said he was going for a piss, I asked him to take care where he did it as he couldn't be trusted to find a bucket in the dark. The last thing he said as he vanished into the night was, 'And you just take care some thug from the shanties doesn't mistake you for a salt lick and whisk ya off as a treat for his cattle!'

After what seemed like a very long time, even for Jiggs, I heard some noise coming from the direction he'd gone in. Some of the older ones suggested we ought to investigate, though I was certain Jiggs would soon return, maybe having come off worst in a scuffle with the warthogs who shared the waterhole with us. I'd tease him about it, he'd insult me some more and then stumble off to bed whilst I made a final check to see that the nets were good and secure. I liked to do that alone, listening to the night sounds and counting stars if the sky was clear. Even the skeetos' buzzing was good to hear; it meant the world was still alive, if not well, and there was maybe some hope still.

But Jiggs didn't come back. A group of us searched for as long as we dared, knowing that any wild beasts or bandits would get bolder at night and our torch oil would not last indefinitely. Eventually, after following a muddled trail of footprints in the dust, we found the small, dark shape of Chapstick circling round and round and mewling at the top of her voice. She wouldn't let me pick her up but reluctantly followed us back to the camp where, for a long time, she and I waited for Jiggs to come home.

3 MEMENTO MORI

My sixth scratch on the wall, to mark my sixth day. Around it there are names scrawled by those who could write, rough symbols carved by those who couldn't. Next to most of them someone has added the letters RIP. My stomach heaves and I need to sit down. I'm glad to be distracted by one of the Guardians bringing me fresh water.

'Here you are, Ten. Try to make it last; the springs are drying up and there's no way of knowing when the next rains will come.'

'Akara,' I mutter, as Ridrick-Oola fills the small pitcher on the floor by my bed. 'My name is Akara d'Fiuri and I don't belong here.'

'No, of course not, Ten,' says Ridrick wearily, as if she has heard the protest a hundred times before. I clutch at her sleeve and make her look at me; there are beads of moisture sitting on her brow and upper lip and she stinks of sweat. I don't suppose she owns more than the clothes she's wearing and they will not have been washed for a long time but I try very hard not to show my distaste. I'm no longer in a position to feel superior about my own personal hygiene.

'Please, Ridrick-Oola,' I say as respectfully as I can, 'You must believe me. I have documents to prove my birth, my registration and the name of my Patron.'

'And where are these wonderful documents?' Ridrick asks as she shrugs my hand away.

'Lost. Or stolen,' I admit. 'But I swear they exist! And my Patron was called Malakai. He was a very important man.'

'And where might he be, this important man?'

'Dead,' I respond, reluctantly.

'Then he's not much use to you, is he?' says the Guardian. I don't think she meant to be cruel, but was merely stating a fact.

Once Ridrick has gone, her odour lingering in my nostrils long after she's left, I ask myself why I'm wasting time agitating, once again, over my name. No-one here cares what it is; I'm just a number: *Wake up, Ten. Time to slop out, Ten. Breakfast's coming, Ten.* What worries me most is how quickly I'm getting used to it and that soon it will become the only identity I recognise. That's why it's so important for me to write things down, before I forget.

I know I'm very lucky to have paper; it's in short supply and expensive, not usually available for the likes of us in here. Adoption Centres can't rely on anything they don't produce themselves or can trade, because there's too much competition in this region for too little already; in my three comfortable years with Malakai I had almost forgotten how bad things were elsewhere. So it pays to ingratiate yourself with as many of the Guardians as possible and to exploit whatever strengths or weaknesses they have. For instance, the one they call Sourface - whose real name is Adelmo - is aloof and condescending but considers himself an artist and has access to paper, pencils and charcoal. On my second evening, as he was collecting my supper dish, he told me that he found my face interesting and that he would like to sketch me. I would have laughed, except that it hurt too much, 'Why would you want to draw me, looking like this?'

He shrugged, 'Why not? Things don't have to be beautiful to be interesting.' He looked down at my hands clutching the two scraps of paper he'd given me earlier, when I wanted to demonstrate that I could write, and said, 'I could bring you some more of that if you liked. If you were co-operative, that is.'

'What do you mean, co-operative?'

'If you'd pose for me.'

When I didn't answer immediately he shrugged again, 'No matter. There are plenty of others here who'd be happy to oblige. You're really not that special, Ten.'

I handed him the enamel plate and wooden spoon, both scraped clean, and tried hard to read his face. I wanted the paper very badly, but not at any cost. 'I don't know,' I said, still hesitating. With a sarcastic twist to his mouth he said, 'Believe me, Ten, I'm only interested in your face,' and he looked me up and down as if no one who wasn't mad would consider anything else. It occurred to me then that, in a locked room, I was at his mercy anyway whether I was posing for him or not, so just as he turned to go I said, 'Very well,' and tried to make it sound as though I was doing him a favour. He didn't respond except by nodding, as if he knew all along that I'd agree, then he drew the screens closed, pulled the door shut behind him, secured the padlock and left without another word. As I heard his footsteps depart down the passage I began to have doubts again. Why would some lowly Guardian be interested in wasting such a valuable commodity as paper drawing a doomed inmate? What could he possibly want, or expect, in return for the extra paper he had promised to give me?

As it turns out, he doesn't seem to want me to do much other than sit still and keep quiet. I stay clothed and, as the evening cools, I'm allowed to wrap a sackcloth blanket around myself as long as my face stays uncovered. When the last of the Visitors has gone and Sourface has finished his shift I find a reasonably comfortable position for myself propped up on my pallet, back against the wall, and I pose. I shift periodically to relieve the stiffness and Sourface tells me not to fidget, but otherwise we hardly speak now. The first night I asked if I could lie down instead, as that would be kinder to all the bruised and battered bits of my body, but he said, 'No, I wouldn't be able to see your features properly. Just sit up and face me.' It was hard that first time to feel so exposed with nothing, not even my hair, to hide behind so I started to tell him things, partly to distract myself but mostly because it still feels so important for someone to know. For a while he listened without comment as I told him about leaving my home in the the north, my mother taking me to Maidentown to sell me and how I still couldn't comprehend how I had arrived here all the way from Malakai's estate in the north west. I started to describe the luxurious surroundings I'd lived in and the position I had held but at that point he put down his sketch in exasperation and said, 'I've heard quite enough, Ten; I imagine the entire block knows your history by now. Do your swollen mouth a favour and rest it. Please.'

So now we just sit quietly; he squats on the stool inside my cubicle and sketches away for half an hour or so then rolls up the paper he's been working on, slides it up the sleeve of his robe and places any unused sheets next to me on the bed. I slip them immediately under my pillow and wait until he's left before taking them out again. They are random in size and origin and some of them are creased and torn, but there are always some new sheets among them, freshly pressed from algae pulp, cotton or hemp, and I smooth them all out, put them in my preferred order and then count them. Sometimes I sniff them – trying to inhale their history as if it might help me to come to terms with my own.

Sourface never shows me what he's drawn and, though I

am quite curious, I've never asked to look. I'm trying to learn how to rest my mouth.

Sweet Mariam, the Guardian who first attended to me when they brought me in, has a soft heart and she cries a lot. The worse your condition and the more hopeless your chances of being claimed or adopted, the more you can get out of her by way of favours and little treats. It must be testament to my dismal prospects that I am one of her pets.

Then there's Gareff, one of the longest serving Guardians and a desirable ally because he works on The Kennel's farm, with particular responsibility for the vegetable garden, the pigs and the bees. On the days when he brings produce into the kitchen he strides importantly up and down the block, looking pointedly into every stall as if deciding which of us deserves favour; if you're chosen he produces a pot of honey from the pocket of his apron and makes a big show of feeding some to you on a spoon through the door mesh. He likes you to kneel down and lift your face to receive it because he says that means there's less chance of any being spilled and going to waste, but it's a performance, a way of displaying his power. I wouldn't do it even if he wanted me to, which he won't because he despises me. He calls me The Queen Bee and, according to Thirteen who claims to see everything from her stall opposite mine, he spits in my food. I know she's a trouble maker, so that may not be true, but there's no doubt about Gareff's animosity towards me; he's an uneducated low caste and will resent the fact that I can read and write because it marks me out as his superior.

I know I should take more care not to show my dislike of him because jealousy makes for a dangerous enemy, but it's hard. If he'd been a server in Malakai's household he would have been reprimanded or even dismissed, but as it is I try to avoid meeting his eye until I can learn to hide my feelings more successfully. If he stops by my door he says the same thing every time, 'And how is our Queen Bee today?' but he doesn't want an answer; he peers at my face, wearing an expression of mock sympathy, and then shakes his head sadly, 'Such a shame, such a shame...' It's all just another performance. If I'm to survive here it seems I need to be smart by appearing humble and meek which, as I learned from fourteen years with Mamma and three with Malakai, is different from merely being obedient. Swallowing my pride goes against everything they both ever taught me.

At night, when I can no longer see to write and my hand is too cold and painful anyway, I spend sleepless hours wondering about dying and if it's possible to escape. Perhaps, if I keep my eyes and ears open, I will spot a Guardian being careless – dropping a key or forgetting to lock a door. Then if I got as far as the outside there would be the Guards to deal with: if they're mercenaries they might be susceptible to bribery, but I have nothing worth offering. I am imprisoned here until I'm adopted or destroyed. That is the way of it.

And yet I'm told there are worse places, further east or south in the desert, in Detention Compounds where re-homing is not an option. Strays are rounded up and penned in barbed wire corrals where they are left to fry in the sun and starve. It's rumoured that at night the centres are opened to let wild animals in; they eat their fill of the dead and the dying and the vultures pick over the bones. What little the birds leave is cleaned up by insects until the bones can be used by Guards or scavengers to grind down into paste or animal feed, or carved into tools, jewellery and instruments that they can sell. Nothing goes to waste.

Here, we are housed in the decaying grandeur of old dog kennels, part of a once magnificent royal palace whose buildings are now crumbling and decrepit, patched up with whatever can be found to repair the results of landslides and subsidence. When the ground here quakes, more pieces fall off. The land is still very unstable here, which is why it is only considered suitable for the likes of us; if we get swallowed up it is assumed no-one will miss us.

The Guardians and the Guards are not much better protected, although they sleep in what remains of the splendid mansion itself, with the remnants of rich hangings and tapestries, painted frescoes and marble sunken baths. They are doubtless grateful to work in exchange for board and lodgings, but who recruits them, and how, I do not know.

Even in our stalls there are still patches of gilt on the cracked ceilings, evidence of mosaics on the floors and beautiful illuminated murals in the passageway depicting feasts and hunting parties, from a long ago time when beasts were plentiful enough to be killed for sport. The sundial on the end wall has little flakes of gold paint peeling off it which catch the light through the open ceiling above and I watch morbidly as the shadows move relentlessly towards the ending of another day.

'Stall Ten: juvenile female for adoption; details unknown'. When they finally take the screens away and put me on show that, and the physician's report, will be all the information provided for prospective adopters. It won't be enough. Adopters want to see a Profile; they need the reassurance of some background about the individual they might be considering taking home with them. And if they're going to put you to work they certainly need to know that you're healthy and going to be worth the adoption fee.

*****

My full name is Akara d'Fiuri. On the day I was born I was registered merely as 'Fiuri's dottir' until, eight years later, Mamma re-registered me with the full name she had finally chosen for me. She had settled on an old name meaning 'beautiful angel', because that was how she intended to market me when the time came. I already held great promise, with a strong body, good teeth and radiant skin. My head, underarms and pubis boasted healthy, lustrous hair and I learned very quickly to give the impression of being compliant and sweet natured when required. When I had my first bleed at the age of twelve, my mother's face broke into a rare smile: if I was potentially fertile then my value escalated and the dates and duration of all my subsequent bleeds were recorded along with every other relevant detail of my life. My mother kept scrupulous records, including my birth registration certificate showing the date as 1st May, 2075. But as that, along with all my other documents, is missing you will just have to trust me on that and everything else I'm going to tell you.

I am seventeen years of age; my exquisite Eurasian mother was Fiuri d'Ursoola and she was probably one of the first genuinely healthy babies to be born in the northern region of the new country. That was twenty six years after the cataclysmic solar eruptions of 2025, which her own mother, Ursoola, had survived by sheer good luck and tenacity.

'She was seven,' Mamma told me, 'and in those days rich people sometimes used to travel just for pleasure. She was on a trip with her parents and visiting some local caves; when the caves collapsed in the aftermath of the catastrophe her parents were killed and she found herself lying under a pile of rubble next to their bodies.'

'What happened then, Mamma?'

'She cried out for days apparently and eventually someone found her,' she replied.

Although some places escaped the worst of the effects, being on the dark side of the earth at the time, there was devastation everywhere. The solar flares blasted all technology, caused oceans to overheat, volcanoes to erupt and tsunamis to drown entire countries; but here and there survivors found pockets of land intact, with oases of drinkable water and plenty of ruined buildings to be plundered for useable materials. The air quality was extremely poor for many years and the remaining animals and humans adapted to their new conditions with varying success. My Grandmother seems to have coped very well, displaying a resourcefulness which her daughter, born twenty six years later, inherited. My mother, according to her own account, was left to fend pretty much for herself as a child and, typically, chose her own name and the singular path to her future as soon as she was old enough. She didn't tell me what happened to Ursoola; being Mamma, I don't suppose she cared.

My pappa, accredited on my birth certificate, was called Kennedy d'Mya. All Mamma would tell me about him was that he was young and very handsome and that he left before I was born. I think it's very likely that she drove him away, which is another thing I should never forgive her for, but it does leave me able to imagine him being the perfect father if she'd allowed him to be. In my mind he has all the qualities my mother despised because, as she was forever telling me, 'Kindness and compassion are weaknesses, not gifts; they have no value in themselves.' With Mamma, everything was always about its value and she would be bitterly disappointed to know that I, the best and most beautiful of her children, now has none.

Now I'm officially an itinerant, so far from my last home in the lush, fertile region of North West Scardland that I still don't even know how I got here to the eastern region, and so far south. Malakai always told me that the East was completely arid and virtually uninhabited, except by people so outlawed by poverty, sterility and disease that they had nowhere else to go; but now I wonder whether he, like my mother, simply told the truth that suited him. Perhaps he said it to make me realise just how lucky I was, and to discourage any thoughts I might have had about running away. Why, in the name of The Divinities, would I want to run away to this, where the reality is a thousand times worse than anything I might have imagined.

4 THE LOSS OF INNOCENCE

Jiggs didn't return and everyone was concerned, for a while. But people were always coming and going - getting sick and dying, or moving on in search of something better elsewhere - so it wasn't long before he was pretty much forgotten by everyone except me, Surrana and Chapstick. The little ones who had been used to romping and playing with him found other distractions and new playmates and the crowds that had gathered to watch him fight drifted away, back to the regular fight pits in the shanties and at Maidentown.

I looked for my friend every day whilst I was out foraging or hunting, and every day his cat followed me. She still hissed and spat at me if I went near her but became my shadow, pacing cautiously behind me wherever I went, eating the food I gave her as long as I kept my distance, and being a constant reminder of the companion we had both lost. The scuffed up tracks that we'd found the night he disappeared were soon erased by the sand storm that blew up the following day and there were no other signs anywhere that gave a clue about what might have happened to him. The only thing I found, snagged on a gorse bush where the winds must have blown it, was a page from a real newspaper from the old days – the print still legible after more than forty five years. It was an important and valuable find and we were so desperate for food that I knew I had to sell it; but I showed it to the others first and then copied it out so Surrana could use it as a history lesson for the little ones. One of the Elders claimed to have been alive at the time the story was written and to remember it well, but no one believed him. I sold it to a very rich man in Maidentown who wanted it for his collection, and that money fed a dozen of us for a month.

'HEBRIDEAN HERALD
January 21st 2037

SCOTLAND BRACED FOR FINAL WAVE OF REFUGEES

The Scottish mainland is preparing to be cut off for good from England as the Northern Passage continues to flood. The melting waters of the North Sea have been rising steadily since the first climatic disasters of 2025, and it is understood that the most recent crop of solar storms has completely devastated a large area of the North European land mass, leaving the survivors from the Western Hemisphere who had fled there dispossessed once again.

Scottish Ministers are in crisis talks and have elected Dr. Astrid Galway BSc. Hons to the newly created post of Humanitarian Registrar in an attempt to track and control the influx of yet more refugees. Dr. Galway has issued a statement which has caused some controversy amongst more liberal ministers, who view her attitude with alarm; Scotland, she believes, should no longer support the numbers of sick and starving who are seeking its help and hospitality. 'We must draw a line,' her statement says, 'and only offer succour now to those who can enrich us in some way – through the skills and strength which will enable our ravaged country to recover. The harsh reality is that the world's resources are extremely limited and our own survival will depend on us making some difficult and unpopular decisions. I say this with a heavy heart but it is the truth.'

'That attitude,' says Angus Morrison SMP for Lomond, 'is taking us further down the road to an Orwellian scenario. These refugees are not merely useless dependants as she implies, surely they enrich us already with their culture and diverse knowledge? I've been into the camps, which is more than Dr. Galway has I'm sure, and they are full of desperate men, women and wee bairns who are here through no fault of their own, seeking our help. I can't condone, or even understand, such callousness on her part and that of the ministers who elected her.'

Whilst that debate continues, we are still asking our readers to donate what they can to the Refugee Rehabilitation Centres. With the continuing rise in temperatures, and very limited transportation to the mainland available, they are not currently accepting any perishables. Our own connection to, and communication with, the outside world is increasingly imperilled but we will continue to publish for as long as we are able. Meanwhile we urge you all to take care and hope that your own personal gods may keep you safe.'

On the other side of the page was a list of Donation Drop Off sites and the most urgent items needed: clothes, camping stoves, babies' nappies and so forth. I cannot imagine anyone giving such things away now; they are luxuries that most of us cannot afford and some have even died in the process of trying to steal. I've seen the bodies in Maidentown's punishment pens – their hands cut off and the bloodied remains waiting to be fed to the pigs.

Myrah, the girl Jiggs had fought so hard to win, fulfilled her early promise and began her bleeds; as soon as they became regular her father began preparations for her sale, just as I'd predicted. She had been left in her mother's care at the camp for several months while the father conducted business elsewhere. Whatever that business was, it quickly made him a wealthy man, buying him higher caste status, fancy clothes and new lodgings in Maidentown near the market square. He boasted that he would be able to watch Myrah being auctioned off from his rooftop garden without having to dirty his expensive new sandals on the common thoroughfare. I heard Myrah and her poor mother crying and pleading with him often before the night he finally took his daughter away but the man had no mercy in his heart, only greed. Surrana cried too, saying she knew what it was like to give up a child, and hugging me close as if I might be lost to her again. As she wept on my shoulder, telling me again and again how precious I was to her and asking for my forgiveness and understanding, I felt a change in me, as if I had quite suddenly accepted that I must become the man I had promised her I would be and the brief childhood I had enjoyed with Jiggs had evaporated along with him somehow, leaving me to grow up. When at last my dick grew, my balls dropped lower and my voice no longer squeaked Surrana cried again and said, 'I knew it! I knew this would happen, my beautiful boy,' and we both admitted to hoping that I might be one of the few, the very few, who could mate successfully and one day breed children of my own. It was a time of exciting dreams, confusing new feelings and treacherous thoughts, because I finally began to understand what had driven Jiggs to fight.

For the first few weeks after Jiggs' disappearance I didn't think about much else; even the foraging trips were really just an excuse to go and look for him. I knew he'd want me to look after Chapstick so, although I never got a hint of affection or gratitude from her, I did all I could to keep her safe and feed her when she was hungry – even picking out the juiciest bugs from the death traps and cooking them for her if she wouldn't eat them raw. Scrawny, scruffy and bad tempered as she was, Chapstick was almost revered within the camp. The little ones were endlessly entertained by her and the older ones saw her as a sign of hope, a symbol of survival. Her stubby tail would twitch as she watched me with her one good eye and, in the absence of anyone else, I would talk to her whilst I sat mending nets or fiddled about making things.

'Where's he gone then, Chapstick? What do you think has happened to him?'

The tail would twitch but she had no answer.

'Warthogs got him maybe? That old boar is big and mean and even Jiggs didn't like to mess with him. But there'd have been something…you know…something there to find if he'd been killed. One day, one day Chapstick, I think we'll find him.'

We'd sit in silence for a while, the sun beating down and the air hot around us and full of flies. Chapstick would snap at the flies and I'd swat the skeetos, always afraid of being bitten and getting some terrible sickness or other, but I never once got a skeeto bite and my skin, although it remained pale, didn't bruise or mark or get infected the way some of the others' did.

'I think you have a certain natural immunity,' Surrana said, 'and I think you'll be strong and healthy like your father. It won't matter what you look like one day, as long as you're fit enough to survive. And maybe,' she added, stroking the soft, blonde hair that was just starting to appear on my head and around my chin, 'maybe you'll be fertile like him too. Oh, I hope so my son, I do hope so.'

I didn't tell Surrana, although she was my mother and I loved her, what I already knew: that something incredible was happening to me that should have made me happy but brought me terrible shame and guilt as well. Oddly enough, it was Chapstick that I confessed to, perhaps because I knew she didn't care.

As well as looking after Chapstick I decided I should protect Myrah for Jiggs' sake too. With her father away, she and her mother might have found it hard fending for themselves but, shortly after his departure, the father sent two men to provide for them and to guard Myrah who was becoming increasingly valuable. The threat of kidnap was always there but I think what he most feared was that she would try to escape.

I visited her camp several times a day and, as I saw her becoming more and more unhappy, I wondered if she was just afraid of the future or if she was as sad about Jiggs as I was. I tried to talk to her about him but she was hardly ever alone and, in the end, all I could do was watch her and foster hatred for her father and what he was about to do. I watched her so often and so closely that I found myself thinking about her even when she wasn't there. I told myself I was taking my role as protector seriously as I imagined her naked at the waterhole, her slender limbs dipping in and out of the water and those exquisite almond eyes closing as she rinsed her hair. She had small, firm breasts that I noticed would swell every month in time with her bleeds and my dick would swell at the thought of touching them, running my long pale fingers over her walnut brown skin and caressing every curve. I would spend hours awake on my mattress at night, mentally tracing the remembered lines of every pattern on her skin: the tattoos her mother had made by tracing charcoal into tiny incisions to disguise unsightly marks and the scars from infected insect bites. She was as close to perfect as almost anyone I'd ever seen and eventually I admitted to myself that I loved her.

Wanting Myrah for myself was as hopeless for me as it had been for Jiggs, but that didn't stop me from becoming more and more infatuated with her. I tried to convince myself that I could win her but I knew in my heart that, without the fortune I would need to buy her, her father would never ever consider it. I was an unregistered low caste with nothing to offer but a pasty looking skin and a few blonde hairs. The useful things I had a knack for finding and the clever things I made could be easily acquired elsewhere by a man with his wealth, and I didn't have the muscle to earn money fighting, though I'd have been willing to try. On two occasions when he had visited he had seen me hovering nearby and had spoken to the men guarding his daughter; after that I got threatened and chased away if they caught me anywhere near her. I never got the chance to tell her my feelings before he took her away and she became yet another person that I had loved and lost.

So the only one who knew was Chapstick and she wasn't any help at all.

"Fukk you, you stupid creature,' I would say, 'Fukk you and your way of looking at me as if I should feel guilty. He's not here, is he? He doesn't know and he won't find out unless you tell him. And you'd have to find him first.' Then I'd get up and make another useless trek into the scrub or another camp further off, asking if anyone had seen him or heard any news and hoping that I might find him this time. But perhaps not hoping quite as fervently as I once had.

When Myrah's father had removed her from their camp, in the dead of night when I probably mistook the distant screams for jackals fighting, I told Surrana I was going to start heading further afield to trade. It seemed she looked at me knowingly but said nothing, except to advise me to be careful.

5 MAMMA

My eyes hurt and so does my hand. I've been clutching a pencil too tightly and I need to flex my fingers and loosen the support around my wrist. I can't resist looking in the mirror again, checking the cuts and bruises and nudging my tongue into the gap where I lost a tooth; I'm worried it will become infected. I wish Beetle were here; he'd search through all his jars and pots and find some magic balm to heal me. He'd put clove oil on my gums and arnica juice on my bruises and somewhere amongst the flasks and phials there'd be an ointment for the cuts. Or he'd concoct something, like he did for Mamma when she got her terrible allergic rashes and nearly went mad with the itching and the pain.

The physician is still quite sure that most of the external damage you can see would fade, given enough time. Internally I'm intact – that is to say unmated – and somewhere are all the precious certificates which prove that, until a few weeks ago, I had as high a value as it's possible for a woman to have. Sweet Mariam is able to sound almost convincing when she assures me that we can be very optimistic about my prospects, even without documents.

The gap in my teeth is too far back to be noticeable and my hair will grow again; maybe not quite as thick and glossy as it once was when I had oils to nourish it and the luxury of fresh, clean water to wash it in every day, but that doesn't concern me. What I really want now is to be able to see properly and to have a belly full of good, healthy food so that my ribs don't stick out and my buttocks don't hurt when I sit down. All my life my mother encouraged me to be vain and all along I knew that my beauty was just a form of currency; it was what she used to secure Malakai's Patronage and with it the life of luxury I took for granted. Now that I'm damaged and my looks are spoiled, perhaps forever, I know I have very little to offer. A disfigured skin has little defence against the sun, or against infection; and if my body is in shock and my next bleed does not arrive then I'm not fertile. If I can't work, fight or breed then I will be useless and no one will be prepared to adopt and support me without good reason. Even my brother Beetle had gifts which made it worth our mother keeping him, although she could still hardly bear to look at him; what talents I have are of no consequence if I am no longer even pleasing to the eye.

At the moment I look as if I've been fighting in one of the pits outside Maidentown and didn't win. My left eye is covered by a fraying fabric pad crusted with dried blood and tied on with a muslin bandage which keeps slipping. They've promised to find, or make me, a proper patch but until then I must make the best of it. Many inmates come in with injuries but we learn very quickly not to make a fuss; there seems to be no pain relief available and if you scream or complain too loudly you are deemed Unfit and taken to the room at the end of the passage to be dealt with. Everyone tries very hard to be at their best during the day time when the Visitors come, and at night the numbing cold takes our minds off our physical pain.

So far, hidden behind a screen and a sack curtain, I've

had little to do with anyone except the Guardians. I listen to the rise and fall of the Visitors' voices and their comments when they stop to speculate about me. If Mariam is with them she tries to encourage them, 'This one, she been badly attacked but she's good girl and gonna be better soon. Maybe you come back again to see her tomorrow or next day? She's clever, I think; maybe do writing for you or look after children and teach.' If Ridrick-Oola is with them she is brief and blunt, 'We don't know much about Ten but she's literate and has some education. She'll go on show soon, you can look at her then.'

But if Gareff is on duty he deliberately discourages them, 'I wouldn't recommend you waste your time with this one; she's badly damaged and,' lowering his voice, 'not to be trusted. You'd do well to look at Six if it's a young, solid female you're after.'

Sometimes, when I hear what some of the Visitors sound like and their plans for whoever they adopt, I pray they don't come back and choose me. If they do, I will have no say in the matter: if they can afford the fee and manage to put their mark on the agreement they will become my legal Patron, just as Malakai was. It is a trade like any other.

I think of Mamma and the first time I asked the question, 'Why? Why is it like this, Mamma? Why must I belong to someone else? Why must I leave home?' She looked at me with cold, dark eyes and said, 'Do not question, Akara. Things are the way they are and the best and safest thing you can do is to be compliant. Arguing against it is not helpful and it is not wise.' *It is not the behaviour I require of you if you are to achieve a high price for me.*

I'm tired now and some of my wounds have started to bleed again; I look in the cracked, grubby mirror and am reminded of what a mess I am. I need to rinse out the dressings and re-bandage the parts I can reach but I don't have the energy. Besides, The Kennels will be closing soon for the night and no one will be able to see me.

My seventh day, early morning and we've just finished slopping out; the stench is foul and the Guardians cover their faces with scarves; inmates use whatever comes to hand or just turn their heads away and hold their breath.

Regardless of the unappetising smells around us we're ready for breakfast when it comes. It's usually broth or warm coconut milk with a large chunk of dry, salted bread which is fresh and very filling. The night Guardians hand over to the day ones and they have brief conversations about how the night has passed, who amongst the inmates has been tearful, or disruptive, or in the worst pain. Charts are chalked with new marks and if there are medicines available they are handed out, but sparingly. This morning I was given a smear of aloe vera balm for my bruises and my new eye patch. It is made of padded calico, shaped to fit comfortably and secured round my head with an adjustable, soft leather band. I am very excited and spend a long time at the mirror fiddling with it until it's in the best position, although nothing I do makes me look less threatening. I try smiling but my mouth is still misshapen and it still hurts too much to be worth the effort.

It was Sourface who brought me the eye patch, 'I'm sure it will look very fetching, Ten. I look forward to seeing it on you later and I may well draw you again,' he said, in a tone that suggested I should be grateful. I gave him a look, but didn't say anything..

The Guardians are made up of a mixture of castes. Some, like Sourface, even seem quite educated and - apart from Gareff - are patient and not deliberately unkind. But the Guards, without exception, are ignorant brutes. When the wagon collected me six days ago it was already crammed full: ten or more of us had been collected in the space of half a day. 'You're lucky,' one of the Guards informed me as they heaved me on, 'Got room for one more bitch, if that's what you are,' and he pulled up my undergarment to check, 'Though *I* wouldn't want to fukk you,' he added and laughed. The other three joined in with the banter, 'You haven't seen your cock upright since the day you got it, Spiro!'

'I don't suppose she'd want to fukk *you* much either,' another said, 'Not if she could see you, anyway!' and, as I drifted in and out of consciousness, I heard them carry on in that way for the whole journey. Now I know that I could instead have been found by one of the Detention Compound wagons I suppose I should feel fortunate.

*****

And that's what my mother told me too on the morning of my fourteenth birthday, as she brushed my hair and stood me in front of a mirror so we could both admire her handiwork. 'Akara,' she said softly, 'you are one of the very lucky ones. You have beauty and talents and you have me for a mother.' She rested her hands on my shoulders and, for a moment, I closed my eyes and tried unsuccessfully to imagine affection in her touch. Mamma had never laid a finger on me in anger, mostly for fear of leaving a mark, but she'd never shown me the slightest tenderness either. Not once during my childhood did she let me make the mistake of believing that she loved me. 'Love is for weak people,' she told me repeatedly, 'Weak people do not survive in this world.'

If I received any affection in the first four years of my life I don't remember it. Maybe Nula, my eldest sister, cuddled me occasionally but I doubt she'd have been allowed. She'd gone by the time I was six, anyway. Hal was next: seven years older than me and out working in the fields most of the time until he too went to auction; I don't even really recall what he looked like. Then came Ash, whom I loved in spite of his disfigurements - he was so sweet and funny and kind. He worked outside and with the animals, and Mamma rarely allowed him in the house, but he'd sneak up to a window if she wasn't looking and pull funny faces to make me laugh, or bring me things he'd found when he was digging the earth or quarrying for salt. One day, I think it was my fifth birthday, he gave me a little silver coloured ring, but after a while it began to discolour my skin and Mamma forbade me to wear it, so I just kept it under my pillow and put it on at night. The day I went to auction I threaded a leather thong through it and put it around Beetle's neck, I knew Mamma wouldn't care about it staining *his* skin because she didn't think he was worth anything anyway.

Ash took his meals outside and slept with the mules in the stone barn, so until Mamma began letting me out more often we didn't get to spend much time together, but when we did I was so happy. I'd beg him to lift me onto his shoulders and gallop around the yard or, better still, let me ride one of the mules. Of course Mamma was furious with us both if she caught us, but she only ever punished Ash. She would send me indoors with just a look before ordering him to the barn and picking up a switch from the goat pen as she marched after him. After that there would be silence for a long time until she came back, flushed with anger and her knuckles white from holding the switch so tight. Very occasionally, if Mamma was occupied elsewhere, Ash would take my hand, hold a finger to his lips and we'd creep right out of the yard into the scrubland beyond. As well as the excitement of being on an adventure with Ash there was the thrill of danger too: the promise of seeing the snakes, scorpions and insects that Mamma had spent all of my seven years warning me about and telling me to avoid. Ash would stalk barefoot and silent with his eyes peeled for threats on the ground while I skipped behind him, swishing away at the air with a palm branch and treating the whole thing as a game.

Then one day a hornet landed on my arm and got caught in the crease of my elbow; I screamed and Ash swiped it away but it was too late, I'd been stung. As my arm began to redden and swell he scooped me up and carried me home, stumbling as he ran but not stopping once. As soon as we got close to the house he began to yell for Mamma and she must have heard the panic in his voice because it was the first time I'd ever seen her run, rushing out of the house with her hands still wet from doing laundry. As soon as Ash could catch his breath to tell her what had happened, she ordered him to carry me inside whilst she sent Tanya to fetch lemon juice and vinegar. Ash laid me down on Mamma's mattress in the corner of the main room and stood back while Mamma collected what seemed like every potion, ointment and tincture we had in the house and knelt down beside me, looking angry and fearful all at once. I was in a lot of pain and was crying uncontrollably, something I was never normally allowed to do because crying makes you ugly, but Mamma let me holler away until she'd applied lemon juice to my arm and soaked a clean rag in honey and vinegar for me to suck.

With the rag in my mouth I watched through my tears and sobs as she mixed up bits of this and that into a paste, which she spread so liberally my entire arm went green. Mamma never had Beetle's later gift for healing but whatever she did that day worked, I gradually calmed down and the excruciating pain faded to a dull throb. All the time Ash stood by the bed, his pale face almost grey with shock and his blue eyes filling with tears; when Mamma was sure that I was definitely recovering she raised her head and looked at him. He nodded, turned and left the house. Mamma followed him shortly afterwards and must have been away a long time because I think I'd fallen asleep by the time she returned.

The next day, Ash had gone; he'd simply disappeared. I

don't know what happened to him, Mamma refused to discuss it, but since he was too young at thirteen to have been sold legally, I hoped he'd just run away and would come back one day. I missed him terribly and couldn't understand how he could have left me without saying goodbye. I think that was the first time my heart got broken.

My sister, Tanya, was four years older than me and she hated Mamma. They were forever arguing and Mamma couldn't tolerate anybody answering her back the way Tanya did. One day Tanya refused to do something our mother had told her to do and Mamma slapped her. It was one of the most shocking things I'd ever seen because my sister was very lovely to look at and I knew Mamma had always had high hopes of getting a good price for her. I saw the ugly red mark left on Tanya's golden skin and the look of disbelief on my sister's face before she thrust her face towards Mamma and spat at her. Two days later a couple from one of the nearby camps turned up with a handcart and a brace of goats. They left the goats and four or five sacks full of utensils, pots and baskets in the yard and took my sister away. For once, she didn't argue, and she didn't look back as she left. Mamma watched her go, then turned to me and said the goats would be a lot easier to look after.

Tanya and I had never been close so I didn't much care when she'd gone; by then I had Beetle to look after anyway and, between him and my books, the gap that Ash had left was nearly filled. My little brother became the centre of my world for the next four years and he was more like my child than Mamma's. If our mother had ever stood a chance of turning me into the replica of herself that she wanted me to be, my love for Beetle put paid to that; the more she discouraged our affection the more I resisted and the more I resented her.

Perhaps if she had explained things to me earlier I would

have had some sympathy for her, or at least more of an understanding of why she was the way she was. Instead, she waited until our very last day together, waited until those last intimate moments in front of the mirror to share some of her story, before then taking me to auction and handing me over to a complete stranger.

'You may not realise it now, Akara, but you have been very lucky. I wish that I'd been blessed with a mother like me.' I think that may have been the only time I thought my mother might cry; she met her own eyes in the mirror and let her hands drop from my shoulders.

'When I was born, in two thousand and fifty one, the world was a great deal harsher than it is now, believe me. Populations had been depleted and diseased already by the earlier pandemics, and after the sun exploded the land was smouldering, the waters had been poisoned and the air was so short of oxygen it was hard to breathe. There was very little to eat, because hardly anything would grow and so many animals had died. My mother didn't care about anyone but herself, she fukked for food and spent my childhood whoring around and aborting babies. I was alone and had to fend for myself. You've never had to do that.'

I watched her perfect, symmetrical face in the mirror and tried to read her expression. Her words were full of bitterness but her face was almost blank. After sun damage, she would often remind me, displaying emotion is the quickest way to ruin your beauty; frowning, crying and smiling 'too much' or 'unnecessarily' were discouraged from as early as I can remember.

My exposure to the sun was limited to what was necessary for building up my resistance to it; I spent most of my early childhood indoors, or covered from head to toe if I went outside. Being cooped up, although I hated it, had one great benefit because it meant I learned to read. Mamma taught me, having learned some from her own mother and one or more of her lovers, and with her usual foresight had collected a small number of books so that her children would be as literate and as cultured as would make them useful and worthy. I loved to read, devouring and rereading every book, teaching myself to write and gaining a knowledge of the old world beyond even what my mother chose to teach me.

By the time I was eleven I was also developing physically in a way that we both knew was going to set me apart; I would catch Mamma looking at me speculatively sometimes and it chilled my heart. I knew which way the wind was blowing and that in three years time I would be going up for sale; if she kept me intact till then, concentrated on refining my skills and reined in my wayward streak, she would have created a very desirable commodity indeed.

'As soon as I could,' Mamma continued, tilting a jar of olive oil and spreading the contents thickly over her hands, 'I left my mother.'

'Did you run away?' I asked, lifting my head and holding out my arms ready to receive the glistening juice. She was right to be proud of the colour and texture of my skin; it is an evenly tanned shade of toasted almond and it has been well looked after to keep it supple and smooth. I was lucky not to have inherited my mother's sole physical flaw which was the hypersensitivity of her skin; it made her particularly reactive to certain things including horse hair, sheep's wool, the detergents we used to clean out the animal pens, and insect bites. By a strange twist of fate it was her allergies that kept her bound, reluctantly but inextricably, to Beetle; although she never admitted her dependence on him or uttered a word of gratitude.

'Did you run away, Mamma?' I repeated.

'No, I didn't have to run, my mother wouldn't have cared enough to try to stop me. But I knew I had to be sure

I was ready to leave and well enough equipped to survive on my own. The world is a hostile place, Akara – it always has been and it always will be – but it was still in chaos, with no authority or organisation and certainly no protection for a fifteen year old girl on her own.'

I presented my naked back to her, arms outstretched and enjoying the sensation as she massaged in the oil. It was a ritual we performed at least once every day, my thirsty skin always ready to receive the moisture, and it was the only time my mother caressed me. As I stood waiting for her to continue her story I had a sudden jolt of realisation: that this would be the last time she would touch me like that. After today I might never, ever see my mother again. She had spent fourteen years ensuring there was no emotional bond between us: grooming, disciplining and educating me without a single demonstration of maternalism, and yet I felt an almost primitive tug at my heart and in my guts at the thought of leaving her. I pushed the thought away, not only because it was a betrayal of all that she had taught me but because it also carried with it the fear of an unknown future.

'What did you do, Mamma?' I asked, trying to distract myself.

'I followed my mother's example and got pregnant. With Nula, the first of my children,' she added.

I barely remembered my oldest sister, she had been sold when I was about six years old as I said and, to the best of my knowledge, has not been seen or heard of since.

'However,' Mamma went on, 'Unlike my mother I had a plan. I had spent months, even before coming of age, looking for the right man; that is, a man who was potent and could get me pregnant with a healthy child. There were other camps not far from our own and some of the men from them used to visit my mother because she was known to have certain skills.'

'What skills?'

'Knowing ways to make a man's cock rise, using plants and potions and other artistry. Your grandmother had a gift that way. Many men cannot function as they should, Akara; they are riddled with disease, raddled by the harsh life and shrivelled up by that relentless sun.' Her graceful hand gestured vaguely towards the sky. 'Most women are the same – weak, worn out and barren. So I used to go to their camps, make myself useful helping to forage and cook and so on, befriending the women and keeping my eyes and ears open. One of them, Shana, had a healthy looking baby and a man who was very good to her and who I knew had never visited my mother. He kept Shana well provided for with a sturdily built shelter and they ate well.'

'He sounds like a good man.'

'He was a good provider,' she corrected me. 'Anyway, as soon as I was certain I was pregnant by him, he and I left together for good.'

It took me a moment to fully understand. 'You took him away from your friend? From Shana?'

'I did what I felt I had to do. She wasn't really my friend.'

'But she thought she was,' I argued. This was met with silence, one of our mother's favourite responses to anything she didn't like to be challenged on.

'What happened then?' I persevered.

'A year after Nula was born I gave birth to Hal and three months later the man left.'

'Why? Where did he go?'

'I don't know and it doesn't matter. What's important is that he left me with this roof over my head and the wherewithal to survive. Akara,' she said with an urgency in her voice and a spark of something in her eyes that I couldn't translate, 'you need to understand what's important in this life: self preservation. It's the primary objective and it's the principle behind everything I've ever done for you. You're not like most of the others, you have something special, something extra. I think you have the capacity to do more than just make it from one day to the next, Akara; I believe you can thrive and it's what I want for you.'

Now, with time to think back over that conversation, I wonder why she didn't see the similarities between herself and her own mother whom she had called a whore. I wish that I had put it to her that they were both driven by the same imperative to survive – exactly as she was instructing me to do. And exploiting her daughter to improve her own situation was surely no better than her own mother's wilful neglect?

I said none of that to her, of course. Instead, I picked up the little phial of Frankincense from the table and applied a drop, as Mamma had taught me, on each pulse point, behind each knee and in the hollow of my throat. It was a precious perfume and not to be used profligately so I was surprised when Mamma took the phial from me and gently dabbed my temples and behind my ears with more. 'Today it is important that you stay calm, Akara. The Frankincense will help to ease your nerves.' But I didn't mistake her words for kindness, 'Fear will make you sweat, and sweat smells. Do you understand, child? You must present yourself as poised and proud and fully aware of your worth. You are my jewel, Akara; the best and most beautiful of all my children. And that's a good thing for both of us because somebody's going to pay me a lot of money for you; and when people pay a lot of money for something they tend to take care of it.'

Then she dressed me in the very finest clothes I had, gathered up my documents and a few personal belongings and took me off to Maidentown market to be sold.

6 MAIDENTOWN

So the shadow on the sundial tells me it is around five o'clock and another day is over, at least as far as Visitors are concerned. The shifts began their changeover at about six in the morning, as usual, but I was awake long before then, struggling to keep warm under the thin blankets and hurting in all the usual places, although the pain is considerably less than it was. I emptied my slop bucket into the gully that runs along the front of my pen and stood back while the night workers washed it down; it is always a smelly, messy, noisy operation and deeply humiliating. The stone floors, with their chipped mosaics, are mottled with the stains of decades I should think, even going back to the days when a nobleman's dogs lived here in a luxury I'm sure they didn't appreciate. But that was many years ago, before subsidence skewed the floors and scavengers stripped the place of every usable, portable item. The clay tiled roof it may have had has long since gone, replaced by rusty metal bars and the tattered tarpaulin and plastic which traps the stifling daytime heat and fails to insulate against the bitterly cold nights. It is only weighed down by bricks and rocks, so when the typhoons come we will probably all drown. Or be killed by falling masonry if we have a major earthquake.

I am in the last but one in the row of stalls, each about two paces wide and four deep; a luxurious amount of space for a single dog, no doubt, but claustrophobically confined for a human being. There is just enough room for a wooden pallet to sleep on, a stool which normally accommodates the enamel washbowl but is serving me now as a desk, and the slop bucket. There is also a rickety folding screen which provides some privacy when using the bucket, washing ourselves or changing our clothes. You may imagine that most of us who find ourselves here do not arrive with much. The Guardians provide us with what they can – a bundle of items which have been found or donated or handed on from the inmates who didn't need them any more. They are washed or aired as often as possible, darned and mended neatly, and serve to remind me yet again of what I once had and have since lost.

*****

I used to love visiting Maidentown, right up until that final trip. Every six months or so, when the big markets were held and Mamma knew it would be at its busiest, she would take me with her so that we could trade goods and she could show me off. We would load up the biggest cart with things to barter or sell, hoick a big, thick canopy over it and harness the two fittest mules. I think I was seven the first time Mamma took me with her and it must have been not long after Ash disappeared because I remember Mamma made sure to dress me in a long sleeved robe so no one would see the evidence of the sting on my arm. She'd smothered it in some of her vile green ointment and every time the itching started up she would stop the cart and smother it again. 'Don't scratch, Akara,' she commanded, 'Scratches leave marks.'

That first trip to Maidentown was the day Hal was sold.

I barely remember him, except as a vague, boyish shape helping to hoist things in and out of the cart, to feed and water the mules when we stopped at intervals during the half day journey and a voice – not yet fully broken – saying 'Yes, Mamma,' and 'No, Mamma,' but not much else. As we got closer to Maidentown the route became busier with one or two carts and riders on donkeys or camels, but mostly people on foot. It was entertaining for me, sitting safely up on the cart and sheltered from the sun, experiencing so much that was new and exciting; it was only as I got older that I appreciated how pathetic most of the sights were. The people were almost all thin, tired and bowed with the weight of whatever goods they were carrying to sell. Some of them approached us and held things out, offering 'best prices' for sale or exchange, but Mamma ignored them all and, if they got too close, would simply say, 'Hal,' in a firm voice and he'd jump down from the cart and shoo them away.

As I got older I also became aware of other strangers coming up to us: men and women in litters or fancy wagons and accompanied by servers with teams of mules, camels or goats. Usually an individual would approach respectfully first, say something to Mamma and she would nod and stop the cart. Then the litter or wagon would pull alongside and whoever was in it would have a conversation with my mother.

'When will she be ready?' the stranger would ask, peering into the wagon to look at me.

'Not for seven years,' Mamma replied that first time.

'Documents?'

'Of course. She is, and will be, perfect.'

'How much?'

Then Mamma would look them up and down and sometimes a withering expression would come across her face as if they could be nowhere near good enough or rich enough to have me. But occasionally she would grace them with one of her rare smiles and say, 'When the time comes I'll let you know.'

As time passed and I became more conscious of myself and my worth I began to enjoy the attention. I would sit proudly next to my mother and copy her expressions, following her lead if she smiled at someone and summing up the quality of their clothes and the extravagance of their caravan. I was most impressed by the camels. I'd never seen one before and Mamma told me they had come from a long way away, brought across the dried up sea beds which suddenly made easy passage between distant lands. But the waterways had soon flooded again with melted water from the north and now Scardland was an island, cut off from whatever remained of the rest of the world. The camels seemed to me majestic and exotic and I longed to ride on one, imagining myself perched gracefully on an embroidered saddle and hearing the lovely tinkling of the bells and tassels hanging from the bridle as we loped across the desert. I determined there and then only to be bought by someone who owned camels, because I was still naïve enough at that point to believe I had any choice in the matter.

Maidentown itself exceeded everything I might have imagined about it, being bigger and busier than anywhere I'd ever been. Unlike the scruffy little tented camps Mamma sometimes took me to when she needed to buy or sell things locally, Maidentown was a mixture of structures; there were old stone buildings mixed in with wooden shelters, mud huts and even upturned carts serving as dwellings; everywhere you looked there were makeshift stalls, gazebos and pavilions built with anything people could lay their hands on. There was colour and bustle and noise: people shouting; animals bleating, whining and shitting everywhere; hawkers selling everything from coloured stones to henna dyes. And there was music. Oh, the music! Sitars, kettle drums, fiddles and kalimbas; flutes, nose pipes and guitars – there was so much noise. I loved it – the sounds and the energy of the place filled me with a new and thrilling view of the world, far removed from my sheltered and disciplined life at home. In Maidentown there were people singing and dancing; there were groups gathered around charcoal braziers eating and drinking things I longed to try; and there were dozens of tents, constructed of precarious looking poles and yards of colourful fabrics, with mysterious individuals perched on stools outside beckoning us into them. The whole place was alive and thrilling and I could hardly contain my excitement.

As our cart rumbled along the main thoroughfare Mamma would be unusually talkative, 'Knowledge is valuable in a place like this, Akara,' she told me. 'You need to know who is safe to trade with and who is not. There are many dangers and I can only warn you about some of them. You will have to develop trustworthy instincts and use your brains, child.'

Two things I learned very quickly: firstly, that Maidentown contained debauchery and despair as well as delights, and secondly that my mother was very well known and respected, if not liked. This second fact probably kept me largely protected from too much experience of the first. As we travelled slowly down the dusty track people would nod and greet us; almost everyone who spoke used Mamma's full name, and only if she responded by stopping the cart and replying to them would they continue the conversation.

'Greetings, Fiuri d'Ursoola.'

'Greetings, Annis. What have you to show me today?'

'Ah, my lady, I have beautiful fabrics all the way from The Promise Land and some very special jewellery. Come and see.'

'I may stop on my way back from the square, Annis; Hal is being auctioned today and should fetch a good price. We shall see.' Then she snapped the reins, cluck-clucked the mules and moved on. Without waiting to be out of earshot she said to me, 'The Promise Land is a myth, Akara. It's a made up story to raise the price of something which has no other provenance, do you understand?'

'Yes, Mamma,' I replied, but as I had no idea what a myth was and there were too many distractions to incline me to ask, the warning passed over my head.

That first visit blurred into many of the subsequent ones until I was three or four years older. I'm afraid I don't remember Hal being sold – I can only imagine it from watching later auctions and from my own experience seven years afterwards. I'm certain that we would have continued to the end of town, where the track opened up into a large square with an imposing two storey, sandstone building facing us at the far end. It would have been crowded, blisteringly hot and noisy, with most attention focused on the large wooden platform in the centre of the square. Mamma would have registered Hal and he would have been led away to the holding pen to wait with the others. I guess Mamma would have started mingling then, speaking to people she felt were worth speaking to, and talking up Hal's price.

I have no idea what Hal's sale fetched that day, or whether we stopped at Annis' stall on the way back. I'm sure we would have called in to a cantina though, because we always did. My mother would have been offered one of the best available tables and I daresay I sat beside her, fascinated by the scene around me. Maidentown had four or five cantinas: large and sturdy shacks with well shaded yards and one or two outbuildings housing stills, presses and the piles of fruit and vegetables that were fed into them. The yards were invariably guarded by large, ferocious looking dogs, secured on lengths of chain which extended just far enough to cover the areas most likely to be vulnerable to theft. Since the dogs themselves were at least as valuable as what they were guarding, there would usually be one or two burly servers to protect the dogs.

As to the customers in the cantinas, they were only ever of the higher castes – Mamma would not have mixed with anyone less - and the spirits, beers and teas would have been more expensive and better quality than the street sellers sold. I would sit quietly, sipping mango juice or chai and watching the carnival of activity in front of me, intrigued by it all.

'Where do they all come from, Mamma?'

'All over the place. Maidentown is famous for its markets and its six monthly auction.'

'Why do they all speak so differently? And they look different too. Why are some of them dark and some white? And some of them are mottled and pock marked, as if they're afflicted or even diseased.' Having been lectured so vehemently and so often on the superiority of a healthy skin I was confused now to see so many imperfect individuals dressed in fine clothes and being treated with the same deference as us.

'They must have personal wealth enough to be here but they have no true value in themselves,' she said, keeping her voice low.

'What's so bad about the way Ash looks then, Mamma? There was nothing wrong with him except for having no hair – you could have just kept him covered up.'

She almost hissed at me, 'Don't mention Ash again, he is dead to us now.' But still, in my heart, I believed that he had run away and, if it were possible, he'd find a way to rise in caste to be like the men and women I saw around me there – easy, confident, powerful people with the means to be in control of their own lives in spite of their impediments.

As I got older, more observant and aware, I noticed that Mamma never paid for our refreshments in the cantinas.

There was always someone – man or woman – quick to provide us with whatever we wanted; eager to find favour with our mother and always full of questions. Tanya was with us for at least three markets before the day she spat at Mamma and was exchanged for the goats, and on those occasions the enquiries were mostly about her. She was much admired, having inherited our mother's fine bone structure and delicate physique, but the questions I heard most often were, 'Is she strong?' and 'Will she be fertile?' Mamma, in her cool and arrogant way would always reply, 'As strong as you'll ever need her to be,' and 'She will be like me, probably late to have her first bleed but the bearer of many healthy children, I am certain.'

I would look at Tanya, sitting straight backed and outwardly impassive, knowing that she was storing up anger for the journey home. Then, once we were away from the main town, she would turn to Mamma and call her a monster, clenching her fists in frustration and bringing down all the curses she could think of.

'I hate you, Mamma! One day the Divinities will punish you and I will be glad.'

'The Divinities have already punished me by sending me a daughter who doesn't appreciate what I've done for her. The sooner I can be rid of you the better. Now drink some water and cover yourself back up; crying has made you dehydrated and you're worthless to me with a shrivelled up skin.'

The rest of the journey was usually travelled in silence.

The cantinas in Maidentown were the very first places I ever saw men with hair on their faces; some had growth above their upper lips and soft, sparse down on their chins, some even had long, luxuriant beards which they decorated with beads and feathers. Once out of the blazing sun the men and women would unwind their turbans and cast off thick, heavy layers from their shoulders, exposing their faces and arms. Most of them had numbers tattooed on their wrists, which Mamma explained were their registration numbers. I wanted to know why I didn't have one, since I knew that I had been formally registered and all my records were kept in order. 'I made the decision to keep you unmarked, Akara. Sometimes the tattoos become infected and it was a risk I wasn't prepared to take. Your Patron, when you get one, may think differently, which will be their choice to make.' Seeing that I was also fascinated by the intricate henna designs painted on some of their hands, arms and necks she continued, 'They're very pretty but they're often used to cover up some blemish or unsightly scar. I want potential buyers to see your perfection, Akara.'

Trips to the town were also the first occasions when I learned about men and women being used to fight for people's entertainment. The fight pits were always on the outskirts of the town, held in old quarries beyond the shabby areas of shanty dwellings which Mamma usually avoided. She explained to me that Maidentown had grown up around what had once been a huge landfill of rubbish, exposed when the big solar catastrophe split the earth and then plundered of anything which could be of use. All that was left now were fly ridden, rat infested dumps that still attracted the truly desperate, in search of something they could trade or eat. If the rats could be caught then Mamma said they made a decent enough meal for someone who was starving, but not for the likes of us, 'They're filthy and diseased, Akara. If you see one you must not go near it. Do you understand?'

'Yes, Mamma,' I replied obediently, wondering why, in that case, she had brought us anywhere near them. On two or three of our visits to the town that I recall, we had wound our way through the maze of shacks, tents and rusty vehicles to one particular place where Mamma would pull up next to the ancient remains of a battered bus. It had long since lost its wheels, mirrors and anything else that could be removed, and rested crookedly in a patch of scrubland under the shade of an enormous kigelia tree. Mamma instructed Tanya and me to stay hidden in the cart, 'Don't move from here while I'm gone. Don't look out or speak to anyone. If you feel in danger then call out and I'll hear you. I won't be long.'

Then she wound her scarf securely around her face and head so that only her eyes were showing, pulled a heavy hessian bag from the back of the cart and stepped down into the dust. She ignored the inquisitive stares and begging hands that followed her and the scrawny, listless men, women and children who were clustered under the shade of the tree. She headed straight for the curtained gap in the side of the bus where once the door had been and disappeared swiftly inside. 'Where's she gone?' I remember asking Tanya, 'What's she doing?' But Tanya just shrugged and said, 'I don't know and I don't care. I only wish she'd never come back.'

I would sit quietly then, disconcerted by the unfamiliar surroundings and the disturbing sounds. I could hear the ugly shouts and cheers from the quarries and only imagine what was going on there, wondering once again why our mother had thought to bring us to this horrible place.

After about ten minutes Mamma would return and the hessian bag would be hanging from her shoulder, empty. She'd make a big thing of brushing the dirt and dust from her clothes before climbing back onto the cart, checking that we were still safely inside, and driving away as quickly as she could.

But apart from a few brief, disturbing moments such as those, Maidentown continued to enthral me, and of course Mamma knew all the best places to go for the highest quality goods and the most reliable traders.

Once Hal, and then Tanya, had gone and Mamma was loath to leave me unprotected in the cart, she would let me join her and watch as she traded. I had to remain covered up as long as we were outside and exposed to the sun, but once we were inside a cantina or well shaded stall I was allowed to remove my headwear and the soft, cotton mittens protecting my hands. That way I could feel the rough texture of the hessians and the smoothness of the exquisite silks, try the sweet smelling creams and the healing ointments and best of all, I could sample the confectionary. There were counters full of sweetmeats made from honey, nuts, cocoa and vanilla nestling alongside little packets of peppermint and sugar cane and golden baked biscuits. There were coffee beans roasting and filling the hot air with their rich, aromatic fumes. To my initial surprise, Mamma encouraged me to try them all. I could have been forgiven for thinking they were treats, rewards for good behaviour, but she soon explained, 'It is important for you to recognise and appreciate the best, Akara. One day your Patron may send you to shop in the markets and you will be expected to be familiar with things and to know what and how to buy. Hawkers will come to your door and try to cheat you if they think you are naive. Knowledge is always power. Do you understand?'

'Yes, Mamma,' *I understand and I won't forget. But that won't stop me pretending that you bought me this wonderful stick of nougat because you love me.*

On the way home Mamma would make me rinse my mouth with spearmint bark to clean my teeth and freshen my breath whilst she listed out loud the things she had bought, sold and bartered that day. And so my education continued; but who she saw and what she did in the burned out bus remained a mystery to me.

7 BEHIND THE SCREENS AND BEYOND

I went on show two days ago. So I'm up for adoption at last and still looking like a savage but feeling very much better in myself. Sourface has brought me a lot more paper, for which I'm very grateful because it keeps me occupied, and I'm becoming accustomed to the rhythm of this place which means I'm keeping calmer and less inclined to panic, though sometimes it's hard not to. In the ten days I've been here there have been two exterminations to my knowledge. One and Five have gone but, as I can't see beyond my immediate and opposite neighbours, I didn't know them. I heard them being taken though, within days of each other; one whimpering and the other fighting all the way. It is the worst thing in the world to hear and is always done at night so that the rest of us have time to get over our distress before being seen by Visitors next day. But the memory never leaves you, the terrible sound of a human animal being dragged unwillingly to their death. It inevitably reminds me of the fight pits.

Jiggs Munro occupies the stall on my right; he is Number Eleven. When I first arrived and was too preoccupied with my own condition to really notice or care he was simply a heap of rags lying on a pallet as far into the corner as it could go. What remains of the stone walls separating the stalls is so full of gaps and badly patched holes that we have better views of our neighbours than we probably should and as the days passed I started to take more notice. Thirteen is the old woman across from me who is a trouble maker. In spite of the best efforts of the Guardians she is a mess; if they wash her she immediately rolls in the dirt and cackles with glee at their dismay; when they attempt to brush her hair she squeals like the devil and shakes them off. She has hardly any teeth but that doesn't make her mouth any less foul and she spends most of the day whispering obscenities at the wall. Unsurprisingly the Visitors are disgusted by her and she stands no chance of being adopted, which means that tomorrow she reaches her Due Death Date and will be gone.

Jiggs Munro, on the other hand, is so quiet you would hardly know he's there. He stays curled up on his bed for as much of the day as he can get away with and the first time I saw him standing up I thought my one good eye must be deceiving me. He is the most enormous creature I have ever seen, quite pale skinned but so covered in tattoos and bruises that, at first glance, you might believe he is black. His body is very thick set and muscular, almost as wide at the shoulders as it is tall and, although his head is bald, he has thick, black stubble on his chin and black eyebrows that almost meet above his very crooked nose. The man is a giant but has the softest, saddest voice I have ever heard.

It was no surprise to learn that Jiggs had been a fighter. He belonged to a cartel of men and women for whom he made a great deal of money until he began losing fights. Then they abandoned him in some deserted place, bloody and beaten from his latest defeat and with nothing to his name except the clothes he was wearing. When an Adoption Centre wagon found him he tried to refuse to be brought here, preferring to be left to die; but he was too weak to resist and they were convinced that they could find him a good, kind home. When Visitors come he retreats to his pallet and I can hear him moaning quietly into his pillow.

We don't get many Visitors. Most people can't afford an adoption fee or, if they can, they go to an auction where they can view the individuals, ask questions and see valid documents. Genuine, quality goods are not expected to end up in a place like The Kennels.

But today someone wanted to see Jiggs. A small woman, holding the hand of a young boy, paused by Stall Eleven long enough to read the notes on the chalk board. She had already discounted me, smiling sympathetically as she passed but clearly not in search of whatever it is I might have to offer. As usual, there was a Guardian hovering behind her and today it was Ridrick-Oola.

'What's this one's story?' asked the woman in a quiet voice.

'Ex fighter,' Ridrick replied, taciturn as ever.

'Yes, I see that from his notes. What about his character? I'm looking for a menial, someone strong to help me with the heavy work. But it also has to be someone I can trust, someone who will be good to my boy and be safe to be left with him when I have to go away.' She looked down at the child by her side who beamed up at her and said, 'Can we see him?'

Ridrick grunted, shifted her considerable weight and called through to Jiggs, 'Get up, Eleven, someone wants to look at you.' The massive shape raised itself from the bed and stood, head hanging, as far away as possible.

'Oh, poor thing,' said the woman, her hand to her mouth in shock at the sight of his injuries. Jiggs didn't move, he didn't even raise his head to look at her.

'Talk to her, Jiggs,' I urged, sensing that this woman might be his one and only chance.

'Be quiet, Ten,' Ridrick admonished, 'This is nothing to do with you.'

'But, Ridrick-Oola, I know -'

'Quiet!'

I sat down and reluctantly held my tongue, but I could see the woman was hesitating and, as she met my eye, she said, 'I would need to hear him speak.' Then, addressing Ridrick, 'Do you have anyone else who might be suitable to show me?'

Ridrick shook her head, 'I'm afraid not, but I do think this one would be perfect for you. He's never given us any trouble and he really deserves a good home.'

'Then I may come back tomorrow and try again.' She put a hand against the wire mesh and peered into the stall, 'Please talk to me, Jiggs Munro.' But Jiggs just stood there and the woman sighed and turned to walk away. Just as they began to walk down the passage the little boy looked over his shoulder, and Jiggs finally looked up. The sweetest smile crossed his face, the first one I had ever seen him raise, and the little boy grinned back. He said something to his mother, she bent down to reply and then they left.

After she'd escorted them out Ridrick came back and spoke to Jiggs who had, by then, returned to his bed and covered himself with blankets in spite of the suffocating heat.

'If they come back tomorrow, Eleven, which I doubt, you must at least make an effort. Did you hear me, Eleven? Do you understand?' There was no response from the blankets and Ridrick waddled off, leaving her distinctive smell behind her.

Do you understand…do you understand… One of my mother's most repeated phrases. My heart constricted at the thought of her. *Yes, I understand, Mamma. Sometimes too much and sometimes not enough.* How do you comprehend a world like this one, where a mother sells her children and a grown man cries into his pillow because he thinks his life is not worth living any more?

I've sat for a long time, thinking and writing, and the

day has drawn to a close. We've had our suppers, slopped out again and waited for the night time candles to be lit. They don't last for long and it's a struggle to read or write by their meagre light anyway, even if you have the advantage of two working eyes, which I don't.

My eighteenth day and a lot has changed in the last week. I think, like Jiggs, I cried myself to sleep that tenth night. In the morning, ashamed of myself, I took care to wash as best I could, comb the sparse little tufts of my hair and tidy up the stall. I was determined to make a good impression. The mirror tells me now that I'm healing well, but back then I could well understand why there had been no interest in me and I knew that, in Ridrick's words, I must at least 'make an effort.'

I spent the first hour of that morning talking to Jiggs, once I'd finally persuaded him to leave his bed.

'You must try, Jiggs. Please. The woman seems nice and she could offer you a good home.'

'You don't know that, Akara,' said Jiggs in his soft, sad voice, 'People canna be trusted.'

'But Jiggs, you only have one week left before your Due Death Date; you can't just give up. I know it's a risk but it has to be better than death, surely.'

'You don't know that either. I've spent twelve years of my life in hell,' he reminded me, 'I'd rather die than go through that again. They kept me in a cage half the size of this and forced me out every day ta fight. I had ta hurt other men and women and sometimes I killed them. The first time I lost a fight they beat me. The second time they tied a rope around my neck and led me miles out into the scrubland before beating me again and leaving me for dead.'

He squeezed his eyes shut to block out the memory and I stretched my hand through the gap to reach for his. But he shook his head and I let him go back to his pallet; there was nothing more I could say.

The hours went slowly that day, and only one Visitor came as far as our end of the passage. It was not the woman from the previous day. That evening Thirteen was taken from her stall; she deliberately pissed herself first, staring me full in the face as she did so and clapping her filthy hands together whilst she chanted, 'You soon, missee high and mighty, you soon.' I tried to look unmoved, as my mother would have instructed me to, but in spite of the old woman's bile I could not. She was pathetic but there was something rather magnificent about her defiance and I admired her spirit. Who knew where she'd come from and what she had been through before ending up here? With a guilty jolt, I realised I didn't even know her real name.

As she was led, giggling and cursing, to the room at the end of the passage I looked into Jiggs' stall and could see the heap of blankets shaking. He had his hands pressed to his ears but I knew there were sounds in his head he could never shut out.

The next day, my twelfth, Jiggs' Visitor came back. She stood in front of his stall, with Mariam hovering nervously beside her, and pulled back her hood so that Jiggs could see her entire face; it was shockingly blotched and pitted but her expression was open and her voice sounded sincere. I liked this woman with her no nonsense manner and her quiet firmness and I was glaring at Jiggs, willing him to see sense.

'Jiggs Munro, I'm here to offer you a home if you will take it.'

Silence.

'I've taken a long time to think about it because you are a big risk. I'm a woman alone with a young son who, for some reason, seems to have taken to you and his welfare is more important to me than anything else in the entire world. Are you hearing me, Jiggs Munro?'

A slight nod of the head from Jiggs, who was finally upright on his bed.

'I know as little about you as you do about me. We will both have to take a lot on trust. Can you read and write?'

Mumbling.

'Speak up, I can't hear you.'

'Yes, lady, a little.'

This surprised me; I had never thought to ask him.

'That's helpful. Are you willing and able to work hard?'

More mumbling.

'Was that a yes? If so, you will have good food to eat, a soft bed to sleep on and honest friendship.'

I think it was that last word that did it for Jiggs. He stood up, lumbered to the front of his stall and burst into tears.

'Very good, then; that's settled,' said the woman, 'I'll go and arrange things.' She pulled up her hood, nodded at Mariam who was almost beside herself with delight, and went off to do the paperwork and pay her fee. Her last words were directed at me: 'I'm sorry,' she said.

As they went down the passage I could hear Mariam chattering all the way, 'Yous made good choice, he's good man. Will be kind to your son and you will be happy.'

Jiggs was released a short while after that and he did try to say goodbye. 'I hope...' he began to say, but couldn't finish. 'I know,' I said, 'Don't worry about me, I'll be alright. And I'm so very happy for you, Jiggs; I think you will have a good life now.'

I really think he will, but I shall miss him.

If Jiggs Munro is the biggest man I've ever seen then Banjo is certainly the handsomest. He's in stall Nine, the one on my left, and I find myself thinking about him a lot, especially since Jiggs left and I have more time on my hands. I pretend to be doing things – washing out a bandage or shifting the screen around - over by the wall between us so that I can spy on him through the gaps. I do it quietly, not wanting to draw attention to myself because I don't want him to see how hideous I am.

Banjo is perfectly proportioned, with skin like smooth chocolate and a face like one of the gods painted on the murals in Malakai's bath house. If I close my eyes when I'm near him I can smell the healthy tang of fresh sweat on his skin after he's exercised, which he does by walking laps of his stall and counting press ups on the floor. I watch his muscles twitching and quivering as he moves and I want to touch them and feel them ripple under my fingers. He wears a red and gold embroidered bolero, open at the chest, and loose pajama pants cuffed just below the knee. His arms and lower legs are bare apart from an ornate silver chain around his left ankle. Though his clothes are a little dirty and the bolero is frayed at the hem I can see they are good quality and he refuses to let them out of his sight to be laundered or changed. I think he washes them out himself at night sometimes.

When Visitors come he stands like a magnificent statue, posing with legs slightly apart and arms folded, and waits until he's spoken to. If someone asks him a question he answers politely in a deep, rich voice but otherwise stays silent. Everyone admires him and almost all the Visitors ask to see his documents, but once they have they immediately seem to lose interest. I don't understand why he hasn't been adopted but as long as he's here I can enjoy looking at him and it takes my mind off other things.

Another thing I can't understand is why Sourface has shown no interest in drawing him. Yesterday, when the Guardian came to me with more paper and a freshly sharpened pencil, I plucked up the courage to ask him. He shrugged, 'He's of no interest to me.'

'But why?' I lowered my voice, 'He's so perfect.'

'I have my reasons, Ten. And now, if I can distract you for long enough, I should like to draw you. And I'd like you to remove your eye patch.' He settled himself on the stool and got out his materials; when he realised I hadn't moved he looked at me quizzically.

I shrank back against the wall. I had only been taking the patch off when absolutely necessary, to bathe my eye or late at night when I wanted to let the cooler air get at it. I didn't want anyone to see me without it and, posing in my usual position on the bed, I would be visible to Banjo through the gap in the wall if he chose to look.

'Why would you want to draw me like that?' I argued, 'This is how I'm going to look from now on, why draw me any other way?'

'Always questions with you, Ten. Once again, I have my reasons.' He paused, then added pointedly, 'How is your own drawing going?' It was his way of reminding me that I owed him for all the paper he supplied me with, so I retreated to my pallet and sat, hoping that Banjo would not choose today to suddenly be curious about me. I took a deep breath and slowly undid the little buckle on the leather band around my head, letting the patch fall away into my hand and keeping my head low.

'Look at me, Ten,' said Sourface, not unkindly.

When I looked up and faced him I expected him to wince or even turn away, but he looked at me steadily and said, 'It's not so bad, Ten. There will be scars and I doubt you'll ever see with that eye properly again, but it's not so bad.' Then he adjusted himself on the stool and began to draw.

I thought I'd detected a softer tone to his voice than usual so I decided to push a little.

'Why has no one claimed Banjo or adopted him?'

'You're very interested in Nine, aren't you? Why would that be, I wonder?'

I couldn't think of a plausible reason other than admitting to my infatuation with him, so I didn't answer. We sat in silence for a while before I ventured another question.

'What should I be doing, Adelmo d'Afrar, to stand a chance of being wanted by someone?'

'Well, the fact that you can read and write is helpful. What other skills do you have?'

'I can dance. And sing a little. And I'm fully intact - I feel sure that I could bear healthy children once I'm completely well again.'

'Have you had a bleed since you've been here? Can Mariam or any of the other Guardians vouch for it?'

'No, not yet, but - '

He waved a hand dismissively, 'What else?'

'If I had my documents you would see.'

'But you don't have them, child. And it's no good sulking, Ten; it's a fact.'

'I know,' I grumbled, 'I don't need to be reminded.' I expected to be scolded for impertinence, but instead Sourface smiled kindly and put down his drawing to look at me directly. He studied my scowling face for a moment and then sighed, 'It's true that certificates and records are important, Ten; but even documents aren't everything you know. Nine has documents, but in his case they won't help at all.'

'Why not?'

He leaned forward and in little more than a whisper said, 'Because Banjo's Patron bought him to breed from and he failed to impregnate her. And whilst his documents are all up to date, and perfectly in order, his report has nothing good to say about him. I'm afraid he stands no more chance of being adopted than you do.'

8 HIDE AND SEEK

Of course Surrana guessed that I was going to look for Myrah, but that wasn't all I had in mind. There was no escaping the fact that the watering hole was drying up and, along with it, the already meagre supply of animals that depended on it. The vegetation around the camp was rapidly shrivelling and every morning there were fewer insects in the nets. I knew that we would have to move on and that we had no choice but to follow other desperate outcasts to one of the very places where we were least welcome.

The closest boomtown to the camp was Maidentown, which I'd first visited when we were selling pots of piss to the tanners who'd set up on its fringes. It had seemed exciting and fun when I was with Jiggs but now, exploring it more thoroughly on my own, the smells and sounds frightened and disgusted me. The outskirts of any town attract the lowest castes, the roughest trades and the most unpleasant activities that must all be kept away from the sensitive ears and noses of the upper castes living and conducting business in the centres. But at least in the shanty district I was not alone in being afflicted and my pale skin, blue eyes and white hair did not attract too much attention; almost everyone was damaged or disfigured in some way and the White Disease so common that most sufferers did not even bother to cover themselves up. But as you got into the town itself that changed and I soon learned that leaving myself exposed was both humiliating and dangerous.

The first time I went, uncovered, with some small trinket to sell to one of the traders on the main thoroughfare he simply turned away from me. I went on to the next stall and was told to leave before she reported me to the Registrar and had me thrown onto a charnel pyre.

'Fukk off and fry!' the woman spat at me, 'You and your filthy kind should all be burned. Go on, back to the hole you came from.'

Her shouting attracted a crowd and soon there was a mob surrounding me, keeping their distance in case I infected them but ready with stones and rocks to throw if I didn't get on my way. 'There's nothing wrong with me, I'm as good as you are,' I shouted back and I was ready to stand up for myself and fight, but I thought of Surrana and how she would manage without me if I was injured, or died, and I bowed my head and ran. I was angry and ashamed of myself and couldn't face anyone when I first got back to camp. I went to Gordie's Creek and sat on Jiggs' favourite rock, letting myself get chilled to the bone as the sun set and night fell. Chapstick perched nearby and watched me cry, mewling every now and then to remind me that she hadn't been fed.

Eventually I got sick of the cat complaining and we walked back to camp. Some of the older men and women were hunched over the fire, talking, whilst most of the others were gathered round them in groups, listening and looking anxious; Surrana was amongst them. She beckoned me over and I joined her, leaving Chapstick to be fed and fussed over by some of the children who hadn't yet gone to bed.

'Things are very bad,' Surrana said, 'worse than I realised.'

'I know,' I said, taking her hand, 'but don't worry; I'm going to take care of you, I promise.' And it was that promise that kept me going after that; if I couldn't be a friend to Jiggs, or a hero for Myrah, then I would be a provider and protector for the new mother who was all that I had left in the world, as far as I knew.

So I returned to Maidentown every few days, but always from then on covered from head to foot and trying to be as inconspicuous as possible. I didn't expect to see Myrah, as I was sure she had long since been sold and probably taken elsewhere by her Patron, but I looked out for her anyway. As for Jiggs, I had no idea where he might be, but certainly not in Maidentown or I was sure he would have found a way to get back to the camp by then. Now I was searching for something else: a new place for us to live that would be safe and secure, and with opportunities for me to provide adequately for Surrana. But the more I discovered about Maidentown the more I realised how limited our choices were because of the way I looked. Surrana had registration documents and an acceptable appearance – she could have offered herself as a server at least and been taken into someone's household. But I had no status and nothing obvious to offer, which meant I didn't even get the chance to prove I had a fully functioning dick. If all I could do was use my gift for procuring and bartering then we needed to be close to the Maidentown markets to trade, but also near to people and places that could supply me, and that meant living in the shanties.

Even in the shanty towns some settlements are better, or a lot worse, than others. I explored most of them in my search. Areas that had shady trees and a nearby, reasonably reliable water supply or reservoir were the most desirable of course, but already overpopulated. Away *from those, and further out, were the squats that had built up around old quarries and rubbish sites, both of which had long since been plundered of anything useful to someone like me. They were also the places where the fight pits were set up and I had no intention of going anywhere near them. As it was the awful sounds often drifted across, even into Maidentown itself when the air was particularly still and clear, and gave me a sick feeling in my gut; reminding me of times and feelings I didn't want to be reminded of any more.*

I reported back to the camp after every trip, being honest about everything I'd seen and heard. I usually managed to go back with some food as well, though there was never enough to go round. We kept the children fed as well as we could but people were getting weaker every day, falling sick and dying. The skeetos brought malaria and few of us were strong enough to survive it. The burial mounds became piled high with rotting bodies that even the jackals, the ghostly scavengers of the night, would not come near. Only the vultures and insects came back to our camp to feast.

In the end Surrana and I agreed that we must take our chances in the shanties. No one wanted to come with us; those that were left in the camp were already too weak to travel or preferred to stay where they were, not trusting that we would meet with the kindness and tolerance we were hoping for. My mother and I packed up all that we could into our wooden handcart and distributed what was left amongst our neighbours. When I went to pick up Chapstick she backed away and hissed at me.

'You'll have to leave her behind,' Surrana said, 'the children will look after her.'

'Oh, I know,' I said, 'and she's perfectly capable of catching things for herself now, I've seen her do it. But she was Jiggs's cat and I think he'd want me to keep her with

me. Just till we find him again.'

We spent an hour or more trying to coax that fukking cat into the cart. She hissed, she bit, she scratched; she arched her back and circled round us on her tiptoes with an evil snarl on her face and eventually we gave up.

'Fukk you,' I said, 'Surrana's right, we should leave you here. You can fukk off and fry, for all I care!'

Surrana and I each took a handle of the cart and began our slow and painful journey towards town. We had piled the cart as high as we dared and every bump and jolt risked us losing something. After every fifty paces or so we paused, caught our breath and looked back to see if we had left anything on the track. Eventually the camp became just a distant collection of shapes on the horizon; we stopped to take one last look at it, squinting to make it out in the orange haze, when there, suddenly, was the cat - galloping towards us like a little black demon and mewling for something to eat.

Chapstick lived a good long time with us in Maidentown. We were there for seven or eight years and she died just before we had taken the final decision to move on again. The only time she ever allowed me to pick her up was when she was dying; I sat with her in my lap and heard that funny growling sound in her throat that Jiggs always said meant she was happy.

9 BEETLE, ASH AND MALAKAI

I was about five when Beetle was born. Who helped Mamma with the birth I don't know; maybe Tanya, possibly even Ash. Perhaps she managed all by herself, having had so much practice. Nor do I know who Beetle's pappa was as I don't recall a male in the household at the time apart from my older brother; but whoever he was Mamma must have considered him suitable, and then been horrified when her poor little deformed baby was born. Although apparently healthy in every other way, Beetle had an oddly formed right leg which I believe might have led Mamma to abandon him at birth if she had not seen a purpose in keeping him for my sake. Tanya never displayed any interest in him at all, except when instructed to by our mother, but I loved Beetle from the very start and begged to look after him.

Mamma refused to give her new-born a proper name and he was never registered; he started crawling at four months and Mamma said he looked so awkward he was more like a scuttling dung beetle than a human child. So that's how he got his name and, although it was Mamma's milk that fed him, it was my voice that sang to him, my arms that held him and my hands that changed the cloth nappies he wore until he was almost six. In every other way he was remarkably advanced and quick to learn and this, along with two other reasons, was why our mother kept him.

The first reason was that she saw in me a natural instinct to nurture and recognised the value this might add if I was bought to be bred from, or to look after another woman's children.

The second reason was that Beetle had a gift for healing. From the time he could walk he was fascinated by plants and flowers and quickly learned all their names and their various properties: which ones were poisonous, which were edible and which could be turned into medicines. As soon as she recognised this gift Mamma naturally began to exploit it by selling the liniments and creams at Maidentown market, where they soon became quite famous. When Beetle reached the age of seven he was allowed to come to the markets with us as long as he stayed hidden under the sackcloth cover of the cart; we knew no one must ever discover that our mother had a failure in her brood, since her entire reputation was built upon her ability to bear perfect children.

If someone needed to be examined in order to choose the right remedy for their ailment, Beetle would be allowed to do so as long as he never let anyone see his leg; it had to be kept covered at all times and, since he couldn't be seen to limp, he had to remain on the cart. Mamma would arrange him at the front on cushions, with a large blanket draped over his lap and his apothecary boxes set beside him. His little childish face would peep out solemnly from under his hood and I would think how sweet and adorable he was, dispensing medicines with all the confidence and authority of a wise old man.

I gradually came to realise how exceptional we d'Fiuri offspring were, compared with the undernourished, sickly individuals I saw in the outskirts of the town and on the highways as we travelled to and fro. Most of them carried signs of the White Disease, although that in itself didn't shock me any more. I had always known it wasn't catching, unlike some sicknesses, but Mamma's attitude towards the poor, ragged children of Maidentown went beyond contempt; it was almost like fear – as if hunger and desperation really were contagious. 'Don't look at them, Akara. And don't ever touch them. Do you understand?'

'Of course, Mamma.'

But one day, when I was still very young, I had an encounter which would have made Mamma very, very angry had she ever found out about it. It happened when Ash took me on one of our forbidden adventures beyond the croft, not long before the time when I got stung, and we had ventured too far into the bush. As usual Ash was concentrating on the ground and I was skipping along beside him, lost in my own little world. We had long since dismissed rumours of wild animals roaming the area since we had never seen any but the insects were, as usual, a constant irritant and distraction. Of course, after the encounter with the hornet I took greater care and once Ash had gone I lost the desire to explore anyway; I preferred to stay at home with Beetle and between us we concocted a pungent skin lotion which seemed to repel most things – including Mamma. She complained bitterly at the smell, but since it proved so effective she encouraged me to use it, especially at night when even the thickest mosquito nets were not entirely effective, and whenever I was outside - except, of course, when we were going to the camps or to the markets when it would not have been appropriate for me to smell 'like a boar's backside,' as she put it. Very occasionally, if my brothers were busy elsewhere and the sun was low in the sky and at its weakest, I was allowed to run and play freely in the yard entirely naked. Mamma believed this maintained my even colour and helped build up my resistance and the sessions were strictly regulated according to the revolutions of the mules around the grindstone: three circuits and I was called in, thoroughly inspected for bites or sunburn, moisturised and covered up again.

Mamma was a firm believer in respecting nature's power, but not worshipping it. She had no time for sects or religious groups, especially those which congregated in Maidentown and detracted from what she considered to be the more important business of trading. Naturally I was fascinated by them, intrigued by their sometimes bizarre headdresses, melodic chants and the intoxicating smell of incense which seemed to hang like a shifting cloud around them all. I would see them gathering for ceremonies in front of their shrines and makeshift altars, offering up prayers and harvest sacrifices.

'Why waste good food?' Mamma would say, 'The fruit will only shrivel and the grain will scorch and be no use to anyone. It will make no difference to the sun, and the rains will come when they're ready. People' she added, 'are stupid, Akara.'

'Yes, Mamma,' I agreed; but I watched them anyway and found myself envying them. They were comfortable hugging each other, holding hands or draping an arm casually around one another's shoulders, and it seemed natural in the way that I had been with Ash and then Beetle, but never with my own mother. I found myself looking out for other families and studying their behaviour but it was hard to make comparisons. The wretched poor seemed to have no energy for affection and the higher castes, almost without exception, seemed to be of my mother's conviction that love had no place in the world.

But I wanted to tell you about the day that Ash and I encountered the mad woman and how I first learned that my half brother was not the only one of his kind. We'd been beating our way through a swathe of tall, dry grass – our eyes fixed downwards in the hope of spotting treasure that hadn't already been salvaged by someone else. Ash always had a bag slung over his shoulder to collect anything which could be turned into something useful or ornamental: shards of tin, bleached bones and pottery were good finds, and shells, feathers and snake skins were highly prized and could be sold or bartered. Valuable discoveries from the time before the catastrophe were rare, having long since been swallowed up by the shifting earth or discovered by earlier foragers; but that day we'd done well. We'd come across an old car seat which was still sturdy enough to sit on and Ash had camouflaged it with grass and rocks so that he could come back for it later. Then I spotted something glinting in the dust: a shiny, gold metal bottle top shaped, where it had long since been flattened, in a corona like the sun. Ash had been delighted with it, promising to turn it into something pretty for me when we got home.

So we had been very absorbed and perhaps had walked further than Ash had intended. I was probably tired and hungry but I wouldn't have complained; if Ash was prepared to keep going then so was I. Suddenly something stumbled through the grass ahead and before we could react and run, stopped dead in front of us. It was a woman, bare breasted and panting and looking every bit as wild as the animals we had been warned about. She was as pale as anything I had ever seen, not mottled or pockmarked but with patches of reddened skin peeling here and there, and threads of bright blue veins running like a network of streams across her body. She had not a single hair on her head or face – no eyelashes, brows or anything - but a fine, blonde down peeping out from her armpits. We all stared at each other for a moment, speechless with surprise. It was the first time I had seen someone almost as hairless as Ash and I suppose it was the first time he had too. After a while the woman moved towards us with a raised hand and Ash pushed me behind him.

'Don't be afraid,' said the woman, looking agitated, 'I'm not here to hurt you, I just want to look.' She seemed intrigued by Ash, as if he was something strange and special but not repellent, or maybe it was because she recognised their similarity. When she lifted her hand tentatively to touch his face he flinched but stood his ground, I think he was determined to show he was not afraid. The wild woman came closer, cupped his face in her hands and giggled delightedly. She looked at me, but only briefly, 'Pretty' she murmured, but it was Ash she meant. Then she turned round and ran off through the grass, back the way she had come.

Ash immediately took my hands in his and knelt down to speak to me as earnestly as he had ever done, 'We mustn't tell Mamma about this ever, Akara. She would never forgive me for putting you in such danger. And,' he added, knowing this would be the most effective warning, 'she would punish me really badly.' 'Yes, Ash; I understand,' I replied. Then he lifted me onto his shoulders and carried me home. We never spoke of it again and, of course, not long after that came the incident with the hornet when I think Mamma must have punished him very badly indeed.

I met Malakai for the first time on the day he bought me, though I'd seen him talk to Mamma on a few occasions before then. As I approached my fourteenth birthday Mamma held increasingly long conversations with high caste people, particularly in the cantinas. She would settle me on the kilim cushions, in the light most flattering to my face, and leave me with blended tea or sweet syrup to sip while she conducted business. I was not allowed coffee or anything to eat which might make my breath unpleasant and I had a large palm leaf fan to help me keep cool. If I did sweat I was instructed to use one of my small cotton handkerchiefs and to dab, not wipe. At home, Mamma spent hours teaching me how to carry out every action with the grace of a dancer and to always, *always* behave as if someone was watching me. 'Even in the water closet, Mamma?' I asked disingenuously and was met with such a look that I resolved never to test Mamma's sense of humour again; she simply didn't have one. To begin with it felt silly having to treat every single movement as if it was significant and might be being observed, whether it was scratching my nose or lifting a spoon to my mouth, but I remembered how my lovely sister Tanya used to achieve it somehow and through copying her it eventually became second nature to me too. Besides, if Mamma caught me doing something wrong or fidgeting unnecessarily she would give me one of her fierce looks and I feared those more than anything.

Needless to say I rarely received praise from my mother, but I discovered for myself that all our hard work was paying off because I learned the art of listening to conversations whilst appearing not to, and heard a great deal more than Mamma ever would have told me herself. There were many enquiries about me, and particularly about the price Mamma expected to achieve for me at auction. 'She will sell for as much as I can get for her,' Mamma would say, 'and there is a great deal of interest in her.'

'Can you be certain she will breed successfully?' asked one man who was accompanied by a tall, thin woman dressed in a finely embroidered robe, with a collection of colourful beads around her neck and wrists. 'I'm looking for a mate for my son when he comes of age.' He indicated the small boy between them who looked to be two or three years younger than me. 'My daughter,' said Mamma, 'has been a woman for nearly two years and her bleeds are very regular, she also has a mother who has produced six healthy children of her own; the chances are excellent.' How convenient, I thought, to acknowledge Beetle and Ash when it suited her to. The little boy glanced shyly in my direction and I smiled at him; he smiled back, but his mother looked me up and down with a disdainful expression on her face as if determined to find me lacking. I could feel my back straighten automatically under her scrutiny and sense Mamma silently urging me to lift my chin and not be intimidated. Then the woman turned away from me, addressed my mother with more questions and ignored me for the rest of the conversation. Although I couldn't hear much of what was said after that I knew they must be considering me because they talked for so long and Mamma showed them my documents, which she wouldn't have done unless they were serious buyers. Afterwards she said to me, 'You did well this morning,' and I was so happy to have pleased her. Encouraged by her good humour I asked, 'Who was the man in the second cantina we went to? The one who stayed covered up the whole time.'

'His name is Malakai. He's come all the way from the north west and says he intends to buy a good many servers at today's market. I shall want to watch, to see if he's as good as his word.'

'Is he interested in me, Mamma?'

'He says so, Akara, but I've told him he will have to wait and bid along with everyone else.'

I thought about this for a while, wondering first about the unnamed little boy and then about Malakai, the covered up man with the dark shades over his eyes; I knew that shades generally signified a certain degree of wealth since they were so hard to come by and cost a great deal, and this inspired another thought, 'Does Malakai have camels, Mamma?'

'I don't know yet. That's something I may find out this afternoon.'

And then, as if there was the remotest chance that she would care I added, 'Because I'd like to go to someone who has camels.'

Meanwhile, out in the cart, Beetle was learning things too. He would peek out through the flap whilst Mamma and I were elsewhere and watch and listen as Maidentown bustled around him. Mamma always left the cart on the main thoroughfare for safety and there was plenty to keep my little brother entertained. Once we were safely home he'd tell me all about what he'd seen and heard and the hours we spent alone together were my happiest. In spite of everything, Beetle had been a cheerful baby and grew into a sweet natured little boy: kind, inquisitive and eager to please. His twisted leg didn't cause him any pain and we used to support it with a splint so that it was easier and quicker for him to move around. I'd been teaching him to read - something Mamma didn't object to as it meant he could now write down the recipes for all his potions and creams – and my clever little brother was quick and eager to learn.

Mamma usually acquired paper from Sinn Rhys The Peddlar, one of the few visiting hawkers she trusted, in exchange for a jar or two of the delicious honey which was one of our main trading currencies. The success of our productive hives was a source of great pride to Mamma, but also her biggest torment. When Ash disappeared Mamma was forced to tend the bees herself, not wishing to risk Tanya or me getting stung. She would wrap herself up in several layers of clothes and netting, but somehow one or two always managed to find a way in and sting her. Then her eyes would redden and swell up and her body would be covered in burning, itchy bumps which drove her half mad. Nothing she tried gave her relief, until the day her least favoured child came up with a remedy. Beetle must have saved her life more than once when she was stung so badly that she could hardly breathe through her swollen throat, but I never heard her even say thank you. As soon as she considered he was old enough Beetle was put in charge of the hives and as far as I know he wasn't stung once.

The bees produced more honey than ever under Beetle's care and we began taking some to market, along with his remedies and our goats' milk cheese which we kept wrapped in dampened muslin cloths to keep cool, along with the poultry eggs. There was something comforting and hypnotic about the gentle rattle of the clay pots and stone jars as we trundled along and Beetle and I would often doze for the first part of the journey, his head in my lap, quite content under the shade of the sackcloth. Then as we neared the town the noise and smells around us would wake us and Mamma would expect us to be alert, and for me to be ready to display myself if required.

One of Beetle's favourite occupations when left on his own in the cart was to study the posters which were nailed to large wooden boards on the edges of the main square. Some were notices of coming auctions and markets, others were put there by people looking for missing servers or Protégés and were usually headed 'LOST, STOLEN OR ESCAPED'. Then there would be a list of identifying features and sometimes a likeness drawn beneath it if the person could afford an artist to create one. Poorer people had to rely on their own skills and, since most couldn't read or write or buy good paper, their notices were badly drawn and generally ignored. I suppose people would visit an Adoption Centre if they wanted someone back badly enough and thought they were worth the fee, but I didn't know about places like this back then. I did once ask Mamma if we could put a poster up for Ash in case anyone had seen him, but she silenced me with a look and I knew better than to ask again.

The afternoon we went to watch Malakai at the auction he spent a great deal of money and even Mamma was impressed; he bought four men and a woman, all of whom he inspected personally beforehand whilst the Registrar hovered beside him. When he and the Registrar went inside to exchange documents and money, Mamma bought a pitcher of fresh water and we sat under the awning of a nearby cantina, waiting until Malakai came out. As soon as he emerged, accompanied by a server holding up a large parasol, Mamma approached him and they stood for a while, talking earnestly and occasionally glancing my way. When I was certain they weren't looking, I would look across to Beetle waiting on the cart, his little face peeking out from the curtains of the canopy with wide eyed curiosity and his usual cheerful grin.

On the way home, as the day faded into a powdery dusk and a slight breeze began to stir the dusty air, Mamma looked to the sky and predicted a sand storm. That meant all the animals would need to be brought in to the out-houses, if we could get back in time, and everything secured as much as possible; losing livestock, crops or possessions was a disaster we could not afford. What preparations we needed to make were all Mamma could think and talk about for the rest of the journey, so I didn't hear more about Malakai until the next day, by which time the worst of the sand storm had swept past us on the horizon. Even so, it was a scary night. We'd covered the mouth of the well with a tarpaulin weighed down with rocks, but it cracked like a whip with every gust of wind and I knew – in spite of her expressionless face – that Mamma was worried; if our water supply got exposed to the dust and became contaminated we were in real trouble because our lives depended on it. Everything clattered and banged so alarmingly that, as soon as he was sure Mamma wasn't looking, Beetle left his wooden cot and crept in with me. I drew the curtain around my bed and we cuddled, whispering to each other for comfort until exhaustion overtook us and we slept. The last I saw of Mamma she was sitting quite still, her exquisite face lit by one flickering oil lamp, just watching, listening and waiting. I don't think she slept at all that night. In the morning she and Beetle let out the livestock and cleared up the scattered debris. Everything was coated in a fine film of acrid orange dust, blown from the south and tinged with a strange, almost metallic smell. I offered to help but Mamma said no, I was to stay indoors pressing hemp oil or churning milk and taking care not to stain or bruise my hands.

'Malakai is very keen to have you, Akara, if you remain in perfect condition. He says he doesn't want to breed from you but to keep you intact as his Protégé and hostess; that way you remain an investment as well as an ornament. It will be a very comfortable and prestigious position by all accounts, since he has a great deal of wealth and a fine home with plenty of fertile land and fresh water. You will be lucky to have him as your Patron if he decides to buy you.'

'Yes, Mamma. Does he - ?

'Don't ask me, Akara. He hasn't bought you yet, so whether he has camels is neither here nor there.'

10 BANJO

At the end of my third week here two significant things happened: Banjo finally spoke to me and I learned a secret.

Sourface was not on duty for several days and I started to worry that I would run out of paper; I've been learning how to write and draw with my left hand and I'm getting quite good at it. I've also been trying to remember the songs and poems I used to recite to Beetle, copying them out and illustrating them.

'Where's Adelmo?' I asked Mariam, knowing she would be the Guardian most likely to tell me.

'He sometimes get sick, cariad,' she told me in her sweet, lilting voice, 'Took himself to be safe, keep sickness away from here.'

'When will he be back?' *When can I get more paper?*

'When he's better,' said Mariam, reasonably. She was busy putting new straw down on the floor; it was by no means fresh but considerably better than what she had swept up and taken away to be burned. She had also borrowed a blanket from Jiggs' empty stall, which I was surprised had not been immediately re-occupied, and put it on my pallet with the forecast that the nights were getting much colder and she was hopeful there would soon be rain.

As she said it, she lifted a small gold cross on a chain from around her neck and pressed it to her lips, 'Please the Divinities,' she whispered and then slipped it back inside her robe. She was wearing one of her towering, turban like head dresses which was so heavy that, every time she dipped her head one way or another, it was in danger of toppling off. She spent so much time holding it up or pushing it back into place that I wondered how it could possibly be worth the effort, although watching her battle with the precarious creations on her head was one of the few things that made me smile and I think that pleased her.

'So pretty when you smiles, Ten. Try smiles when Visitors come so they see how good you are.'

'It makes no difference, Mariam; no-one is ever going to want me.'

'They will, cariad, they will,' and she reached out to place a hand on my head, bristly now with its growth of new hair. 'You smiles more and people will want you,' but I'm not convinced. She finished bustling around the stall, tidying and cleaning as if she were my server rather than my gaoler which, in my old life with Malakai, she would have been. Then, after making one more adjustment to the floppy headdress, she looked around nervously before tucking something under my pillow. As she closed and padlocked the door behind her she put the tips of her fingers to her mouth and shook her head. I nodded and waited until she was out of sight before going to my bed and reaching under the pillow to find what she had left there. It was a small handful of brazilia nuts.

This act of kindness and generosity overwhelmed me and I could only sit and stare at this unexpected bounty, pondering how much she must have paid or traded for such delicacies and wondering how I was going to open them.

'Give them to me,' said a voice nearby.

'What?' I looked up, startled, expecting to see Gareff or Sourface by the door.

'Give them to me,' Banjo repeated and he thrust his arm through the gap in the wall between us. When I didn't reply he withdrew his arm and his handsome face replaced it, 'I'll open them for you.'

'How?' I said.

'It's easy. I only need to wait for the right moment so I don't draw anyone's attention.' When I hesitated he added, 'Neither of us would want Sweet Mariam to get into trouble, would we?' and winked at me. My heart fluttered at the wink. I went to the gap in the wall to pass the nuts through and he snatched them away so quickly I immediately regretted it, thinking he had tricked me after all. But then a voice by the door made me realise why Banjo had been so quick to pull away and how bad it could have been for us if he hadn't.

'And how is The Queen Bee today? Not writing I see.' Gareff's eyes darted from my face to the gap in the wall and I stepped forward to distract him, 'No, Gareff, I'm short of paper. I was hoping Adelmo would be back soon.'

'Ah, of course. I'm sure we all hope that, Ten. Meanwhile the world must be deprived of his little pet's scribblings; what a tragedy for us all.'

I was surprised to hear that I was considered a favourite of Adelmo's; it was not the impression he had given me and I wondered whether it was just another excuse for Gareff to dislike me. His gaze swept slowly round my stall and back to the hole in the wall. I don't know if he noticed, as I did, that Banjo had quietly replaced some of the loose bricks in the gap, but if he did he said nothing. He merely sighed dramatically, as if somehow very disappointed in me, and made a big show of taking the lid off the pot he was carrying and inhaling the aroma of the luscious honey inside. Then he turned slowly away and shuffled the few steps to Banjo's stall where, with another exaggerated gesture, he held out a small piece of dripping honeycomb. I guessed Banjo dropped to his knees because I heard Gareff murmuring, 'Good boy. You're a good, sweet boy,' before continuing down the passage, dispensing honey to the chosen few as he went.

There was silence from Banjo's stall then. I suddenly imagined him sitting and sucking at the honeycomb, maybe dipping *my* brazilia nuts in its sweet stickiness, and I was angry. Most of all I was angry with myself for trusting him just because he was so beautiful. I'd wanted to feel the touch of his hand, and it was beyond simply needing the comfort of human contact; Banjo stirred something new in me, a different longing from the one I had for Beetle or Ash, and I realised Mamma was right: feelings made you weak.

I sat on my pallet for a long time, staring at the marks on the wall that counted down my days and feeling utter despair. Of the five Visitors we've had in the last six days only one paused for long enough to take a proper look at me and it was just out of curiosity. If Banjo, who is as perfect a creature as it's possible to be, cannot get adopted then what chance do I have?

The day faded and a welcome chill settled on The Kennels; there is usually about an hour each evening when the fierce heat of the day is replaced by a delicious coolness, before the temperature begins to plummet to near freezing and we long for the sun to come up on another blistering day. Mariam came back with a supper of lentils and soya beans in gravy and, forgetting her earlier kindness, I refused to take the bowl or even look at her. She spoke to me but eventually, getting no reply, she placed the bowl on my stool and left. Still I sat, with so much hurt and anger and fear inside me that I didn't know where to put it, except on paper; but I had lost the urge to write. I wrapped myself in blankets and tried to hug myself to sleep.

I didn't rise to empty my slop bucket when the night Guardians came to flush down the gullies and I could hear them asking each other, 'What's the matter with Ten? Is she ill?' They tried to rouse me but I didn't respond. Someone came in, bent over and shook me roughly but I didn't move. 'Well,' the Guardian said, 'I'll empty the slop bucket for you this time, but tomorrow you see the physician if you're no better. Do you understand, Ten?'

Yes, I understand. And I know that if I'm considered too sick to be worth adopting then my Due Death Date will be brought forward and I'll be taken down the passage to be exterminated. I don't care. I really don't care anymore, so please just leave me alone.

I heard the heavy mesh door clang shut, the contents of the bucket slosh into the gutter and the Guardian return. He put the bucket back in the corner and replaced its wooden lid, for which I should at least have thanked him - especially as I was perfectly capable of doing it myself. The evening noises of clattering buckets and banging doors continued until, finally, we were considered settled for the night. I heard someone further down the passage whimpering and wondered if it was their turn to die tonight; but the unnatural hush that usually signals an extermination didn't occur, the wall torches outside our stalls were lit as normal and Kennel life continued its strange, predictable rhythm.

Then, once again, I was startled by his voice. It made my heart thrill, in spite of my fury with him, and though I kept silent I lay rigid on my bed waiting to hear it again.

'She's right,' he repeated. 'Mariam. She's right.'

I shifted slightly on the pallet, just to let him know that I was awake, but still I didn't respond.

'You look much better when you smile, Ten. You should do it more for the Visitors.'

I'm listening.

'I cracked the nuts for you.'

I lifted my head at this and turned to face him, not sure whether to believe him, but there he was at the gap, with more of the stones and crumbling mortar removed so that

94

his entire upper half was visible, and his arm stretched out towards me. I stood up and walked over to him and he carefully dropped five shelled brazilias into my hands.

'How did you do it, Banjo?' I must have seemed more incredulous than grateful.

'It was easy. I told you it would be. I just bashed them with a stone when all the other noise was going on.' I suppose I must have had a rather stupid expression on my face because he peered at me curiously, 'Haven't you ever cracked a nut?'

'No,' I replied, honestly, 'I was never allowed to. Someone else always did it for me.'

He laughed, and I thought he didn't believe me.

'It's true,' I said, in my coldest voice, 'I had people like *you* to do the menial tasks.' His face fell and then took on an expression of such wounded pride that I was ashamed; he had been nice to me and I had insulted him. I didn't know how to apologise without making things worse. We both stood for a moment, saying nothing, and just as he was about to turn away I held out my hand and said, 'Please take one. It was very kind of you and I'd like to share them.' After a moment he took it and nodded, though he didn't smile. I watched him bite into it, his teeth brilliantly white against the creaminess of the nut, and I was overwhelmed again by his beauty. We ate two more of the remaining three nuts and the last one I saved for the occupant of Twelve.

Twelve, the stall diagonally opposite to my right, is occupied by a female child., as far as I can tell. It is hard to be sure because very little is visible of the tiny figure shrouded in rags, apart from an enormous pair of dark eyes. Whenever I look across, those eyes seem to be watching me, but the child never speaks. All the time the old woman in Thirteen was ranting and cursing the little girl took no notice, as if she couldn't even hear her although she must have done. Maybe she is mute, no-one seems to know. She eats, she sleeps, she pisses and craps and does what she is told but never says a word. Finally, that night, I had something I could offer her and, when I'd made sure she was watching me as usual, I tried to throw the nut into her stall. But it bounced against the wire mesh of the door and landed on the floor of the passage, perilously close to the gully. I was sorry to think of it going to waste, but more alarmed at the thought of it being discovered. Mariam had trusted me with her secret – the cache of delights she kept in her oversized headdress; even if she had acquired them legitimately it was certain that she should not be sharing them with inmates. I wouldn't be able to forgive myself if she was found out because of my stupidity and the poorness of my aim.

'Can you reach it?' I whispered as loudly as I dared, 'Can you get your arm through and reach it, Twelve?'

The little girl just stared at me, not a flicker of understanding on her face.

'Please, Twelve. Try to put your arm through the wire and get the nut.' I gestured as I said it, trying to demonstrate what I wanted her to do. Banjo joined in with encouraging words too, but I knew he was fearful of disturbing Eight, who couldn't be trusted not to give us away.

'Just pick up the fukkin' nut,' growled a voice from the stall on my right; I had no idea there was anyone in there. I hadn't been able to see into Eleven since Jiggs had gone and the Guardians had been in to repair and patch up the stall while it was empty. I was completely unaware that it had been re-occupied. When had the new inmate arrived? How could I not have known?

Banjo and I were both stunned into silence, but the little girl blinked as if suddenly woken up, eased her slender arm under the bottom of the stall door and retrieved the nut; then she wiped it on the hem of her robe and began to nibble at it.

I looked into Banjo's stall and he shrugged and shook his head; no Kennel gossip had reached him about our new neighbour, it seemed. I tried a tentative, 'Hello?' and was met with a surly, 'Fukk off and let me sleep.'

Banjo and I didn't speak again that night but I still went to my pallet elated. We had eaten contraband together and he had forgiven me, I think, for my ill chosen words. I sat on the bed, hugging my knees and watching Twelve nibble at her brazilia nut, making it last for as long as possible. When I eventually lay down to sleep she was sucking her fingers, her eyes closed and a little smile on her face.

In spite of all the thoughts of Banjo in my head, I dreamed that night of Malakai. I dream a lot about him. Mostly I relive the last few, awful days before he died and I wake up sweating, in spite of the cold.

The next morning, Sourface appeared. He looked the same, no better or worse than he had when I last saw him. I must have been emboldened by what Gareff had said because I felt brave enough to tease him, 'Why, Adelmo, I thought you had abandoned us.' He gave me a sideways look, as if he detected some change in me, and I did feel different. I had no greater hope of being adopted, no real expectation of Banjo liking me as much as I did him or of him finding me in any way desirable, but I had rediscovered some of my spirit.

'Have you been writing, Ten?' Sourface asked and, to my delight, produced a large sheaf of paper which he placed on the stool.

'No, Adelmo. I'm afraid I had very little paper left and no idea when you might be coming back with more. Are you better now?' I got another sideways look.

'I'm much improved thank you, Ten. And I see that you are doing well which is good – I had heard that you were sick yesterday and might need to see the physician today.'

'Oh no, Adelmo. I made a remarkable recovery

overnight, please don't make me see the physician.'

He considered me for a moment. 'Well,' he said at last, 'in that case I'll see if I can arrange some outside exercise for you.'

My heart leaped. The thought of some light and open air after three weeks of suffocating under the tin and plastic of my roof was intoxicating.

'They must think you're worth it,' said Banjo after Sourface had gone.

'Have you been out?' I asked him, as if I wasn't aware of almost everything he did.

'Yes, once. They'll take you in the coolest part of the day, just before changeover probably. But don't get too excited. You'll be on a long lead and the Guards will be watching every step you take. If you look as if you're going to try to make a run for it they'll stop you. And if you struggle they will kill you.'

After a few moments considering this I moved close to the wall and said in a low voice, 'Has anyone ever escaped, Banjo?'

'There are stories, but I don't believe them.'

'Would you ever try?'

'No. I think it's impossible. And I will be leaving here anyway.'

'Really? How can you be so sure?' I thought back to what Adelmo had told me.

'My Patron will miss me and she'll come to claim me back.' He lifted his chin proudly and said it as if there could not possibly be any doubt. Before I could stop myself I blurted out, 'But I thought -' and he looked at me so sharply that I took an involuntary step back.

'She will miss me, I tell you. She paid a lot of money for me and she'll realise that she made a mistake giving me up.' And with that he moved away and I knew that I'd offended him again. I felt crushed, and thoroughly confused by the extremes of my emotions, which seemed to be entirely under his control

Somehow the prospect of exercise lost some of its appeal after that. Banjo went back to pacing up and down his stall, and the afternoon passed without Visitors and only the sundial and hunger marking the time. I picked up the new paper Adelmo had brought me, smoothed it, smelled it and counted the ragged sheets; but even that did not bring its usual comfort and I had no urge to write. With Twelve still mute my only company was the farting and snoring from stall Eleven and a tiny green lizard which had paused on the wall beside me. But after a while it scurried away, slipping through a tear in the canvas of the roof towards the ochre yellow sky. There was no sign of clouds heralding the rain Mariam hoped for and the air was still thick and sticky, sitting like a film on my skin and smelling like decay.

As Banjo had predicted, Sourface came for me at sundown. By then I had determined to concentrate on looking forward once again to my exercise break; I had tidied the stall, taken off the last remaining dressings on my arms and legs so the air could reach my limbs, and shaken a pomander vigorously over my empty slop bucket. The cloves, bay and orange inside were dried up and ancient but there was still a faint fragrance clinging to them and, once the torches are lit, the smell of burning oil helps to disguise the permanent reek of bodily functions hanging around us. My mind drifts often to the perfumed rooms I left not so long ago, to rose petals scattered on the floors and beds, and the cloying smoke of incense burning constantly in the water closets. The memories of those three years of luxury, which I took so much for granted, sharpen the misery of my conditions now and the longing to return to them is a physical pain in my gut.

'Are you ready, Ten?' Sourface and another Guardian had appeared at the door, a length of rope in their hands which, between them, they tied around my wrists in such a way that, if I pulled or wriggled, the rope would tighten uncomfortably and begin to rub. It felt very strange coming out after nearly twenty three days of confinement and seeing the passage stretch before me; my recollection of the first day of my arrival had contained very little detail and I paused by my stall in an attempt to take it all in. Sourface tugged at the rope, not brutally but enough to get me moving, and we began to walk down past the stalls, the occupants in each watching our progress in a way that was oddly reminiscent of the day Mamma put me up for auction. This time though there was no accompanying murmur of appreciation or admiration, only a desperately sad curiosity on their part and a terrible feeling of shame on mine. *How have you come to this, Akara?*

As we approached the bottom end of the passage a terrible thought struck me. Ahead was the heavy, reinforced door to the extermination chamber and I suddenly became convinced that they were going to take me through it. I began to pull back and the rope bit into me, burning flesh that was still tender and not fully healed. More memories washed into my head and I began to panic. I could hear Sourface's voice through the blood singing in my ears and it was calm and firm, 'Stop it, Ten. There's no need to be afraid. Stop pulling and take a deep breath. We're going outside now, one step at a time. That's it, we're almost at the outer door. There.' And there we were indeed, out in a large open courtyard with the first hint of cooler air meeting my face.

I stumbled a bit and the other Guardian gripped my arm to steady me. Sourface offered me water from a small trough on the wall, scooping it up in a wooden cup and holding it to my lips; it was hot after sitting so long in the sun but I welcomed it, managing to hold the cup by myself and remembering to thank him. Once again though I had disgraced myself and all I wanted was to get back to my stall and be alone.

But I had been brought out for exercise and Sourface was determined I should have it; he guided me around the yard, warning me to be careful of the uneven paving underfoot as his hand hovered under my elbow in case I stumbled again. I could feel the eyes of several Guards on me, each of them holding sticks or metal bars and ready to use them if necessary I was sure. They had nothing to fear from me. I was in no condition to attempt escape – not by scaling walls or running anyway; if I'm to leave this place it will have to be through my own wits or someone else's mercy. That evening in the yard I talked myself into regaining some dignity, reminding myself of my heritage and asking myself, *what would Mamma tell you to do? She would tell you to be observant and to use your brains if you can no longer rely on your beauty. She would tell you to be strong.*

So I began to look around me properly, noting the height of the walls around the courtyard, the barricaded archways to the left and right which connect to the passages of stalls, and the graceful metal gates at the entrance which have somehow escaped being looted or repurposed. There was an elegant fountain in the centre of the yard which would once have fed the magnificently mosaiced pond beneath it; perhaps there had even been fish. It was larger than Malakai's, but his had cascaded continuously with gravity fed water, while this was dried up and cracked, full of dust, debris and the Guards' saliva as they took it in turns to spit gobbets of foul brown juice into it. Jiggs had told me that Sativa and tobacco leaves are part of the Guards' pay, and I'd be surprised if they could show one healthy tooth between them. They are unreliable and mercenary, but they are cheaper and easier to acquire than dogs and swiftly replaced if they die or move on.

I was walked twice around the perimeter of the courtyard and, although I felt feeble, I knew I was regaining my strength. I raised my face to the darkening sky and took deep breaths, inhaling the freshest air I had known in twenty three days; my ribcage still hurt but it was worth the discomfort. I asked Sourface to roll up the sleeves of my shift so that the scabs on my arms were exposed and he said, 'What about the eye patch? Shall I take that off?'

I think if we had been alone, if the Guards had not been there, chewing and spitting and smirking at my obvious distaste, I would have agreed, but I shook my head.

'You can take the rope off though, if you like,' I prompted, and got the expected sideways look from Sourface, 'Of course, Ten,' he replied sarcastically, 'And then perhaps we could unlock the gates for you and all come and wave you off.'

'Yes, that would be nice, Adelmo,' I found myself enjoying the banter, and I suspected Sourface was too because I thought I saw the faintest hint of a smile on his lips, 'I think I should bathe and change my clothes first though, it wouldn't be appropriate for me to travel in these,' and I indicated my grubby shift and the threadbare slippers that were too small for me; the stitching rubbed uncomfortably against the hard, cracked skin of my heels but I pointed one foot gracefully as if it was still encased in the soft suede sandal it was used to. There was an odd moment then, with Guardians, Guards and me all looking at my feet, and it somehow seemed very comical; I wondered what they were all thinking as I flexed and straightened first one then the other, balancing carefully because my arms were still stretched out in front of me tethered by the rope. I suppose to them it was just a silly piece of amusing entertainment, but in my mind I was back on Malakai's estate, dancing round the room with Emanuel and feeling as if I had the world at my feet instead of dirt.

A tug on the rope brought me back to reality, the moment was over and Sourface was leading me back inside. Continuing the banter I said grandly, 'You may escort me back to my quarters now, Adelmo,' and I even attempted a haughty wave at the Guards, which didn't quite work with tethered hands. They stared at me and I could hear them spitting behind me as we stepped into the building. Just inside the passage we passed another inmate heading towards the courtyard for exercise; she was a girl about my age, flanked by two Guardians but tied by only one arm because the other was missing. I was about to say something, to exchange a greeting or even just a smile, but her expression as her eyes met mine, and something in the unnatural quiet, stopped me; after a few more steps, I realised what it was: there was a small candle being lit in the sconce outside the extermination room. Someone was about to die.

11 TO MARKET

My twenty sixth day and I can't help wishing that Mamma had given me something else to believe in apart from myself. The night Eighteen died, when I passed her stall on the way back to mine after my exercise, Mariam was sitting with her and they were both praying over Mariam's little gold cross. I could tell that Eighteen had been crying, but she seemed quite calm by the time I saw her; her hands were clasped in Mariam's and her eyes were tight shut. Sourface ushered me along without comment until we were back at my stall and the door had clicked quietly behind us; 'Sit down, Ten,' he said. Surely he wasn't going draw me tonight? It was too dark, and even he must see how disrespectful it would be to Eighteen, facing her last moments at the far end of the passage. I perched on the edge of the pallet, ready to protest if he brought out paper and pencil, but he merely pulled up the stool and sat down, his knees almost touching mine and his long, thin face looking grimmer than ever.

'We do our best you know, Ten. But you have to make an effort too.'

'I thought I was,' I replied, genuinely surprised and stung by the criticism.

'Perhaps you did. But it is not helpful to keep reminding everyone of your past status. I'm afraid you have to accept that you no longer look high caste or beautiful and that you need to demonstrate other qualities if someone is going to be tempted to adopt you.'

I was too stunned to speak.

'You need to make yourself agreeable to Visitors, if not to us. I'm prepared to listen to your fanciful chatter but others – people who it is best not to antagonise - find it aggravating and disrespectful. You must appear less arrogant and ... difficult. Unless your provenance is proved somehow it is not something to boast about.'

Recovering my voice I raised it, angrily, 'How dare you say that to me. Everything I've told you is true. Why should I pretend to be less than I am – I don't belong here and you know it, Adelmo.'

He looked at me for a long moment and then shook his head, as if I was missing some obvious point and perhaps I was. How could I have misjudged that moment outside so badly, when I thought he had understood my silly behaviour and been amused by it? How stupid of me; I felt utterly humiliated and that infuriated me further. I was so enraged that I momentarily forgot myself and I dismissed him as if he was a server, 'Go away, Adelmo,' and, when he didn't move, 'Go away!'

'This is just what I mean, Ten. You do yourself no favours by insulting me,' he said in a low voice. Then he rose without another word and left me, closing and bolting the door very quietly as he went as if to emphasise that he, at least, had remembered what was happening at the end of the passage and had more consideration for Eighteen than to shout.

That night was another long and sleepless one and, to begin with, all my thoughts only served to feed my anger. Mamma had said I was the best and most beautiful of her children, hadn't she? And hadn't I achieved what was rumoured to be the highest ever price at auction? I had belonged to a Patron who knew the value of perfection and had never let me forget it; how was I supposed to now accept that all of that meant nothing? Worst of all, I realised, was the thought that Banjo had heard everything and, if he now thought even less of me, then Adelmo was entirely to blame.

I must have lain awake for an hour or more raging at Adelmo in my head, too self engrossed to spare a thought for Eighteen until a distant voice called out 'And so be it,' signifying that the sconce candle had been blown out. One by one the passage torches were lit and the Guardians made the first of their regular rounds to check on us. I didn't see Adelmo, but Mariam stooped and called softly to me, asking 'Are you quite well, Ten?' Her voice was thick with emotion, I knew she would be very upset about Eighteen and I was aware that I hadn't thanked her yet for the brazilia nuts. 'Yes, thank you, Mariam,' I sat up on the bed, 'Mariam, may I talk to you?' but she had already gone.

Was I really so unlikeable that even the sweetest and most soft hearted of the Guardians no longer had time for me? I felt utterly alone and vulnerable, with the added misery that even my memories were tainted now by self doubt. I cast my mind back to other occasions, before The Kennels, when I had felt this wretched and there were only two. Even the days following Ash's disappearance had not been so hopeless because I was only seven at the time and hadn't know for sure that he wouldn't return. So that left the day that Malakai died, and the morning of my fourteenth birthday when I woke knowing that I would be sold and must leave home forever.

*****

Mamma came to my bed at dawn, wanting to bathe and

groom me before the sun rose too high and we both began to melt. 'You can sleep on the way to town,' she said when I began to grumble; I wasn't used to rising early because Mamma liked me to get a full eight or nine hours sleep as a rule. Beetle was up already, simmering oats in milk and chopping dried fruits ready for our breakfast. I hadn't seen him for two days; Mamma had kept us apart, knowing how we loved each other and warning me that I was not to cry when we parted because, 'I will not take you to auction with a puffy face and red eyes. Do you understand?

As soon as I sat to eat, Mamma sent Beetle away and served me my breakfast herself. I watched her as if she were a stranger, this woman who had brought me up for fourteen years, and wondered whether all mothers were like her. And if so, why did it not feel right and natural for it to be that way? If I could love Beetle, my half brother, like he was my own child then why could our mother not love us? So much of what she did for me was good, I could see that – the way she protected and nourished me, the way she taught me everything that she thought was important and useful for me to know, and the way she worked so hard to get me whatever I needed. I looked at her hands, blistered from doing chores and still rough with callouses from rooting around in rubble and rubbish for the books she'd found me to read. How could all that be done without affection or warmth?

I didn't feel hungry, only sick with nerves at the thought of what lay ahead and distraught at the idea of leaving behind my beloved Beetle who was now nowhere to be seen. Mamma didn't force me to eat but she insisted on me drinking a full tumbler of milk, claiming it would line my stomach for the time being and I could have food later, if I felt like it. I sat miserably at the table whilst she gathered up olives, cheese and flatbreads, which she wrapped in cheesecloth and placed in one of several baskets containing everything necessary for our journey. Then, from the wooden cupboard in the corner she produced a large lidded box, beautifully constructed from palm leaves woven around a wicker frame, and said, 'I've made this for you, Akara and put your most personal belongings in it; you won't need much because whoever buys you will certainly provide you with the finest clothes, perfumes and jewellery. However, there are some of your favourite books which are of no use to me or your brother, as well as your two best shifts, a kaftan and some scarves. You're to dress in your most becoming bodice and silk trousers once you've bathed, which I suggest you do now. I will draw up the water and finish filling the tub, you may come out when it's ready.' She looked at the box, not at me, whilst she made this speech, her hands constantly stroking it as if smoothing imaginary wrinkles and bumps.

As soon as she had gone outside I lifted the lid and peeped inside. My tortoiseshell hairbrush and comb lay on top of the clothes she had listed and beneath them were the fabric bound copy of A Child's Collection of Favourite Verse and my illustrated translation of The Rubaiyat of Omar Khayyam, both of which she had given to me on the day I was officially registered in Maidentown at the age of eight. I remembered how delighted I had been at the time and what joy those books had brought me ever since; but it was only then, as I wondered at her uncharacteristic display of sentimentality, that it occurred to me to think they must have cost her a great deal. I don't believe those books were found; I think she paid dearly for them in the town on the same day she formally named me.

I closed the lid, lost in thought until a little voice behind me whispered, 'Akara, I'm here. Akara!' and I turned to see my brother. He was beckoning from the back of the room, half hidden by the curtain draped across the alcove where he slept on a cot made from old crates and a horsehair mattress. I had asked Mamma to let him have my room once I had gone, pointing out that he was too old at nine to be sleeping in what was little better than a cupboard. 'He's small for his age, he doesn't need any more space,' was all she said, leaving me none the wiser, but hoping that he wouldn't be there for much longer anyway.

I slipped behind the curtain with him and we hugged, 'Oh, Beetle, I can't bear to leave you. I will make whoever buys me come for you as well, I promise.'

'I know you will. But don't worry, Akara, I'll be alright till then. Mamma may not like me but she needs me. She'll have no more babies now so I'm all she's got.'

'Yes,' I said, 'Remember that, and remind her too that next time she gets stung you might let her die!' We giggled and hugged again. Then we heard Mamma's voice calling from the yard and knew it was time to say goodbye. From the pocket of my nightshift I produced the little silvery ring Ash had given me, threaded onto a leather thong which I placed around Beetle's neck. It was tarnished and green in parts now, although I had spent many hours trying to polish it, but I knew how much it meant to Beetle to have it and that he would treasure it as I had done. He looked up at me and smiled, 'Don't cry,' he said, 'I'll keep it safe until I can give it back to you.'

Mamma called me again and I knew I had to go. I held Beetle to me and told him how precious and special he was and how much I loved him. 'I love you too,' he murmured into my shoulder, gripping me with all his strength until I had to forcibly break away. I tried very hard not to cry but the tears came and I had to pinch myself to stop; Mamma mustn't think that Beetle had caused me to have puffy eyes or she would be angry with him.

I went out into the yard, where she was waiting for me next to the large barrel she had laboriously filled with water fresh from the well. I took off my shift and stepped onto the box she'd put there to assist me so that I wouldn't have to clamber in and risk scraping my legs; then I paused, knowing she would want to inspect my nakedness to be sure there were no new marks, bruises or bites needing attention. With her hands on my waist she turned me slowly on the box, her eyes scanning up and down so that not an inch of me would miss her scrutiny. I felt compelled to speak, 'Thank you, Mamma, for the books; that was kind of you.'

She took my hand and guided me into the refreshing coolness of the water, made silky and fragrant with generous amounts of her favourite geranium and orange essence. 'Kindness has nothing to do with it. I told you, they are of no use to me or your brother, you may as well have them and at least you won't be going to your Patron empty handed.' So that was that; I was to be left in no doubt that Mamma's motives had been anything other than practical ones.

My bath was conducted in silence then, apart from the hums and clicks of the insects around us and the gentle swoosh of water as she sponged my neck and back. When she'd finished, I submerged myself entirely and let my hair float out around me while I held my breath, counting the seconds until I thought she would be satisfied that I was clean. When I emerged she turned to the well and lowered the bucket for water to rinse me, her delicate arms straining to wind the spindle for what must have been the twentieth or thirtieth time that morning. There was sweat sitting on her brow and soaking her hair and she kept pausing to wipe it away, positioning her feet more firmly on the ground each time before grasping the handle and turning it again. Eventually the bucket came up and she heaved it out, taking great care not to spill a drop; I quickly turned away then, for some reason anxious not to let her know that I had seen her struggling.

I climbed carefully out of the barrel and Mamma rinsed me where I stood, the moisture instantly evaporating off my skin in the rising heat. Then Mamma took her turn, dipping in and out of the tub with her clothes on so that they would get cleaned too. Afterwards we stood side by side for a while, our hair dripping down our backs, drying in the sunshine. I was already taller than her and with her slender frame and small, unlined face she looked more like a child than a woman who had borne six children; it was hard to believe she was thirty eight years old. I wondered whether she might yet find another man, not to breed from because she was well past child bearing age, but to provide for her. I had seen men and women looking at her, even as they talked about buying Tanya or me, because there was no denying her loveliness and she always took great care to hide any little tell tale signs of her skin condition and her hands were always gloved. What would she do once I'd gone and she had no children left to raise for sale? Perhaps being so dependent on Beetle she might learn to care for him, except that I would soon be taking him away from her and then she would have no one.

'Come, Akara, it's time for us to go inside and get you ready; there is a great deal still to do.'

'Yes, Mamma,' I replied obediently, and I stopped concerning myself with her future and returned to worrying about my own. Mamma wrapped a towel around me and told me to put my slippers back on. Then, as we walked back towards the house, she called out, 'Go and bathe, Beetle,' and my little brother came hobbling towards us from the goat pen, 'Yes, Mamma. Should I tip the water in the goats' trough afterwards?'

'No, it has oils in it and can't be drunk. Save it and we'll use it again tomorrow.'

Tomorrow; when I would be who knew where, starting a new life with a stranger.

Inside the house Mamma made me stand on an old shearling rug in front of the long mirror and began the ritual of preparing me for market whilst she told me all those things about her own mother, along with the repeated reminders of how lucky I was. Now I see that she was right, but at the time I just felt mystified and desolate.

Once she had finished brushing my hair and oiling my skin she left me to stand for a few moments while she fetched the clothes she had chosen for me to wear. I stood in front of the mirror and and tried to view myself as others might when they watched me being paraded later, but all I saw was a frightened young girl. When Mamma returned I said, 'Do I have to go, Mamma? Can't I stay here with you if I promise to be good and work hard – I could help with the animals and everything and I wouldn't mind.'

'No, Akara, you can't stay.'

'But why?'

She laid the clothes out carefully on the long wooden table, smoothing the fabric and fussing with it and taking so long to answer that I thought she never would.

'Because,' she said eventually, but without looking at me, 'you will have a better life elsewhere and one day you will appreciate that what I am doing is for the best. This is the way of things, Akara, and it's best not to question them.'

Now here I am, three years later, still not being expected to question things; still being told what to do and how to behave by people I once could have summoned with a click of my fingers. Lying in the dark, still seething at Sourface's comments, I slowly began to pass beyond impotent resentment and to experience a new sense of active defiance. If my mother thought I had something special, that I had the capacity to thrive, then I must stop feeling sorry for myself and prove her right.

But back then, as I slid my arms into the sleeves of the gold silk choli Mamma held out for me, I was resigned to my situation and my fate. She fastened the brocade buttons of the bodice, nodding approvingly at the fit, and guided my legs one at a time into the shalwar pants, checking for missing beads or loose threads that might need repairing.

'Perfect,' she announced and she lifted my chin and positioned me so that I could admire myself in the mirror. In spite of my reluctance I was impressed by what I saw: a slim, flat stomached girl with high, firm breasts encased in a gold and red embroidered costume which complemented her glistening skin. Her hair was thick and healthy, her nails long and unbroken, and her eyes large, bright and clear. Mamma had done a good job.

'Keep those slippers on for the journey so we can keep your best ones clean until we get to the Registry building; no one will see your feet until then. You may put your earrings, necklace and bangles on once we're in the cart.'

'Yes, Mamma.'

'Beetle!' she called and went to the door to call again, 'Beetle! Hitch up both mules and get the canvas up.'

'It's done, Mamma,' my brother replied, and I could see him through the window, already loading the feeding bags and binding the animals' hooves in cloth ready to soak them with water at the very last minute. My heart began thumping then, the final minutes before leaving were upon us and I was swamped with misery. I stood rooted to the spot as Mamma went backwards and forwards with baskets and boxes; she collected skins of drinking water from the stone larder where they had been hanging to keep cool and checked that Beetle had loaded all the merchandise she intended to sell. Once she was sure everything was ready she told Beetle to go and tend to the beehives, knowing he would then be well out of sight as we left. He hesitated for just a moment but her face was set in an expression that we knew only too well; there was no point arguing. I watched him limp away and then turn, just as I reached the doorway. Simultaneously we raised our hands to our lips and then gestured towards each other, *My heart goes with you,* the gesture said; and then he was gone.

I think I would have sunk to the floor and wept if my mother hadn't immediately spoken to me so sharply that I actually thought she might slap me as she had Tanya, 'Get into the cart, Akara. You're already sweating.'

So we began the long journey to Maidentown with Mamma at the front driving the mules, mostly in full sun, and me bouncing about in the back, cushioned from the worst of the bumps in the road and shaded under the canvas. Even so she was right, I was hot and sweating and we soon emptied the first three water bottles; we stopped regularly for the mules to rest and be refreshed too, which meant Mamma getting up and down from the cart with feed and buckets and making frequent checks to make sure their hooves weren't scorching. After about two hours, as we joined one of the main routes to the town, things got easier. There were shady trees and grasses lining the sides of the track and we started to come across people travelling, as we were, to the market; there were stalls set up and that meant we could buy fresh water and food. By then, in spite of myself, I was feeling hungry and Mamma exchanged some of our mead for biscuits and fruit from one of the hawkers she recognised. She peeled two oranges and fed them to me herself, taking care not to let the juice drip down onto my clothes, before wiping my face and hands with a dampened cloth. Then she dabbed more frankincense onto my wrists and temples and told me I should now put on my jewellery.

Whilst the mules chomped on their feed Mamma leaned back wearily against the canvas and closed her eyes, in a rare moment of peace. There was something about her when she was resting, a softness which made me want to go to her and rest my head on her breast and feel the gentle rise and fall of her breathing as if we were one. But of course it was an intimacy she had never invited and I had never dared do more than imagine, even when I was younger. I picked up the engraved sandalwood box that contained my jewellery and took each piece out with the reverence it deserved; every one had belonged to Mamma, given to her by one of our pappas – perhaps by my own – and kept for me to wear for the first time on this significant day. I had never seen her wear any of it herself.

I threaded the stalks of the earrings through my lobes; ear piercing was the one mutilation Mamma had approved and she had arranged for it to be done when I was six. An old woman had come to the house one morning, a walking stick in one hand and a brightly coloured carpet bag in the other. She sat me on a stool and suggested to Mamma that she might like to hold my hand, but Mamma called for Ash and I was glad. Even if she'd wanted to, Mamma could not have offered me the comfort that my elder brother could; he crouched beside me, held my hand and grinned reassuringly, as if I was just about to have some wonderful treat.

We both watched the old woman as she lit an oil burner and held a sharp metal pin in the flame, twisting it this way and that to be sure it was sterilised. Then she took some leaves from her bag and pushed them in my mouth, telling me to chew but not to swallow; I looked at Ash and he nodded, 'It's just to make you feel better. Though it's not going to hurt,' he added quickly. Mamma produced the stone pestle and mortar Beetle would later use to grind his potions; the old woman selected a few berries and leaves from a round metal tin and began pounding them vigorously in the mortar until she was satisfied she had extracted everything she could from the pulp. She dipped a small, clean scrap of cotton in the juice and wet my earlobes with it, 'Antiseptic,' she said, 'Stops infection.' It did nothing to numb the pain and nor, as far as I could tell, did the leaves I was chewing because I howled as the first pin went through my left ear and Beetle, who was still only a baby at the time, began screaming in sympathy. Tanya was sent to the alcove to quieten him. Ash squeezed my hand harder, Mamma grabbed my chin firmly and the old woman quickly pierced the second ear before I could jerk away.

I spat out the leaves and turned to Ash, putting my arms around his neck and sobbing. But Mamma would not allow it; she pulled my arms away, Ash was dispatched to finish his chores and I was told that screwing my face up made me ugly and I was shaming her in front of our visitor. I don't think the old woman cared one way or the other; she was rummaging in her bag, cursing under her breath until she found a small leather pouch which she emptied onto the table. There were a dozen or more ear studs, some matching and some not; 'All good. All gold from Promise Land,' she assured us, inviting Mamma to look and choose. From my mother's sceptical expression I knew she had serious doubts about the quality of most of them, but she quickly picked out a pair of small, simple hoops and said, 'These will do to keep the holes open for the time being. Clean them, please.'

'Ah, yes. Best choice. Very good gold from –' but a look from Mamma silenced her. She took the studs and wiped them thoroughly with the noxious berry juice before thrusting them into my newly pierced ears, 'Very pretty girl. Plenty more piercings I think before you sell?'

'No more piercings,' said Mamma firmly, as she paid the woman with a single silver coin before showing her to the door. When she came back to me her face was stern, but she cupped my face gently in one hand, turning it this way and that to look at my ears before nodding that she was satisfied. 'Go and fetch your little brother for his next feed,' she said, 'And you may help yourself to one date, or a fig if you like.' Being allowed to help myself to anything sweet was a rare treat, not only because Mamma was strict about me having too much sugar, but because such luxuries were costly. I slid off the stool and went to the cool stone larder, lingering by the intriguing collection of jars and bottles

containing cheese, butter, preserves and fruit, grateful to be
distracted from my ordeal. At the back of the larder we kept
raw and fermented honey and the mouldy grapes which
Mamma claimed were a special delicacy, along with hemp
seeds, oils and salt blocks. By the time I left home, of
course, the larder was also home to Beetle's herbs, dried
leaves and home mixed remedies – all carefully labelled
and arranged alphabetically. I never saw a better organised
apothecary's store, even in Maidentown; but then, as I soon
discovered, Maidentown did not hold all the world's
wonders by any means.

12 MOTHERS

I was with Surrana the first time I saw one of Akara's posters in Maidentown. We were with a group of friends, talking about the plans for our forthcoming journey, when Adelmo appeared in the square, heading towards the board of notices with a handful of papers, some nails and a small hammer. It was several weeks since I had seen my old friend so I excused myself to go and greet him and we talked about this and that while he pinned his posters. I looked only absentmindedly at the faces as he put them up, admiring his skill as an artist but otherwise not especially curious until I saw her name:

'AKARA D'FIURI, waiting to be claimed from The Borderlands Eastern Region Adoption Centre and believed to come from the north west High-lands via Maidentown.'

It seemed a near impossible coincidence and my spirits soared momentarily, but the drawing of this girl was nothing like my Akara, even allowing for ten years estrangement. The face Adelmo had drawn was of a gaunt and haunted woman, looking older than the seventeen years I knew Akara to be, and wearing a patch over her left eye. The rest of her features, though Adelmo had tried to soften them, were swollen and cut from horrific injuries and I could not believe that Fiuri d'Ursoola's daughter could possibly have ended up in such a condition. Could life be so cruel?

'Tell me about this girl,' I said to Adelmo.

'Oh, she's an interesting one alright. Talks and acts like a princess although she looks like a vagabond. I don't hold out much hope for her,' he continued in his customarily gloomy way, 'but somehow I can't help but like her and I believe her story. Or some of it, at least.'

'How does she explain her condition?' I asked, still afraid to get my hopes up but willing to be convinced.

'She doesn't seem to remember much, other than that she claims to have been a very privileged Protégé whose papers have somehow mysteriously been mislaid. Why do you ask, my friend? Do you think you might know her?'

'Adelmo,' I said in a low voice, 'it is just possible that I do.'

After his initial surprise, Adelmo was delighted to think he might reunite us after all these years, but we both knew it was unlikely. And even if the girl really was my long lost Akara there was no possible way I could pay the adoption fee to release her. Before we parted we agreed to be cautious, both in our expectations and in any future action. Adelmo was already taking risks by feigning illness to leave his duties at the Centre and said it would be some while before he could do so again, 'I will do what I can, Ash, but I must be careful. Neither the girl nor anyone else must become suspicious or I am in danger of losing my Guardianship and being of no use to anyone. Besides, we must prepare for it not to be her but some imposter. The real Akara could be anywhere, or possibly no longer even alive.'

'I know, but do what you can without too much risk, and you know where to find me when you're able to come back. Some of us are preparing to leave here soon, heading south *to look for the Promise Land, but I'll stay here until you're able to get to me with more news, good or bad.'*

'I wish I could believe as fervently as you that there is somewhere better than this, my friend, but I fear you will only find endless desert if you head further south than The Borderlands,' and his slender, brown fingers clasped my pale hand as if we were brothers and my afflictions did not come between us at all.

I went back to Surrana, hardly able to contain my excitement. We said a hasty farewell to our companions and returned to the old bus to talk in private and to hope.

I wonder if Akara would remember the wild woman we encountered one day out in the bush? It turned out to be an important day for discoveries: firstly the old car seat and then the metal bottle top that I've worn on a chain around my neck ever since. It was also the day I met my real mother, although I didn't know it then.

I'm sure Akara wouldn't need reminding about how things were for me with Mamma, how determined she was to keep her favourite child from being tainted by me – the imperfect, throwback who believed he was her son. But we loved each other, Akara and I. She was the one blessing in my life then, such an innocent and happy child, in spite of our mother. I recall how sweet she was when little Beetle was born and I hoped he'd be a comfort to her when I'd gone.

Mamma beat me quite often but never so badly that I couldn't work. For me the greatest pain was in knowing that she could take a stick to her own son. The day Akara got stung and Mamma blamed me for it I knew what to expect. She followed me out to the barn, cracking the switch behind me to remind me what was coming. When we were inside she waited for me to raise my arms as usual, ready to wrap the ropes around my wrists and secure me to the rafters, but I didn't. I turned to her and spoke against her for the first time in my life.

'Mamma, don't do this. You cannot keep punishing me for loving my sister. I did wrong by not keeping her safe and for that I'm truly sorry, but don't whip me. Please.'

I was already taller than her by then, we both knew I could overpower her if I wanted to, but Mamma had something in her that made me afraid, and a look on her face that could hurt more than a whipping.

'Don't dare to defy me, Ash,' she said, 'You are fast becoming more trouble than you are worth to me. Without me you would have starved. Perhaps you think you are ready now to fend for yourself, but I can assure you the world is a more hostile place without someone to house and protect you as I have done.' And she flicked the stick to get me to turn around.

'I will take him!' came a voice from the shadows and we both started, peering to see a half naked figure emerging from the corner. It was the wild woman Akara and I had met only days before, her skin gleaming pearl white as she stepped into the harsh sunlight. She and Mamma looked at each other, each standing their ground for what seemed a long time. Eventually Mamma lowered the switch and said to the woman, 'Have him, Surrana. I have more than done my duty by him and he is nothing but a bad influence now on Akara. Are you really capable of looking after him at last? It seems to me that you are still little more than a savage.'

The woman did look just as she had when we came across her in the bush: bare breasted and lightly sun burned but with something fine and noble about her face now I looked closely at her. It stirred a deep emotion within me – something like a faint recognition which later proved well founded: Surrana was my real mother, half sister to Mamma and the last of our Grandmother Ursoola's children to be born alive. This, and the rest of her story, I learned later, of course – after she had taken me away from

Mamma to the camp she lived in, not more than three miles away from the home I had known for thirteen years.

Mamma had pushed me towards her without a word to me, 'Take him and see how you manage, Surrana. I won't miss him.' But I knew Akara would miss me and I begged Mamma to let me see her before I left. She wouldn't agree, and I have no doubt she didn't pass on my message either. Surrana took my hand and, bewildered as I was, I went with her without protest and Mamma watched us leave. I turned back when we reached the brow of the hill where I used to graze the mules and she was still standing there, tapping the switch against her leg as if daring me to come back and face the consequences.

13 WHAT AM I BID?

The other night, the night I was so angry at Adelmo, I simply couldn't sleep. In the early hours of the morning, by the time all the torches had gone out and the passage was dark, I was resigned to staying awake until dawn. It can be one of the best or the worst times in The Kennels: an opportunity for whispered conversations amongst the inmates without Guardians around, or a waking nightmare listening to the sounds of pain and desperation around you.

The death of Eighteen seemed to have left us all lost in our own thoughts that night because it was unusually quiet, until I heard a persistent scratching which I thought, at first, was my little lizard companion back to gorge on the flies that constantly plague our stalls. But then I heard a tiny voice from the far side of the door, 'Ten, are you still awake? I have somethings for you.' It was Mariam, speaking as soft and low as she possibly could and, as I slipped off the bed to go to her, I could just make out her shape in the gloom.

'Mariam, I'm so happy to see you. I wanted to say thank you.'

'Shhh... No need. I brought you somethings to help, you suck it and it make you feel better.' With that she looked round to make sure it was safe and then reached up to her headdress and pulled something out from the folds; it was a small white pod, similar to ones I had seen Beetle collect for our mother, and with an encouraging smile and a nod she quickly passed it through the mesh to me before rustling off back down the passage.

Once again I had received kindness beyond anything I deserved and in that instant I resolved to be more worthy of it. Perhaps Adelmo was right: I no longer had the right to be proud, or at least not in the same way. I had barely two weeks to summon up the courage either to find a way out or to meet the future with some dignity and I went back to my pallet feeling calmer and stronger. I sat on the bed, debating whether to use the pod or to save it, and decided that I might have more urgent need of it in the future; so I rinsed out one of the muslin dressings and wrapped the pod carefully in that before slipping it safely under the pillow with my stash of paper.

I lay back and gazed up at the roof, high above me and criss-crossed with enough heavy metal bars and rods to discourage all thoughts of escape; there was a faint breeze lifting the corner of one of the pieces of plastic and I thought I could smell the slight promise of rain in the air; the very thought of it was refreshing and, once again, my mind wandered back to a time when I had taken plentiful, pure water for granted.

*****

We rested for half an hour or more on that last stop before Maidentown. Mamma dozed, but like a nervous animal with its ears still pricked in case of danger. If a voice came too close to the cart, or the mules got restless and began to wander, she would instantly be alert. Doubtless many people would know by now that she was carrying valuable cargo and the threat of robbery or kidnap was a constant one; I didn't suppose she would relax until I was sold and safely off her hands. Aside from me and the various things she had brought to trade, there was the jewellery, the worth of which I couldn't even guess at. I put the lapis lazuli earrings in my ears and lifted the choker from its velveteen bed in the sandalwood box; it consisted of numerous gold strands with pendants of precious stones dripping from them and was the most beautiful thing I had ever seen. With the benefit of a small mirror Mamma had hooked up for me to use, I arranged the choker on my neck and fastened the clasp at the back. Even in the shade, the colours glinted and shone, the jade echoed the green of my eyes and the sparkling stones resting just above the neckline of my bodice set off the colours in my choli perfectly. I was, I know, quite a sight to behold.

'Do you need to piss, Akara?' Mamma asked and I was surprised she hadn't thought of it before I put the jewellery on. When we were still travelling through deserted wilderness it had been easy for me to remove my shalwar, hop down from the cart and squat somewhere, certain that no one would see me and with Mamma standing by just in case – but mostly to keep a look out for scorpions and snakes. Now we were nearer Maidentown it would be harder to find privacy and in all my finery I would be an obvious target for thieves, even if I removed the jewellery. It was unlike Mamma not to have thought of it; a sign, I supposed, of her tiredness.

I wasn't in desperate need and knew I could wait until we reached one of the cantinas and the certainty of a proper outside water closet.

'No, Mamma. Thank you.'

'Very well. Then you may put your proper shoes on and come and sit beside me as soon as we reach the outskirts of the town. We've made good time and we'll be able to get refreshed before the auction.'

'Yes, Mamma. Thank you.' Suddenly I felt sick. Up

until that point I had almost been able to convince myself that there was nothing different about this trip from any other we had made. As we left home I had dug my nails into the palms of my hands to stop myself from crying and had not even looked back, in case I saw Beetle's sorrowful face gazing after me. I had been certain that I would be able to persuade my new Patron that we must return for my little brother who, though he may not look able, was clever and gifted in so many ways that they must surely find him useful. But now Mamma had reminded me of what lay ahead and I was afraid. Who would she sell me to and what possible power would I have in my future life? At least my home with Mamma had been safe, if not exactly happy; but I may go to someone who did more than neglect me.

As Mamma click-clicked the mules into action and we got under way, I sat in the back slowly putting on my shoes and the last of my ornaments; the delicate little ankle chains and dozens of pretty bangles that had so enchanted me just half an hour before now seemed dull and cheap. The nausea swirled in my belly and started to rise up into my throat, 'Mamma,' I said, 'I feel unwell.' She immediately stopped the cart and turned back to look at me; I suppose I must have looked bad because she scrambled into the back and held a water bottle to my lips.

'Drink slowly, child. Take some deep breaths in between sips and lie down if you need to.' She put the back of a hand to my brow and shook her head, 'This is not good, Akara, you are very hot and damp.'

'Mamma, I'm afraid.'

She looked deeply into my eyes and shook her head again; she sounded firm, but not angry, when she said, 'Akara, I did not raise you to be afraid of anything. I've equipped you with everything you need to flourish, don't let me down now. This is your opportunity for a good life, please don't waste it.'

She took the little bottle of frankincense and tipped

several drops into the palm of one hand, using the finger tips of the other to dab oil on my forehead and temples. More than that, more than the touch of her calloused fingers on my skin, it was her voice which calmed me; not because it was loving exactly, but because it was so assured. She was the mother whose standards were so exacting and whose demands were so high that her own belief in me couldn't be contradicted. I swallowed some more water and ate some of the sweet biscuit she offered me and the nausea subsided. Mamma sat back on her heels and watched me as I got up and straightened myself. She smoothed out my clothes and adjusted the choker so it sat symmetrically on my breastbone before announcing that I looked perfect again and leading me forward to the front. There were cushions on the seat and we sat side by side for the last part of the journey, shielded from the blazing sun by the large Chinese parasol Mamma had given me to hold. 'Don't bother with protecting me,' she insisted, but it was big enough to shade us both and we drove in relative comfort for the last few miles.

As usual we passed increasing numbers of hawkers and beggars as we reached the edge of the town; there were stalls, wagons and makeshift tents scattered here and there, some familiar faces and a lot of new ones. Of the few children I saw on the ground most were thin and ragged, shyly watching our progress with round eyes and hands tentatively held out for money or food. As usual, Mamma ignored them, but there were others, like me, being taken to be auctioned, mostly riding on mules or in little traps whilst their mothers and fathers walked in the dust, and I noticed Mamma observing them, assessing their worth and judging what I would be up against at market. There were very few girls and Mamma pronounced herself satisfied that none of them was as beautiful as me, 'You see, Akara, you are a queen amongst peasants; you will make me proud today.'

'Yes, Mamma, I will try.' *Really I will try. But I would*

much rather not go.

By then I knew there was no turning back and I let myself be entertained by the distractions around me. Mamma did not seek out the site of the burned out bus on our way into town - whether she did on her return journey I'll never know - but drove us straight onto the main thoroughfare. It seemed even busier than usual, which pleased Mamma of course because it meant more wealth, more Patrons, more bidders at the auction. There were people everywhere, a lot of noise and a great deal of bargaining going on. At one point the crowds were so thick that we had to halt by one of the yurts which I had not been aware of before; it had a large poster of a male phallus outside and a very striking woman standing by the curtained entrance having an intense conversation with a small group of women. There was a great deal of nodding and the occasional laugh before they all went inside and the curtain was dropped. As the striking looking woman secured the ties to prevent any more customers going in, she looked directly at my mother and they exchanged nods.

'Who is she?' I asked, as the throng cleared and we moved on.

'Her name is Carolan.'

'What does she do? What was she selling?'

'She sells Man Magic; Woman Magic too.'

'Oh, like Grandmother!' and I could see Mamma was annoyed.

'No. Ursoola never got paid for her services; she was just a slut.'

I expected to have to press for more information but, to my surprise, Mamma continued unprompted.

'Carolan is Patron to men who can help women have children, and to girls who can help men who have difficulty achieving pleasure. The women you saw just now will all be hoping to breed; they will either be wealthy or who have Patrons who are, and they will be paying Carolan for the services of a fertile man.'

We pulled up outside the largest of the cantinas then and Mamma started to get down to hitch the mules. I stopped her with one last question, 'What about the men who go there, I don't understand what they want?'

'They will probably be impotent. They want Carolan, or one of her Protégés, to use remedies and skills to arouse them, and perhaps to stimulate their potency. Now, get down, Akara and come inside.'

It did not occur to me then, or even later at the auction, but I wonder now how Carolan and Mamma knew each other. It amuses me to think that perhaps Beetle had concocted remedies, under our mother's instruction, for her to sell to the woman with the phallus outside. If my clever little Beetle made them then they almost certainly worked.

*****

My twenty seventh day dawned with an ominous crackling in the sky, which threatened either rain or more solar eruptions. Although we all hoped for rain there was anxiety as well as relief when it arrived; welcome as the water is, it can also be destructive. Ridrick-Oola told me, with some satisfaction I thought, that the last time the rains had come most of the roof had collapsed and four inmates had to be euthanised because of their injuries.

I thanked her for the warning, not sarcastically as I might have done only the day before, but with as much humility as I could and asked what I might do to protect myself. 'Not much,' she responded, 'But you should empty your slop bucket so that you don't get flooded with your own piss and excrement; and if you have anything you value,' her eyes swept the stall as if it seemed unlikely, 'you should protect it as best you can.'

What do I value here? I have nothing except my untidy scribblings and the blank sheets of paper I have stored. A month ago I was rich beyond my wildest imaginings.

*****

Mamma and I stepped inside the cantina and received even more than our usual attention. Dressed in such lavish costume it would have been obvious that I had been prepared for auction, even to those who didn't already know my day had come. The owner cleared a table, lit the oil burner and plumped some cushions before inviting us to sit down; I felt as if all eyes were on us and that everything now depended on me behaving as Mamma wanted me to. I spotted Malakai seated at a table in the far corner, immediately recognisable by his distinctive eye shield; he was smoking from a very elaborate hookah, topped up at intervals by the woman kneeling at his feet, a pretty girl who looked a little older than me and whose glorious curtain of auburn hair hung loose down to her waist. Although she was instantly attentive to Malakai's every need, feeding him sweetmeats and pouring wine, she had a far away look in her eyes, as if she really existed in a different place from the rest of us. I wondered why, with such a beauty at his disposal, Malakai would be interested in me and I asked my mother. She sighed, as if all her years of teaching had been wasted on me, 'Provenance, Akara. She is certainly lovely to look at but she has no pedigree. Nothing can make her any higher caste than she is.'

Several people approached Mamma, offering to buy us drinks and food; she only accepted from those she knew would be serious contenders at the auction, leaving the others in no doubt that I was beyond their means. Malakai, though he glanced over at us occasionally, made no such offer and did no more than nod to acknowledge us. If Mamma was worried she didn't show it, but I noticed she made a point of having very obvious discussions with people in front of him, to make him aware that he had competition. She placed all my documents on the table and everyone who looked at them was impressed, which was no more than she expected. After a while I whispered to Mamma that I needed the water closet, so she gathered up the papers, wrapped them carefully in their leather portfolio and accompanied me to the back of the cantina. As we passed through to reach the yard at the rear I smiled at Malakai's attendant, thinking we might one day be together in the same household but, although our eyes met, she didn't return my smile. Somehow she managed to make me feel foolish, as if I were the lesser person for trying to be friendly, and I resolved not to let my guard down again and to always remember my superior position, as Mamma had instructed.

We walked out to the back; the dogs lying panting in their kennels were too hot to do more than wag a lazy tail as we passed, but the Guards sprawled next to them scrambled to their feet and tried to look alert. The water closet was in a sturdily built wood and metal shack with room for us both inside; Mamma removed my shalwar pants and I sat on the rough wooden seat and did my toilet. There was a water bowl on the stool beside me and Mamma moistened a clean cotton cloth for me to wipe myself; then when I'd finished she told me to go back outside. Mamma never did her toilet in front of me, so I left obediently and waited under the bright green leaves of a Judas tree until she came out. It felt as if she was gone a long time and I was starting to feel a little sick and faint again, struggling not to give in to the temptation to sit down in the dirt. When Mamma appeared she quickly led me back inside and we returned to our table, where there was fresh water waiting and a new crowd of people. Malakai was nowhere to be seen.

The sun was high in the sky and the time had come for us to go. Mamma made sure I was feeling quite well enough before saying, 'We should leave now, Akara,' and bidding farewell to the immediate group around us.

'Thank you for your custom, Fiuri D'Ursoola,' said the owner, bowing obsequiously as his server opened the door for us and we swept past.

I don't really remember a great deal about the rest of the drive down to the main square. I suppose all the usual activities were going on but all I was conscious of was a muddle of noise in my ears and the sweat dripping down into my eyes, making them sting. Mamma kept looking at me anxiously and her grip on the reins was tense. The mules plodded along and I concentrated on watching their firm little rumps swing from side to side, imagining Beetle washing them down when they got home and maybe crying into the flank of his favourite at the thought of being without me. *When I come to fetch you,* I promised him in my head, *I will come on a camel and you will have many animals to love and look after.* Convincing myself that, with a rich Patron, I would be in a position to demand all these things provided me with comfort for the last part of the journey.

When we reached the square there were servers waiting to help us down from the cart and lead the mules off to be fed and watered. Mamma collected what she needed from the back: her personal bag, a pouch containing oils and perfumes and my documents. The palm leaf box with my books and clothes inside was fetched down by the servers, who were instructed to handle it with great care.

With the parasol held over us by another server we walked to the registry building, past the platform where they were still erecting a huge canvas canopy, and the boards full of all the usual posters: Lost, Stolen or Escaped; Missing; Wanted For Theft and Assault. There were lists of animals and goods for sale; notices of forthcoming events – including that day's auction – and a selection of painted phalluses advertising the skills which Mamma had previously explained to me. I looked to see if Carolan's name was there but, as if reading my mind, Mamma said, 'Carolan doesn't need to advertise; she has an exceptional reputation and people who go to her know they will rarely be disappointed and are less likely to catch a disease. It is why her services are costly.'

We walked on and up the four steps into the blessed cool of the registry. I had not been inside since my eighth birthday and, if anything, it seemed even more grand and imposing, with most of its flagstone floor restored and a vast domed ceiling freshly painted with jewel coloured symbols and figures. Texts in languages I didn't even recognise illuminated the dado rails in shimmering gold script. The main hall was scattered with ottomans, cushions and kilims and there were little carved tables dotted around with jugs of water and fruit syrups and tiny bowls of figs, dates and nougat. The Registrar, dressed in an immaculate white robe, was sitting on an engraved wooden chair in front of a large table on which were all the papers, seals and wax of his office. As soon as he saw us he rose and came towards us, bowing and smiling. I'd never seen him up close before and was fascinated by his beard, which had strands of coloured thread plaited through it, and the long coil of hair wound around his head like a coronet and similarly decorated. He had a smooth, brown complexion, not particularly dark but clear and unblemished, and piercing grey eyes. He and my mother greeted each other like equals.

'My dear lady, I am honoured, as always, by your visit.'

'We are honoured to be here, Registrar,' said my mother, as if we had been invited to drink tea and watch some delightful entertainment.

'Shall we take care of the paperwork?' asked our host, indicating the bench where we should sit opposite him at the table. I moved towards it but Mamma stopped me, 'If you don't mind, Registrar, I would like Akara to go straight to the holding room; she doesn't need to witness the paperwork and I'm sure she would like to rest before the auction.'

'Of course, Fiuri; one of my servers will take her and you may be assured she will be well cared for.'

'Mamma?' I reached for her hand, suddenly afraid again. I had not imagined this would be how we would part – quickly and brutally, without more to say to each other.

Mamma pulled her hand away, 'It's quite alright, child. I will see you again later but it's best you go now and compose yourself,' and she turned away from me. Left with no choice I followed a young man in a white pajama uniform as he led me down a hallway and into a large ante-chamber, where there was more seating and plenty of food laid out on low, white clothed tables. I accepted a small cup of water but shook my head at the invitation to eat; my belly was in turmoil again and there was a sour taste in my mouth. As I closed my eyes to stop the room from spinning a voice beside me said, 'You'll feel better if you eat something,'

'How would you know how I'll feel?' I replied sharply, turning too late to see that it was not a server, but a sumptuously dressed boy of about my age holding out a small dish of oat cakes and smiling shyly. His smile faded and, before I could find the words to apologise, he had turned away. I needed to sit down; having humiliated myself twice already that day – first with Malakai's attendant and now with this high caste boy - I could not disgrace myself further by fainting or being sick. I chose a bench next to the wall and leaned back, taking frequent sips of water and dabbing discreetly at my damp skin as Mamma had taught me to do. After a while I felt better and was able to sit up properly and take in my surroundings.

The holding room was a large, ornate chamber divided in two by a thick rope. There were five of us on one side, all extravagantly robed and bejewelled, and nine on the other, all plainly dressed in simple shifts or kurtas and clearly going to be sold as servers. Where we had dishes of fruit and sweetmeats set out for us on filigree trays, the servers had jugs of water and baskets of dry bread. Several of them looked old – in their fourth or even fifth decades – and past being able to do physical work, which meant they must have valuable skills as scribes, artisans or cooks. We all viewed each other with curiosity and, I supposed, some envy on their part.

On my side of the rope the boy who had suggested I eat was now sitting cross legged next to an older girl wearing similar colours to his; they had similar noble profiles too, with elegant, hawk like noses and high brows. But when the boy whispered something to the girl and she turned to look at me I saw that the left side of her face was scarred and discoloured and she immediately hurried to draw her scarf across to hide it. I wanted to tell her that I wasn't shocked, that it didn't alarm or disgust me any more than Beetle's funny leg had done, but once again I couldn't find the words. She and the boy had gone back to talking and laughing with each other anyway and the moment had passed.

*****

Nobody drowned when the rains came to The Kennels, but there was damage done even before they arrived. The winds picked up during the morning and began shifting debris about on the roof, tearing at the sheets of plastic and canvas and making a colossal amount of noise. I think Twelve must have been cowering at the back of her stall because I couldn't see her, and if she called out I didn't hear her. The Guardians were all rushing around tying things down and shouting out warnings to the inmates to put what they could on the beds, including themselves, and to use blankets to shelter under. Even Adelmo broke into a run, hastily removing the clattering chalk boards from outside our stalls and collecting any loose candles and oil burners that were lying about. When they'd done everything they could the Guardians disappeared, all except Mariam who let herself into Twelve's stall and stayed there for the entire storm, which must have lasted six or seven hours.

The wind didn't come alone; it brought with it dust, dead insects and rubbish from the old landfill sites which have been splitting open and spewing their contents for the last sixty five years or so. By the time the wind had dropped and the deluge started my floor was littered with bits of plastic, metal and glass which had blown through the holes in the roof. When the rain came it was so heavy that the straw quickly got saturated and there was nowhere to stand without my feet getting cut by something. At times it was hard to catch breath through the cascade of water and soon the roof was covered by nothing except the rusty iron bars; the sheeting, the rocks, everything had been blown or washed away.

But two good things happened as a result of the storm that day: the water supplies were replenished and Banjo decided to talk to me again.

*****

No one spoke to me on the afternoon of my fourteenth birthday as we lined up to be taken out and auctioned. Protégés were always sold first, while potential Patrons still had plenty of money in their purses and the highest prices could be achieved; servers were left until last, to be bought with whatever funds were left. The first five of us were accompanied by the same young man who had escorted me into the holding room; we followed him along a passageway, through a large, arched doorway and out into the square. My parasol had been removed so that I had nothing to hide behind and could be viewed easily, but the heat was bearable under the canopy and I was no longer feeling faint. We were arranged in order of sale on cushioned benches next to the Registrar who commanded his own dais, chair and table. Next to him on the other side was a large group of people, my mother amongst them, talking, eating and drinking. Mamma had told me, all those years ago when we first came with Hal, that the Registrar made a considerable commission from each transaction, so esteemed sellers and high spending purchasers were treated well; they were seated on the platform, served wine and cake and kept happy. I tried to catch Mamma's eye for some reassurance, but she was busy. I watched her, a slight figure moving gracefully amongst her group: smiling and nodding, or sometimes shaking her head, but always charming in the way she could be when she was negotiating business and charm was required.

Already settled at the most prominent viewing position was Malakai and next to him I was certain I recognised the family who had approached Mamma once about a mate for the young boy. Other buyers began to take their seats; some were familiar to me from cantinas or previous market days, many were not. Last to be seated was Carolan, resplendent in a sequinned gown of red and gold and attracting a great deal of attention from men and women alike, including my mother who had a long conversation with her before going to her own chair, still avoiding me.

At ground level the rest of the square was filled with people gossiping, trading and bargaining, but once they saw the auction was about to start they gathered round the platform to watch. A hush gradually descended, the giant brass gong was struck and the Registrar rose, clearing his throat and raising his arms as if to embrace the entire assembly.

'Greetings everyone; you are all most welcome to today's auction. As usual, I will introduce each individual and those of you who have not already familiarised yourself with their documentation are invited to do so now if you intend to participate. We have already received advance bids on all five and expect today to achieve record prices for several of them. Let us begin.'

We were announced and paraded in turn, with the Registrar referring to our ages, provenance and particular gifts or attributes. The first, a sixteen year old boy, sold swiftly to a local merchant – probably to be traded on at another market. The second, a well favoured youth, was nearly sold to Carolan but went instead to an older woman I didn't recognise.

The boy and girl turned out, unsurprisingly, to be brother and sister and were not to be sold separately.

'It is,' said the Registrar, 'a condition that Gwin and Erin d'Lile be sold together. The boy, recently come of age at fourteen, is sound and promises to be a healthy and potent adult; the fifteen year old girl, as can be seen, has a disfigurement resulting from an accident with scalding water at the age of six. Since it is not a birth defect she too can be expected to achieve healthy maturity. They both have an excellent shared family pedigree.' He looked across to a couple sitting nearby who nodded in acknowledgement.

Both Carolan and Malakai were looking interested; Malakai beckoned to the boy, Erin, who took his sister's hand and went to be inspected. It was impossible to discern any expression on Malakai's face; besides the dark eye shades his face and head were shrouded in a thick scarf corded by black silk. He didn't speak but tried to dismiss the girl with a flick of his hand, he was only interested in the boy. Erin looked pleadingly at his parents and refused to let go of Gwin's hand. Summoning a server, Malakai wrote something on a slip of paper and sent it across to the Registrar.

'Malakai de Montagne,' the Registrar announced, 'has

bid eighteen thousand krona for Erin. However, Malakai, I must tell you that we already have a bid of twenty thousand for the pair and,' he looked to the d'Liles for confirmation, 'they cannot be separated.'

At this, Malakai merely shook his head.

'Very well. Do I have a bid above twenty thousand? No? Then I am pleased to sell at twenty thousand krona to Carolan d'Savoy.'

As the siblings were taken away I looked towards my mother, knowing my moment had come, and at last she was looking back at me with a direct, unwavering gaze that seemed to convey everything she had ever taught me: be strong, be proud, be aware of your worth and, above all, don't let me down now. Keeping my eyes fixed on her face I rose and walked slowly along the platform, pausing as she had instructed me to, by the row of prospective bidders. I can't deny that I felt the power of desirability; there was something intoxicating about being coveted so fiercely by so many. The Registrar held a pile of written bids and announced that, in view of these, the starting price was fifty four thousand krona. There was a swell of noise from the crowd on the ground and they pressed forward to watch; I could hear them commenting and joking as I passed.

'She's certainly a beauty.'

'Ha! My daughter is twice as lovely.'

'Only when compared with your pigs!'

'If I could afford her I'd be bidding.'

'The sun will be cold by the time you've got that kind of money, Caleb.'

It struck me that the conversations were not much different from the ones I heard at the animal sales; I might as well have been a sheep.

But the buyers on the platform were serious and mostly silent. I saw Malakai writing and Carolan looking through my documents once again; and the parents with the young boy were whispering to each other, talking over his head as if his opinion was of no consequence.

Over the buzz of the crowd I could hear the Registrar repeating all the details of my age, my education and my health records – reminding everyone of the regularity of my bleeds and stressing what a promising sign it was of my future fertility. Carolan was nodding, Malakai gave nothing away.

The Registrar kept taking slips of paper, there must have been five or six different bidders even as the price kept rising. Sixty three thousand. Seventy thousand. Seventy eight thousand. The bidding went on so long I was told I could sit down, which I did. A server brought me water and I was given a palm to fan myself with. My mother looked satisfied and I supposed I had done my duty by her.

Still the bids went up and up until the Registrar announced that both Malakai and Carolan had bid ninety eight thousand krona and it was now a contest between the two. Each looked equally determined and I allowed myself to wonder what life might be like with either of them. Mamma had told me Malakai wanted little more than an expensive ornament to show off. If I went to Carolan, I didn't know what to expect but it gradually dawned on me that there would be requirements of me which I didn't fully understand but could guess at. I began to panic.

Looking round at the crowd of faces, I imagined being hired out to any of the men or women there; it wouldn't matter how disgusting, ugly or unpleasant they were; how young, old or decrepit; I would always be at the mercy of my Patron, just as I had always been at the mercy of my mother. If my legs had not been so weak I believe I might have run away there and then but suddenly I saw my mother rise and approach the Registrar. Had she changed her mind? Was she going to take me home after all? I would have done anything, promised anything, if she would only take my hand and say, 'Come Akara, we're going back to Beetle and our quiet little home. You will shovel pig shit all day for the rest of your life but at least you will be home.'

Mamma didn't even glance in my direction; she had a moment's conversation with the Registrar who looked surprised but nodded agreeably.

'Esteemed brothers and sisters,' he said as he rose and extended his arms, 'Unusually, but entirely within her rights, Fiuri d'Ursoola has decided to end the bidding for her daughter.' He paused dramatically, 'It is her intention to accept the final offer of Malakai de Montagne, with apologies to Carolan d'Savoy. This means that Akara d'Fiuri has achieved the highest price ever recorded at this market for an individual. Congratulations, Fiuri d'Ursoola.' There were cheers and some applause. 'This concludes the first part of today's auction. We will return in one hour for the sale of servers and menials. Thank you.'

Malakai remained in his seat but Carolan got up and was clearly angry; she went to the Registrar and they had a very heated discussion, which led to her throwing such a venomous look at my mother that my blood ran cold at the thought of making such an enemy. What had come over Mamma to do such a thing? Carolan swept off the platform and I just sat, looking from my mother to Malakai and waiting to be told what to do. In the end it was the Registrar himself who came to me, smiling broadly and holding out a hand to take my own.

'You should feel very proud, Akara,' he said and I nodded because it was expected of me. 'Come, we will finish the paperwork in the office and prepare you for your journey home with Malakai.'

Home? I had no idea even where that might be.

14 AFTER THE RAIN

The way the rains were responsible for getting Banjo to speak to me again was because a large chunk of our wall crumbled and he could no longer avoid me. When the torrent had eased we all began clearing up; the Guardians came round with brushes and swept the stalls, cleared the clogged gullies and lit every burner, torch and candle that was dry enough to burn. After the eerie silence of the previous night and then the deafening cacophony of the storm, the ordinary chatter of the Guardians was reassuring. The Kennels were returning to their strange normality and the mood, as well as the air around us, seemed lighter. Supper was late and we'd missed our mid day meal altogether because of the storms, so we were all very hungry but, with the kitchens still being in chaos, we were glad of crusts and a watery vegetable stew to dip them in. In spite of the damage around us there was almost a sense of celebration; Mariam could be heard muttering thanks to the stars and Gareff came round with honey and yogurt. The hives had taken a battering, I heard him say, but they would recover and the rain would make everything flourish again. He was in such good humour he even gave me a spoonful of honey, without making me beg for it, and I didn't care that he still called me 'Queen Bee,' with his usual sarcasm.

I savoured the lingering taste of the honey in my mouth as I wrung out my sodden blankets and draped them over the screen to dry; then I carefully unravelled the oiled canvas I had hastily wrapped around my papers as soon as Ridrick had warned me about the coming storm. The first few outer sheets, which were blank ones, had mostly disintegrated but, sandwiched between them, everything I had scrawled on was intact. I almost wept with relief and the realisation that some meaningless scraps of paper are now my most precious possessions.

As I cleaned up my stall I was aware that more of the stonework had collapsed between us, but I didn't look in Banjo's direction, in spite of being intensely aware of his presence as always. Twelve had emerged from the back of her stall, wrapped in a dry blanket which I expect Mariam had somehow found for her, and watched me intently as I tidied up. I smiled at her but got no response. Eleven was also silent, but that was no surprise; I was sure that the first sound to come from him would be a gaseous eruption from one end, or a curse from the other.

'Is your paper alright?'

I looked up from the bed where I'd been separating out the soggy sheets, 'Yes, it is, thank you. Are you alright?' I was concerned to see that Banjo had a deep cut and a bruise above his right eye; his hand reached up to touch it and he winced, 'This is nothing, I believe I'll live. For now anyway,' he added with a half smile.

'I wish I had something I could put on it for you. My little brother had all sorts of potions and creams...' The words caught in my throat and there was an awkward pause while I struggled not to dissolve into tears. It had been a traumatic night and exhaustion was making me emotional. Then Banjo said, in a low voice, 'I expect you miss him. I had a sister, but she died.'

I got up and moved to stand by the wall, resting my hands on the rough ledge between us and thanking the rains for an opportunity to be so close to him. If his shoulders hadn't been so broad he could almost have squeezed through, the gap was now so big. As it was, I could look into his deep brown eyes and almost count the individual lashes on their lids. There were drops of moisture still clinging to his skin and I wanted so badly to touch him and wipe them away that I was afraid the desire must be written right across my face; instead, I talked, 'My brother is still alive, I hope; but I don't know for sure. What happened to your sister?' He hesitated and I thought he might change his mind about telling me, but instead he half turned, leaned against the wall and gazed off into the distance as if was talking to himself. When I couldn't look directly into his eyes I felt safer knowing he couldn't see the emotion in my own, I was so happy to hear him talk.

'Both our mother and father developed White Disease and lost their Patron and our home because of it. We went to live in a camp and my sister, being older, looked after us all until she became ill as well, with malaria.'

I stayed silent, afraid of saying the wrong thing and breaking the spell.

'My father,' Banjo continued, 'had taken care to register both of us at birth, while he still had the benefit of a Patron. When my sister died he decided it would be best to sell me, knowing that I could have a better life away from the camp.'

'How old were you?'

'Fifteen.'

'I was fourteen,' I said, 'My mother couldn't wait to be rid of me.' I think that was the first time I'd spoken aloud to a stranger about the bitterness I felt at her abandoning me.

'I don't believe my father would have sold me if there had been any choice,' said Banjo firmly, but I wondered whether all children try to make excuses for the parents who betray them until, like me, they can no longer deny the truth.

'I know,' he continued, looking at me, 'that Sourface told you something about me.' I couldn't avoid answering him, 'He said... he said you were bought to be bred from.' Banjo nodded, 'Yes, I was sold to a whoremaster and hired out. Do you understand what that means?' I thought about it and remembered Carolan and the phallus posters in Maidentown, 'Yes – women would come to get children by you.'

'Or to be pleasured. Whatever it says in my documents I am not impotent.'

'Then why...? I don't understand,' I confessed, wondering why that alone would lead to him not being wanted if he could still perform in the other ways required of him.

'I may be sterile – not able to father children,' he explained and I flushed with embarrassment that he thought I didn't know what it meant.

'I understand the difference,' I said scathingly; I had seen enough of Malakai's books on the subject to know that sexual congress was not always about the begetting of children, desirable though that was.

'None of the women who came to me fell pregnant,' Banjo continued, 'but more than one of them became attached to me and wanted to purchase me for their own exclusive use. Eventually, the wealthiest of them made the whoremaster an offer he could not refuse; I was only nineteen and still potentially virile, so Isabella,' and his voice softened, 'paid a great deal of money for me.'

The words stirred a memory in me: my mother's voice assuring me that when someone paid a great deal of money for something they tended to take care of it. And yet Banjo's Patron had brought him here and left him in the most miserable of conditions.

A thin trickle of blood began oozing from the cut above Banjo's eye and he wiped it away with his hand.

'You shouldn't do that,' I said, 'Your fingers are dirty and you might infect it.' I looked around for a clean strip of muslin to offer him but everything was wet and covered in dust and grit, 'You should ask to see the physician tomorrow, just in case.' But he shook his head and frowned, 'It's just a scratch.'

'Go on,' I said, prompting him to carry on with his story and to satisfy my curiosity about Isabella, 'What was your new Patron like?'

'I felt very lucky to be sold to her; she was rich, educated and very beautiful. It wasn't hard to enjoy my role and I soon became her favourite, although she had many other Protégés to choose from.'

'So what happened?'

'After two years she was still childless and I knew she was beginning to visit the markets regularly to find a man with a proven record of fertility. I was stupid, I let my jealousy show and we started to quarrel. One day she got angry with me over some small thing which I didn't think was my fault and I made the mistake of arguing with her. She began mocking me and I accused her of being barren.'

'Well, that may have been true,' I said, but he looked at me as if I was deliberately misunderstanding, 'I should never have said so, Ten, it wasn't my place. I'd become too comfortable with her and thought she was fond enough of me that I could say anything I liked.'

'So it was her who brought you here then?'

'Yes, to punish me. And she made sure my records said I was sterile and insubordinate so that no one would adopt me.'

'But why? If she didn't want you herself, why wouldn't she want someone else to have you?'

'Because,' he replied with a confident smile, 'she's going to come back for me. When she thinks I've learned my lesson she'll reclaim me. I'll apologise and things can carry on as they were before, except that I will be more careful.'

He seemed so certain, and so eager to get back to her although she'd been so cruel. I didn't want her to come back for him; I wanted someone to adopt us both. I imagined us going to a large estate, like Malakai's, and being well treated and cared for and perhaps one day, when he had forgotten all about Isabella, we would be bonded for life.

I came out of my daydream and we talked for a while longer, but it was mostly about the storm and how we were going to manage to get any sleep with everything still so damp. Banjo asked me a few questions about my life before The Kennels, but he was distracted and I felt more aware than ever of my spoiled face and the clumsy eye patch which was rubbing on my cheekbone and making it sore. His feelings for Isabella seemed to stand between us, as solid and as undefeatable as the brick walls.

I told him a little more about Beetle but he was barely listening, so it seemed pointless boasting that I had fetched a record price at auction, or that I too might have been the prized property of a whoremistress if my mother, for some reason, hadn't changed her mind and called a halt to the bidding and let me go to Malakai instead.

*****

When the Registrar took me inside after the auction we went first into a small office where my mother was waiting with my documents. After a few moments, Malakai joined us and the three of them sat at a table and took it in turns to sign the sales papers, receipts and letters of transfer. I stood and watched as they talked about me, but I was not included in the conversation.

'Will you get her tattooed with her registration number

while you're here today, Malakai?' asked the Registrar.

'No, I don't want her marked in any way.'

'Well, you know you have seven days' grace in which you can change your mind about that.'

'I won't.'

If the Registrar was offended by Malakai's brusqueness he didn't show it. He was full of smiles and congratulations – to Mamma for her successful sale and to Malakai for his exceptionally fine purchase; I could almost see the glint of krona reflected in his eyes. In fact, of the three of them, the Registrar was the only one who appeared delighted with the day's events. Malakai's face, being covered as always, was a mystery and nothing about his behaviour gave any indication of satisfaction. Mamma concentrated on the papers in front of her as if her life depended on it, her face as inscrutable as ever.

The papers were checked, folded and sealed; Mamma put her copies in a small leather pouch which she then placed on her lap whilst she waited for business to be concluded. Malakai scrutinised his copies and slipped them into a satchel, which he bound securely with a thong and put over his shoulder. Everyone then rose, bowed to each other and turned towards me. Was I supposed to do or say something? I looked at Mamma, expecting as always to take my cue from her, but her face was blank. Malakai simply stood there, his gloved hands folded in front of him, waiting. After a moment the door behind me opened and a server appeared, spoke quietly to the Registrar and left again.

'Excellent! Everything is ready,' said the Registrar, 'Akara d'Fiuri's belongings have been transferred to your wagon, Malakai, and you may take her as soon as it's convenient for you. May I offer you more refreshment before you go?'

'No. We have a long journey ahead of us so I'd like to leave immediately.'

The Registrar nodded and invited Malakai to leave the room ahead of him, gesturing to me to follow but I held back. Mamma hadn't moved so I took a step towards her and whispered, 'Mamma, I need the water closet.' At last she looked straight at me and it seemed to me that her steel grey eyes had never looked colder, 'You belong to Malakai now. If you need the water closet you must ask him.'

'But Mamma – I don't know him, he hasn't even spoken to me. What should I do? Please don't make me go, Mamma.'

'Akara, you have no choice.'

'But I don't want to! I want to go home with you, please Mamma, please!'

'Keep your voice down, Akara – don't shame me now. I've done my best for you today and I expect you to appreciate this chance you have of a good life with a man who will take care of you.' She began to walk away from me but paused, 'Things could have been very much worse. Be grateful, daughter.' And then she was gone.

I looked after her for a moment, not quite believing that she could just abandon me like that, but she didn't return. Instead, the Registrar came back, an anxious expression on his face and beckoning impatiently, 'Come along, child, your Patron is waiting.'

'Please,' I touched his sleeve, 'Can I use the water closet?'

'Yes, yes of course. This way,' and he took me along a corridor to a small, tiled room where he left me with repeated urgings to please be quick and not keep Malakai waiting any longer than necessary.

There was a large gilded mirror on the wall and I stared at my reflection, feeling strangely detached from it. The voices I could hear in the passage had a hollow, distant sound and my legs felt weak. I stumbled a little, turned towards the china water closet bowl and was violently sick.

*****

Banjo and I agreed that it would be wise not to let the guardians see how much of the wall between us had disintegrated during the storm. We patched it up with loose bits and pieces which would be easy to remove whenever we wanted. I was pleased to think that he took it for granted there would be more conversations and reminded myself that, in spite of his faith, Isabella might not come back for him. I went to my pallet and lay there, cold and still hungry, but assured that hair grows, bruises fade and I may not always need to wear the patch. My left eye would continue to heal and, even if I didn't regain the sight in it, maybe it wouldn't look as awful as I'd feared. I was so unrealistically optimistic suddenly that I forgot where I was and how late the hour; I called out, 'Goodnight, Banjo,' and got a whispered, 'Goodnight, Ten,' back.

There was a long, low, rumbling fart from the next stall and Eleven's gravelly voice followed it saying, 'Are you two goin' to fukkin' shut up now?'

'Yes, Eleven,' I replied cheerfully, with a tiny sliver of happiness restored to my heart, 'Good night.'

The aftermath of the storm kept Visitors away for the next two days; we ate, slept and exercised suspended in a kind of limbo of steaming heat as everything dried out. The flies came buzzing in their hundreds during the day, feasting on every scrap of filthy refuse that remained and settling everywhere; they were followed by small armies of lizards who, in turn, devoured the insects. At night we got cockroaches - rippling carpets of them, keeping us awake with their hissing and chirruping. Though she still never made a sound, Twelve was so disturbed by them that she tried to climb the mesh of her door in an effort to escape. The Guardians brought us candle stubs and lit them so we could keep the bugs at bay for an hour or two, but they returned in a relentless tide as soon as the candles burned down and we lost their light. We longed for morning to come and dreaded it too; with every wasted day all our Due Death Dates crept closer and there was a constant tension in the air at our end of the passage, with very little to distract us except each other.

One thing that diverted and disturbed us in equal measure was the sudden activity in the stall to my right. After days of doing nothing but belching, cursing and farting in his sleep Eleven got up from his pallet and lumbered out of his unlocked stall. He propped open the door and began to come and go at will at unpredictable times of day and night. Sometimes he returned with a plate of food, a jug of what smelled like ale, or a mouth full of leaf plugs which he would suck and chew noisily before spitting into his bucket. I sensed it would not be wise to ask questions of Eleven, but my anxiety grew and I didn't know who else might be persuaded to tell us what was going on.

Mariam was absent, probably working in the laundry or the kitchens as sometimes happened, and although Adelmo was on duty I was afraid to ask him anything since his recent harsh words to me. I was very careful to be polite and obedient and even offered to pose again for him, keen to show that I was making an effort as he had suggested. He declined, saying he had all the sketches he wanted, but he managed a small smile as if he recognised that I was trying. The next day he brought me more paper. When I tried to thank him he stopped me, 'I don't need you to thank me, it's good that you are practising your writing, Ten. Just be careful, keep whatever it is safe.' He seemed a little uneasy and later that afternoon I discovered why. Banjo tapped discreetly on our wall with a spoon to get my attention and when I went over to him he whispered, 'I've found out about Eleven. Fifteen just came back from some exercise and saw Eleven outside – he's one of the Guards.'

'What? How can he be?'

Banjo shrugged, 'I don't know. Maybe there's no room for him to sleep in the main building. Maybe he's here to spy on us. Maybe he just loves your company.' I liked him teasing me, so I joked back, 'Ah well, I can understand that; who could resist such beauty?' and I tossed my head in an exaggerated way, hoping he would laugh. Instead he looked serious and said, 'You don't look so bad, Akara. Stop thinking about how you were before and make the best of what you are now.'

That was the first and last time Banjo ever called me by my real name.

15 STARRY SKIES

For as long as I could remember, Mamma had impressed upon me my obligations as a Protégé; I had always known that once I belonged to a Patron I would be entirely at their disposal. I knew I could be put to work, treated well or badly, mated, bred from and sold on. I had no idea what Malakai intended for me. As I was assisted into the litter my heart thumped furiously and I was afraid I would be sick again; I didn't know where we were going or what would happen to me once we got there.

When I'd emerged from the Registrar's water closet there had been a young female server waiting in an ante chamber with a hot towel which she soaked in rosewater to clean my face and hands. Then she dipped a fresh flannel into the bowl, lowered her eyes respectfully and stood waiting whilst I looked at her, mystified. What was she expecting me to do? After a few moments she raised her eyes and smiled shyly at me, 'For below,' she said and nodded at my groin. 'Oh,' I said, suddenly understanding. Nobody but my mother had ever washed or even touched my female parts and I was embarrassed. But the girl nodded and smiled again, gesturing for me to lower my trousers, which I did. She knelt down and with skilled and careful hands she sponged my crotch before soaking another flannel and cleansing my bottom, although I'd already done so myself in the water closet. She dried me thoroughly with a soft white towel, pulled up my trousers and tied them gently at the waist.

When she rose to her feet her eyes were lowered modestly again and she gave a small bow before leaving the room. As soon as she'd gone the Registrar appeared and beckoned to me. 'Are you feeling quite well again?' he asked as we walked out to Malakai's caravan. It occurred to me then that he must be used to terrified individuals emptying their guts in his water closet. I daresay some of them never even made it that far.

Outside in the searing heat, the yard behind the Registry building was a noisy, smelly bustle of activity. Wagons and carts were being loaded, servers were hitching horses and mules and the camel stewards were coaxing the animals to their knees, ready for mounting. I recognised faces from the auction and watched the siblings, Gwin and Erin, clambering onto Carolan's very ostentatious chariot; they were still clinging to each other as their new Patron whipped up the horses and the vehicle made its dramatic exit in a cloud of orange dust. Carolan, judging by the grim expression on her face as they passed us, was still very angry about her earlier defeat and I wondered, once again, what had caused Mamma to stop the bidding in Malakai's favour.

The Registrar guided me towards a collection of vehicles, at the centre of which was the largest, handsomest litter I had ever seen. It consisted of an ornately carved, rectangular wooden frame that was almost as large as the stall I'm in now. It had openings on all four sides, draped with brocade curtains, and was furnished with soft bedding and plump silk cushions which Malakai was already reclining on when I got in; it seemed I had no choice, in such a confined space, but to lie next to him. He was still covered from head to toe, with only his very dark eyes visible. It was impossible to guess his mood or expression; I had only his voice to guide me and that too was almost expressionless and I soon learned that he never wasted breath or words.

'Come,' he commanded, and waved a white gloved hand at me. I'm sure he must have heard my heart banging against my ribs and seen my fear, although I tried hard to appear calm, as Mamma would have wished.

'I won't hurt you,' he assured me.

I still hesitated and, with a hint of exasperation, he added, 'I don't intend to mate with you, Akara; you're too precious to me intact. As long as you don't anger me you have no need to be afraid.' Whether he was telling the truth or not, it was a relief to hear the words and I eased myself down next to him, hearing Mamma's voice in my head telling me to be composed and cool.

'You're young and inexperienced, but I will teach you everything you need to know. You're already beautiful but I can make you perfect.' And with that he instructed the bearers to lift the litter and set off.

There were eight servers in all to carry the litter: two sets of four who took it in turns to carry or rest. They were all young men, chosen to be equal in height and strength so that the poles would rest evenly on their shoulders and provide as smooth a journey for us as possible. Ahead of us were porters accompanying two luggage wagons drawn by fine, well muscled mules; and behind us were two more large carts, pulled by draught horses and containing the servers Malakai had also bought that day. The caravan pulled out of the yard at a much more sedate pace than Carolan had, but drew even more attention and comment. If I hadn't been so scared I would have felt very proud to be part of such a grand parade. We passed onto the main thoroughfare as the sun began to dip and Maidentown prepared itself for evening. Already, as flares were lit and the daytime bustle faded, there was a different atmosphere to the place: a seductive hint of night time activities that I could only imagine, having never been there beyond sunset before. New smells and sounds filled the air and I looked through the curtains, curious in spite of my nervousness. There was music and laughter coming from the cantinas and my eyes were drawn to the last one I had been in with Mamma earlier that day. For a moment I was certain that I could see her in there again, a cup raised to her lips and a man's face intimately close to hers as if whispering in her ear. My heart contracted and I nearly called out to her but what would I have said? *Mamma, it's not too late to take me home. Please, Mamma, I'll be good I promise.* But I could already guess her reply: 'Be good for Malakai. He is your master now.'

So we carried on our way, in silence for more than an hour I should think, until we were well away from Maidentown and heading North West. To begin with the road was quite straight and smooth but it gradually became rougher; the bearers began to tire and stumble and I could actually feel Malakai stiffen with irritation next to me. I had eventually stopped trying to keep a physical distance between us, we were jostled and jolted into touching shoulders and, when Malakai made no attempt to be more familiar, I allowed myself to relax and lie next to him in comfort. He invited me to eat and drink from the treats laid out on a brass tray in front of us and when I offered to serve him he shook his head and said, 'No. We have servers for that, Akara. You must remember your position now as mistress of my household, answerable only to me.' He clapped his hands, the litter stopped and was lowered and a little girl, no more than seven or eight, climbed into the litter and passed us drinks and sweetmeats from the tray. Then she unhooked a smoking pipe from the corner, lit it and passed it to Malakai who sucked on it greedily, dismissing her with a wave of his hand. The girl scrambled out, the litter was raised and we continued on our journey.

Malakai didn't offer me the pipe, but the sweet fumes from it filled the litter and made me drowsy, lulling me into a half sleep for I don't know how long, until the litter came to a halt with a gentle bump.

'Are we there?' I asked, lifting my head from the cushions to look out.

'No,' Malakai replied, 'We will camp here for the night.'

Apart from the torches which the servers were lighting, we were surrounded by the blackest of nights and the starriest sky I had ever seen. The air was clearer than at Maidentown, or back at Mamma's where we were used to looking through a permanent haze of chalky dust. The atmosphere was less oppressive too and it seemed easier to breathe, not exactly fresh but lighter somehow. And the night was alive with noise, not just of the insects I was used to hearing – cicadas, mosquitoes and big winged bugs – but other sounds I didn't recognise, like things rustling and snuffling in the vegetation nearby and a faint, eerie howling in the distance.

'Jackals and hyenas,' Malakai said, 'They won't come near the fires now, but they'll scavenge our scraps when we pack up camp in the morning.' I'd only ever seen domesticated animals and it was exciting to think that the rumours Ash and I had heard about wild creatures still roaming the country were true. I wondered what else might be out there.

The wagons and carts had been positioned in a rough circle around a large fire and an elegant little tent was being erected just in front of our litter; food was being cooked and the succulent smells of roasting pork and chicken were making me hungry, in spite of myself. Servers moved about quietly and efficiently, as if they had done this many times and knew the routine. All the while, Malakai and I sat in silence. I felt awkward and nervous, still unsure of my position and his expectations, but he seemed entirely comfortable – resting back against the cushions with his eyes closed and a hand occasionally raising a hookah to his lips.

Eventually, just as I was beginning to wonder if I would ever get the chance to eat or sleep, a server informed us that food and accommodation had been prepared and Malakai lifted his head to speak drowsily in my direction, 'Go to your tent now, Akara. You'll be attended to. Good night.'

'Goodnight…' I began to reply but I didn't even know how to address him. Should I call him Master, as the servers did? Or give him his full name of Malakai de Montagne as Mamma, the Registrar and others had done?

'You may call me Malakai,' he said, before waving his hand in the now familiar gesture of dismissal and letting his head fall back onto the cushion, as if exhausted from being carried so far.

The opening to the tent was being held back for me so it was clear where I was meant to go. Inside there was a thick mat covering the ground and a heap of cushions, pillows and rugs making an inviting and sumptuous little nest. A flap at the other end revealed a sort of annexe containing a wooden water closet, towels and bowls of scented water. The woven box my mother had made for me had been set down on the mat and the lid opened, but nothing had been disturbed. Having just those few familiar, personal things nearby was comforting and I began to relax a little, reassured that Malakai would not be looking after me so well if he intended to mistreat me. But looking at the box also made me very homesick, even for Mamma, but especially for Beetle. I wondered how he was and what he might be doing now if not already asleep in his little cupboard. The only thing that stopped me from crying was the determination to speak to Malakai in the morning about fetching my little brother to join us.

I was brought a selection of tagines and a jug of watered

down wine – a feast beyond anything I'd been used to – followed by berries, nuts and herb tea. None of the servers spoke to me, other than to ask what I needed, and as I had no idea what else to say to them I stayed silent too, apart from thanking them. However, I learned very quickly that Malakai did not consider it necessary to thank menials, as they were only doing their job, and I soon grew out of the habit myself under his tuition.

I could hear the low murmur of voices outside and the crack and spit of the fire, which stayed lit until dawn; the howls and barks continued throughout the night but came no closer and I fell asleep feeling safe and warm, aware of someone coming and going occasionally from the litter nearby, but not disturbed by it.

In the morning the camp was dismantled as efficiently as it had been set up. The fire was doused and the scraps and bones from supper and breakfast were gathered into small heaps to be left for the animals. I'd hoped to see some and compare them with Mamma's old picture books, but they were shy and all I could make out as the litter was lifted and we resumed the journey north were tiny, dark shapes on the horizon, waiting patiently until we'd gone.

Although the air was clearer the heat promised to be just as fierce and we set off early to avoid the worst of it, but still the bearers had to swap frequently and the mules were changed every half hour or so. It must have been noon before Malakai instructed me to look out and see what was ahead. Up until then we had spoken very little and the last conversation had not gone well. Malakai had greeted me quite pleasantly when I first got into the litter, just as a young male server was taking away his breakfast tray. My Patron was, as usual, covered from head to foot, in fresh robes of royal blue with matching head covering. His eyes, without the visor or shades, looked brighter than the night before and his voice sounded stronger.

'Good morning, Akara. Did you sleep well?'

'Good morning, Malakai. I did, thank you. Did you?'

'I never sleep well. Come, let me look at you.'

I knelt down beside him and he cupped my face in his gloved hands, turning it this way and that to inspect me. My hair had been brushed but I was aware it needed washing and I began to apologise.

'All that will be taken care of. It's important that you are eating and sleeping well. Rest is the best preservative.' I almost giggled, thinking he made me sound like one of Beetle's jars of pickle. His eyes had crinkled at the corners and I guessed that he was smiling so it seemed like the ideal time to bring up the subject of my brother. On Malakai's command the litter was lifted, I settled myself next to him quite confidently and began my plea.

'Malakai, I have a younger brother.' There was no response, but his head was inclined towards mine and he was listening. 'I wonder... I *hope* ... that you might consider bringing him to join me. Us. I know that's presumptuous of me, but I love him dearly and I believe you would find him very useful.'

'Why?'

'Because he's very clever and gifted. He makes medicines and he knows all the best herbs and things for cooking.'

'When will your mother be putting him up for auction?'

'Well, he's only nine. But I don't think she will wait until he's fourteen to sell him officially. I think that she would give him up now if... if she got the right price.'

'Why? Why won't she sell him when he's older and worth a lot more?'

I tried to think of the best way to explain things to him and decided I could only be honest, 'Beetle has a poorly leg that looks a little odd and makes him limp. But it doesn't give him any pain and it doesn't stop him being very good at a lot of things.' I waited for Malakai's reaction, trying to judge from his eyes what he was thinking. He straightened his head and then turned to look out through the curtain on his side.

'We should be on my land in two or three hours. Perhaps you would like some tea or juice?'

I was confused. Had I misheard him? Had he answered me and I'd missed it?

'Malakai?'

'No.'

'No? I'm sorry, I don't understand.'

'I will not buy your brother. He sounds deformed and I like to have only beautiful things around me. Don't ask me again, Akara.' Then he closed his eyes and reached out for one of the smoking pipes. As if by magic, the young server who had taken his tray reached through the curtain and lit the pipe; he must have been walking alongside us the entire time and heard every word. I soon learned that privacy was something I had lost along with my liberty.

16 TRUTHS

By nightfall we had reached my real mother's camp, a collection of roughly built huts near a pool of muddy water that the dwellers shared with a family of warthogs. I was seated in front of a blazing fire with a bowl of hot grits and a blanket round my shoulders, badly shaken by the events and shocked by the story Surrana had told me as we trudged through the sweltering heat to get there.

Fiuri, the woman I had long called Mamma, was born in 2051, barely twenty five years after the Divinity's biggest flares had begun to die down. Surrana was born two years later, by which time their mother, Ursoola, was already sick and exhausted and had fallen prey to a disease she believed she had caught from Surrana's father. By the time Mamma was ten she was caring for her younger sister alone – scavenging, foraging and surviving as best she could, whilst Ursoola had apparently gone quite mad. The two girls were unalike in looks and character but nonetheless devoted to each other; they left their mother, taking their documents with them, and joined a small community which was rebuilding the remains of an old village. At last their lives held some hope and promise. People were becoming more organised and regulated and a caste system was evolving. Mamma quickly recognised the need to conform to the way the wind was blowing and the importance of good breeding in a society that now valued it above all else. Being Mamma she then learned to exploit it. She found herself a provider whom she called her Patron and who fathered her first two children, Nula and Hal, and she took care to lodge their birth with the new Registrar at Maidentown and raise them to be strong and healthy - perhaps she even loved them then, as she loved Surrana. Her Patron laid claim to some decent land out of town, acquired some livestock, planted vegetables, excavated the well and built the shelter that became our home. Then he was struck down with a fever and died.

Mamma was resourceful, she husbanded the farm well and for the next two years the sisters managed by themselves, sharing the work and caring for Mamma's two children between them.

Then one day, when she was eighteen or so, Mamma went to market, leaving Surrana at home with the bairns. There was a young white musician performing in the square and Mamma stopped to watch and listen. In spite of his pallid skin Mamma thought him very handsome and, when he singled her out of the crowd to sing to, she was completely charmed.

'His name was Adam Ocksford and he was so splendid,' Surrana told me, 'Tall, broad and long limbed, with thick, golden hair and clear blue eyes. You have to remember, Ash, that we saw so few healthy men and the caste system was not so defined as it is now.'

'When,' I asked her, 'did being like us become such an abomination then?'

'When more thin skinned people succumbed to sun damage and sickness and failed to reproduce successfully; having an uncorrupted complexion and thick, dark hair became the measure of your chance to survive and breed. You and I are unusual, Ash – you especially – because we

are both strong and well in spite of our physical traits. Even so, my skin burns and peels if I am not careful but you…you seem so perfect and so beautiful to me. I am so proud of you.'

'So, is that why my mother – my old mother - hates me? Because of the way I look?'

'Oh no. Fiuri hates you because you are my son and your father was the man she was in love with.'

Mamma became so besotted with Adam that she returned to Maidentown frequently to see him, finding excuses to go and leaving Surrana to mind her two babies. Surrana became very curious about Mamma's secretive behaviour and one day she insisted on going with her. By then Mamma was convinced that Adam was in love with her and she was eager to show him off to her sister. They gathered up Nula and Hal and set off.

Surrana was fifteen, innocent and just as lovely as Mamma in her way; she even had a fine head of corn coloured hair at that time. Adam could not take his eyes off her and immediately lost interest in Mamma, who was so blinded by love herself that she couldn't see it. She invited Adam into their home, believing that she had found a permanent provider, and only discovered the couple's betrayal when her lover disappeared weeks later leaving Surrana with a child in her belly.

In spite of Surrana's denials, Mamma believed that her sister had deliberately set out to seduce my father and, whatever the truth, could not forgive her; she saw her safely through her confinement and my birth but they barely exchanged a word with each other from that day on. Not long after I was born, my real mother abandoned me with Mamma to go in search of Adam, convinced that she could persuade him to bond with her and provide for us both. By the time she eventually found him she had lost almost all her hair and he claimed not to know her at all. Deserted and desperate, she went back to the only home she had ever known, hoping that Mamma would welcome her back.

During Surrana's long absence, Fiuri had not only survived but had managed to breed and to provide for three more children of her own – Tanya, Akara and little Beetle, each by different fathers to maintain the genetic diversity she was convinced would create the strongest line. Surrana found her very changed: hard, unyielding and unforgiving. Mamma turned my mother away.

'I would have taken you with me then, Ash,' Surrana told me, 'but I had nowhere to take you. At least I knew you would be fed and clothed if you stayed with my sister, although I learned later about the beatings and the way she made you live outside. When I was allowed to join this camp I started visiting secretly to watch you and, after I came across you and the little girl in the bush, I followed you home. Seeing you up close and even being able to touch you after all this time was such a joy to me, Ash. I knew I couldn't leave without you again and I was hiding in the barn today when you and my sister came in.'

17 LA BELLE DAME SANS MERCI

Isabella came back two days ago, just as Banjo said she would. It was late afternoon on my thirty third day and we were all still shaken by the events of that morning. When Mariam took the wretch in Two his breakfast he had tried to escape by pushing past her and running towards the exercise courtyard. He was stopped almost immediately by one of the Guards from outside, and then pinned down by Eleven who had just left his stall and was in the passage already. We could hear Two screaming and crying out, fighting for his life, as they dragged him back and straight into the Extermination Chamber. We heard Mariam, who was also crying, being instructed to light a candle in the sconce and then we didn't hear anything except for her sobbing. We held our breath for what seemed like an eternity, all of us hoping that they had managed to calm Two down and would take him back to his stall. But the minutes crawled by and the whisper passed up the stalls telling us that the candle had been blown out. Two was dead.

There are no second chances here. Poor Mariam was distraught, blaming herself for being careless and giving Two the chance to attempt an escape. But if he was desperate then he'd have tried anything and he would have known the risks. Eleven spent the rest of the morning striding up and down the passage, stopping to glare at each inmate in turn in case any more of us might consider making the same mistake. He was sweating so much that his feet left wet prints on the stone floor, though they'd evaporated before he got back to the same spot minutes later. Eventually I suppose the heat became too much for him and he disappeared.

Nobody said much that afternoon. Guardians brought our mid day meal in virtual silence and, although Banjo and I exchanged looks through the gap in our wall, we didn't speak to each other. There was nothing to say. I didn't think the day could get any worse but, just as I was finally about to start writing, I heard Gareff's voice from the far end of the passage.

'He is indeed still here. There has been a great deal of interest in him Lady Isabella, but no offer of adoption as yet.'

'Good,' came the response in a husky, female voice that I immediately disliked, 'Where is he?'

'Stall Nine. Near the end, on the right.'

I was straining to look through the mesh of my stall, waiting for Gareff and the Visitor to come into view on my left. They took their time and I was able to watch Banjo as he tried to compose himself. He hardly knew what to do, it seemed – whether to sit casually as if he didn't care, or stand with his usual proud, erect posture preparing to be viewed and admired. He didn't look in my direction and I think I knew then that he was lost to me. When Isabella appeared I tried hard not to be affected by the sight of her but failed; she was the most extraordinary and impressive woman I had ever seen.

Isabella was not what my mother would have considered beautiful, but she had such a strong and dramatic presence that it was impossible not to be enthralled by her. She wore a sleeveless, flowing blue and gold batik gown which had a stiff, half moon collar and a hem which swept the floor. Her face, neck and arms were bare, except for a few tattoos and her jewellery: bangles, earrings, necklaces and studs. There was a small gold ring through her nose and one through the right side of her lower lip; when she spoke I could see that her tongue was slit at the tip, and her skin gleamed like polished bronze. Her hair was dyed purple, blue, copper and tangerine and was braided into a cascade that sprang from her head like a vast, glossy halo. None of her features was delicate or even seemed in proportion, but she was handsome, sensuous and terrifying. My mother had been frightening in a small and quiet way; Isabella was tall, arrogant and commanding. Even Gareff was bowing and scraping to her.

'Here he is,' the Guardian announced unnecessarily as Isabella was already standing by Banjo's stall and looking at him. They gazed at each other for a long time, with me quietly going back to watch Banjo through the gap and my heart lurching at the look on his face. I had never seen that expression when someone looked at me – even when I was the perfect woman that Malakai claimed he had created – because it was more than desire or admiration, it was complete devotion. My brothers had loved me, but I saw a different kind of love in Banjo's eyes for this woman Isabella and I was so jealous.

'So,' she said at last, 'you're still here, Banjo.'

'As you knew I would be,' he replied, 'and I knew that you would come back for me one day. I've been waiting.'

'Have you? You look very fit and well, I don't believe you've missed me at all.' She said this with a sly, sideways look, teasing him. Putting her face close to the door, Isabella lowered her voice and even I could hear the seduction in it, 'Do you want to come back, Banjo?'

'Isabella…' Banjo said softly, leaning his forehead against the door as if he didn't have the strength to play her game. His fingers curled round the mesh, making it rattle, but otherwise there was silence while we all listened.

'Oh, Banjo,' Isabella sighed, and her breath must have touched his face, 'if only I could trust you not to let me down again.'

Banjo's head lifted sharply and he raised his voice, 'I swear to you!'

'Swear what? That you will curb that temper of yours and learn real obedience? Promise me that you will give me the child I want? I'm sorry, Banjo, I don't think those are promises you can be certain of fulfilling.' Isabella's voice was loud and clear, as if she wanted everyone in The Kennels to hear and for Banjo to be humiliated. She sighed dramatically again and began to move away, looking around her as if she was bored with that conversation and eager to move on. She saw me and wrinkled her nose as if I disgusted her, but she read the notes on my board. I glared at her, trying to convey my own disgust.

Twelve was in her usual position opposite, watching everything that was going on but making not a sound. When Isabella noticed her she went over and spoke, 'Well, who do we have here?'

'Juvenile female,' Gareff responded quickly, 'We estimate the age to be between eight and eleven but we can't be sure. She has no documents, I'm afraid, Lady Isabella, but if you're interested she appears to be quite healthy, apart from being mute.'

'Which, in itself, might be considered an advantage,' said Isabella, with a look in Banjo's direction.

'Yes, indeed!' said Gareff, laughing ridiculously loudly.

Twelve had shrunk into the corner of her stall but her enormous eyes stayed fixed on Isabella, who beckoned her forward so that she could examine her.

'Would you like to see her close up, Lady? She takes a lead quite well and we could walk her around the exercise yard for you,' the Guardian offered.

Isabella paused, looking back and forth from Banjo to Twelve as if trying to make a decision. Eventually she said, 'No that's not necessary,' and walked back to Banjo's stall. His eyes, like Twelve's, had never left Isabella and relief spread across his face when she returned to him. Isabella's mouth spread into such a broad and lovely smile that even I, much as I despised and was jealous of her, would probably have followed her anywhere at that moment if I'd been him. Gareff hovered beside her, ready for instructions and a hand poised on the bolt of Banjo's door.

'I will probably send someone tomorrow,' Isabella said, still smiling directly at Banjo, 'to collect the female child. That is all.' And she turned and walked away.

'Isabella?' Banjo's voice, quiet at first, rose to a shout when she failed to respond, 'Isabella! Isabella!' I stood helplessly on the other side of the wall, trying to think of something comforting to say. 'Banjo,' I said, 'I'm sure she's just punishing you for a little longer, she'll come back tomorrow for you too.'

'You don't know her.'

'But you're her favourite,' I argued. He gave a sort of false laugh before disappearing from view and I didn't see him again until the next morning.

The Guardians brought supper and I heard Adelmo urging Banjo to sit up and eat, but he refused and the plate clattered to the floor as if he'd pushed it away. When I went to the gap I could just make out Adelmo on his knees, clearing up the mess and muttering about it being a waste. But after that he emptied Banjo's slop bucket without complaint and I thought that was kind of him.

I lay awake for a long while, cold and uncomfortable and sharing Banjo's misery. I called out goodnight several times before giving up. He wouldn't answer me and all I could hear before I finally fell asleep was the creaking of the straw mattress as Banjo tossed and turned, and the usual clicks and chirrups of the night insects. I wasn't aware of any sounds from the other stalls, so even the Guardians had an undisturbed night for once.

I must have slept soundly eventually because I woke with a start yesterday morning and later than usual. The Guardians had begun their shift change and, for a moment, I had an unfamiliar sense of peace and normality. Then I remembered to put another scratch on the wall and was reminded of how few there were left to add. My next thought was of Banjo and I became aware of him tapping gently against the wall to attract my attention. Happy that he wanted to talk at last I took the time to go to the mirror to put my eye patch on and fiddle with the thick stubble on my head. As I splashed water on my face I was convinced that all my wounds were healing well, and what scars I will be left with I can accept. I hope I will get back the sight in my left eye but I don't expect it. The old Akara no longer exists and I must learn to like the new one.

I swilled some water around my mouth to freshen it and stepped up to the gap. I couldn't see Banjo at first but I could still hear the tapping and I called out to him. When he didn't answer I scrabbled away at some more of the loose brickwork and stones to get a better view into his stall.

Banjo was suspended above his bed, the thick silver chain he wore on his left ankle clinking against the wall as he swung slowly to and fro from a rusty bar in the roof.

18 MEMENTO VIVERE

By the time my brain had accepted what my eyes had seen, the Guardians had come in with Banjo's breakfast and discovered him themselves. Adelmo, Ridrick-Oola and Eleven got his naked body down and laid him on the bed, agreeing that he was beyond reviving and had probably been dead for some time.

I heard all the discussions between them as I stood in absolute shock by the gap, unable to take my eyes off Banjo's lifeless body and hoping that he would suddenly sit up and say it was a mistake. He still looked as near perfect in death as he had in life, though there was some bruising around his neck and the old cut on his forehead had burst open again. Ridrick-Oola, in her matter of fact way, pondered over how she thought Banjo had managed the seemingly impossible. Having created a thick rope from bedding and clothes he must have repeatedly thrown it up until it caught around a bar in the roof. That would account for the sounds I had heard which I thought were just his restlessness. Then I was probably asleep by the time he made the noose, balancing his stool on the mattress to climb onto and then kicking it away. It had toppled back onto the bed rather than the floor, otherwise I might have heard it. And, if I had, I might have saved him; instead I had lain only five paces away and fast asleep.

I've seen dead people before, including Malakai of course, but never when they've died by their own hand. It was not the first time the Guardians had dealt with a suicide in The Kennels however, and there was a lot of talk about how it had been allowed to happen again, who had been on that night's shift and who could be blamed. They even asked me if I had heard or seen anything which could have prevented it happening. *Would I have said something if I'd realised what he was doing*, Ridrick-Oola asked me and I could only look at her in disbelief. How could they think I would have let Banjo die? I would rather he went to live with Isabella, knowing I'd never see him again, than to think that he had killed himself because of her.

Hours passed. I couldn't eat, I couldn't draw. I had watched them wipe the blood from Banjo's cut, sponge his arms, chest and legs and remove the silver anklet which Adelmo placed carefully on Banjo's discarded bolero and passed to a weeping Mariam to take away. As Ridrick and Adelmo gently turned the body over to continue sponging I was horrified to see a dozen or more angry wheals on Banjo's back. They were not fresh enough to have been made while he was here in The Kennels but had been hidden under his clothes all the time. I felt sick at the thought of how any man could worship the woman who must have been responsible for such brutality.

The Guardians did not comment on the wounds; they would have seen them when Banjo first came in and are long since past being shocked by anything I suppose. Adelmo and Eleven wrapped Banjo up in the sheets he had hanged himself with and carried him away, leaving Ridrick-Oola to finish cleaning the stall. She shook the pillow and beat the straw mattress with a wooden paddle, bending down to pick up something which had fallen out along with the dust and bits of loose straw. I couldn't see what it was but I suspect it was a small stash of treasures that Banjo had been keeping hidden; perhaps some pods that Mariam had given him, maybe some more brazilia nuts. Without looking inside, Ridrick quickly put the pouch in her own pocket, swept the floor and departed, wiping Banjo's details from the chalkboard outside as she left.

Mariam came with a plate of food and tried to persuade me to eat but I wouldn't. 'You must eat, cariad,' she said and laid a hand on my shoulder, 'Nothing you can do bring Nine back. I knew you like him but he never going to be happy without that lady.' It's only now, thinking about it, that I realise how much Mariam, along with the other Guardians, must observe and understand about us. At the time I just leaned my cheek against her hand and she sat down next to me on my bed while I cried.

In the afternoon, accompanied by a great deal of fuss and noise and two servers, Isabella returned. I don't know who had told her about Banjo but she strode straight up to his stall, which was being cleaned out, and stood looking around her angrily – as if she refused to believe them and Banjo was simply hiding somewhere to tease her. She caught me looking at her through the gap and some message passed between us that I couldn't put into words, but I sensed she recognised her guilt just as I did. There was no shame in her eyes though, only defiance. As we stood there I became aware of a low, insistent hissing from further down the passage which gradually became louder as all the inmates came to the front of their stalls and joined in. Isabella could have been left in no doubt that the hissing was meant for her. I continued to stare at her and her narrowed eyes dared me to join in, but I couldn't; I was too afraid. This woman and I were enemies now, and I knew more than anyone what she was capable of. She drew closer and began to examine me in detail.

'Interesting,' she said, 'there's something about you, in spite of your gruesome appearance... I might consider you.' I don't know what expression she saw on my face then, but a triumphant look crossed hers as she said, 'But not now. I can afford to wait, since no-one else is going to want you.'

Then she turned her back on me and summoned Adelmo from the end of the passage.

'You! Come here. Release the dumb child I've come for and hurry with the paperwork,' she instructed, 'If you'd taken better care of him I would have been able to take Banjo as well; as it is I want his ankle chain and any other items returned to me immediately, before they disappear into one of your pockets.'

Adelmo's expression was unreadable from where I stood and I didn't hear him reply. He stood looking after her as she strode back down the passage and the hissing turned into shouts, the inmates banging any object they could lay their hands on against the walls and doors as she passed. Even then I could not bring myself to join in. Was I afraid that she would single me out for punishment, or did I secretly hope she would come back to adopt me as she'd hinted? The thought was disgusting and sickened me, but the prospect of death was worse.

When Adelmo unlocked Twelve's stall and brought her out the servers immediately reached to bind her hands and lead her away, although Adelmo insisted it wasn't necessary, 'She's an obedient child, she'll follow you if you are kind and don't frighten her.' But the servers shook their heads; they had their instructions.

The raucous noise from the other stalls continued, but Adelmo did nothing to stop it. It took the arrival of Eleven and Gareff to quieten the racket, while I stood silently in shame and self loathing at my cowardice. Twelve, her eyes wide and uncertain, began to follow the servers but gave me one last pleading look. I could think of nothing to do to help her except to offer some advice, 'Be good,' I said, 'and don't make the lady angry. I know she wants a child and if you're good I'm sure she will look after you.' I had nothing else to add as they led the poor creature away, with Adelmo's stooped figure following close behind.

The Guardian came back after a while with a bundle of fresh bedding for Banjo's stall and a clean slop bucket. The floors had already been washed down and everything else prepared ready for a new occupant. I saw Adelmo run his fingers thoughtfully over the rough edges of the gap in the wall and I knew he would get it blocked up; I didn't care. With Banjo gone there was no one I would want to talk to and my life was nearly over anyway. I lay on my bed, asking the gods to please just let me die now; seven more days would just be seven more days of hell so what was the point? I heard my door being unlocked and guessed it would be Mariam with another plate of food and another plea for me to eat, which I would refuse. But it was Adelmo's tall, lean figure which came to stand by my bed and his morose voice which spoke to me.

'Get up, Ten and stop feeling sorry for yourself. It's not your fault that he died.'

Of course I knew he was right, but the honest truth was that in spite of my feelings for him I had betrayed Banjo in the end by not speaking out to the woman who really had been responsible for his death.

When I didn't answer I expected Adelmo to shake his head and leave, frustrated by me once again and realising I was not worth wasting his time on. Instead he persisted, 'You were wise not to cross her, sacrificing yourself would not bring Nine back.'

I turned my head away, hardly bothering to listen and beyond accepting comfort. Eventually, as I'd expected, Adelmo sighed and left, but first he pushed something into my hand and said very quietly, 'Read this.'

It was a long time before I raised my head to look at what he had left me: a small scrap of paper, folded and with just three words written in clear, large letters inside:

KEEP WRITING TEN

I was confused at first; why would Adelmo write something down when he could say it out loud to my face? But the more I thought about it the more I became convinced that the Guardian must have come across the note when he was checking Banjo's stall just now and that Banjo had written it himself and left it in our gap in the wall for me to find. He had been thinking of me at the end and wanted me to carry on with my scribblings. Now it seemed as if I had a way to make things up to him, not by calling Isabella a murderess to her face and risking terrible punishment, but by doing what I can still do. When I first came here Adelmo had said that scribes were always in demand; perhaps my future lies in my hands if I just keep practising.

So, I am writing and drawing again. What remained of yesterday was for mourning Banjo and putting things straight in my head. I ate the supper Mariam brought me and took the little pod she offered from the folds of her headdress, 'It help for you to sleep, cariad,' she said. But I didn't want to sleep; I wanted to think, plan and remember so that today I could write. I added the pod to the one she had given me before, wrapping and hiding the package carefully, saving it for another time. For now, I want to live every moment I have left before my Due Death Date in seven days and, just as my body is healing, my mind is becoming clearer and the memories more frequent and sharp.

*****

Around mid day, with the sun high in an incredibly clear sky, Malakai told me to draw back the front curtains of the litter and look out. His tone of voice was no different from when we had spoken two hours before – neither stern nor kind but definitely a voice not to be argued with. Just like my mother's. Over the course of three years in Malakai's household I rarely heard any change in his expression except when he was slurring with tiredness. Of course it was different at the end, when he was dying and terrified, but on the day we arrived at the Montagne estate it was hard to tell if he was happy or not to be home. His eyes gave nothing away and it was only his choice of words that displayed his pride, 'From here,' he said, 'everything you see is mine. It was all inherited from my maman, who was French. You will learn about her and the estate so that you fully appreciate who you are following and what will be expected of you as its mistress.'

'Yes, Malakai,' I replied, gazing out at the landscape ahead of me. For as far as I could see there was more lush greenery than I had seen in my lifetime – fields upon fields of healthy crops being tended by hundreds of workers. Since Malakai was clear that he wanted me to be educated it seemed safe to ask questions, 'What is it, Malakai?'

'Hemp. The most versatile and useful crop on earth.'

'Oh. What is it used for?'

'Almost everything – building, paper, medicine… In a day or two my foreman will take you on a tour of the estate and tell you more. Beyond these fields there is bamboo, sugar cane and the fruit plantations. Closer to the chateau are the vegetable crops and the livestock.'

I had no idea what a 'chateau' was and he explained, whilst making it clear that the lesson would not be repeated since he did not have the energy to answer questions more than once. I soon discovered that Malakai's pride in his French heritage was quite obsessive and required the entire household to be familiar with some of its language. He would spend hours on end in his library and throw out new words as he learned them, often giving no clue as to their meaning but expecting us to understand. I soon learned not to ask but to go down into the library myself as soon as I could to look them up. Most of the servers were forbidden to enter the library at all so had to rely on guesswork, or being given an unreliable translation by someone else. Since very few servers were literate it became something of a game amongst them to translate Malakai's instructions through deduction and I often caught them laughing at each other's suggestions. They never included me in their amusement; as Malakai's premier Protégé my loyalty to him was assumed to be absolute and they viewed me with suspicion. In time I thought I had earned their trust, and even that some of them liked me, but now the mist is beginning to clear I see I must have been mistaken.

There was a wide, sandy track running through the middle of the fields and at the start of it the litter stopped. The servers put us down carefully, stretching their arms to ease aching muscles and seek some shade. All the other vehicles stopped too and I prepared myself to get out and walk the rest of the way to the chateau, but first I badly needed to do my toilet. I turned to Malakai and began to ask, 'Malakai, I need - 'but he interrupted me with a raised hand, 'Arrangements will be made,' and he flicked his fingers to encourage me out of the litter. Another thing I learned very quickly about my Patron was that he not only did not like to look at people or things he considered ugly, he didn't like to hear about anything unpleasant either.

I climbed out of the litter with assistance from the little girl I recognised from the day before. She seemed to know exactly what I needed and led me off the track into a field where a small area had been cleared. Waiting there was a large container with a hole in the middle of its wooden lid to create a seat; it was obviously a water closet and, before I remembered that I shouldn't, I had thanked her and I then waited for the girl to leave. When she didn't, I realised I was expected to do my toilet with her there. It was even more embarrassing than my experience at the Registrar's, where at least I had been given some privacy for the business itself.

That was one of the hardest lessons for me to learn in those first months at Montagne: that I was hardly ever permitted to be alone. It was not just that Malakai wanted me to be waited on at all times, my every need attended to and often anticipated; it was also that all his most precious possessions were guarded constantly: against theft, damage or – in my case - escape. Left with no choice I sat on the seat and eventually managed to do what I needed to, avoiding looking at the girl as she stood patiently with towels and water to clean me afterwards. As we came out of the clearing I discovered we had been encircled by four guards the whole time, each holding a machete and ready to defend or restrain me as required.

Had I known then what I know now of the world beyond the Montagne estate, the thought of escape would never have entered my head. I was about to become imprisoned in a life of such extravagance and comfort that I believe it was beyond even my mother's ambitions for me. On that day though, I still had dread gnawing at my guts, with so much uncertainty about my future and the bitter disappointment of my request for Beetle being denied. *I will ask again,* I thought; if I am good and obedient he will become so fond of me over time that he won't be able to refuse.

I returned to Malakai in the litter, which remained on the ground and had been extended by awnings on each side to provide more relief from the sun. Laid out on mats were trays of delicacies and flagons of juices and wines, all of which I was invited to try. No sooner had my fingers become sticky than someone would appear with a damp cloth to wipe them; if a strand of hair floated across my face and threatened to stray into my mouth or eyes it was brushed gently away by a nearby hand. I was treated like royalty, as Mamma had predicted, and I very soon became accustomed to it.

As we sat with our feast a wooden cart pulled up beside us; there were twenty or so little baskets piled up on it and a young man on foot waiting for instructions. On Malakai's command the server pulled a string which raised the fronts of all the baskets and a flock of white birds was released into the air – I had never seen so many all at once. There were sometimes exotic birds for sale in Maidentown, but very rarely more than one or two in a cage and they were generally beyond most people's means. Most animals were more valuable than the lowliest server and even Protégés could sometimes be had more cheaply than a fine horse or a cow in calf.

We watched as they circled a few times above us and then they all flew confidently off towards the north. 'What were they, Malakai?' I asked, 'and where are they going?'

'They're homing doves, Akara. They are the signal to my workers that I am close by and most of them will be waiting for us when we arrive.' He called for the remnants of our meal to be cleared away and the litter to be prepared once again for our departure. 'Meanwhile,' he continued, 'we shall have some sport to amuse us for the last part of the journey.' He put a thick leather gauntlet onto his right hand and held out his arm. 'Emanuel!' he called and, from the other side of the wagon a handler appeared with the most magnificent hawk gripping his slender arm. The bird was hooded and its ankles had thin leather straps attached to them; when it was passed to Malakai his arm seemed barely able to support the weight. He swiftly removed the hood and launched the bird into the air with a command which caused it to spread its glorious wings and soar away in the direction of the doves.

I knew enough about nature to be sure that one or more of the doves would not make it home. I looked at Malakai in disbelief, why would he sacrifice any of his birds unnecessarily for this sport?

'It is a simple way of selecting the best and strongest; I shall breed from the ones that survive and ensure the continuation of their superior genes. Besides, the falcon has to eat too, does he not?'

We did not travel together for the remaining two miles. As soon as the first of the doves was spotted, a stable hand at the chateau had been dispatched with horses to meet us. When Malakai discovered I couldn't ride he was a little irritated, I think, and said that for the time being I would have to continue in the litter and he would go on ahead. He was a very skilled horseman and galloped off at speed, leaving me feeling strangely alone without him. He was, after all, both my master and my protector in those days.

19 THE SHANTY

Before we left the camp I had tried on two occasions to go back to my old home to see Akara, but Mamma caught me both times and could still control me with fear – not for myself but for Akara.

'If you attempt to see her again, Ashley, I will have her removed from here. If necessary I will even sell her early to assure myself that she is kept away from you, do you understand?'

'Mamma she is barely eight years old! What harm could it do for me to see her? Just once, I beg you.'

'Akara is special, she will be the best and most beautiful of my own, true children and I won't have her contaminated by aberrations. Go back to your real mother, Ashley; you belong with your own kind.'

When Surrana and I moved to Maidentown it was hard leaving Akara even further behind, but we had no choice and I knew that at least Mamma was taking good care of her, if only for her own ultimate benefit and enrichment.

After several weary days Surrana and I reached the edge of the town. We had been forced to sell a number of possessions in order to buy food and fresh water but had resisted the temptation to sell Chapstick, in spite of some very handsome offers. She had soon given up walking behind us on the blisteringly hot ground and chose to travel on the cart instead, finding shade under pots and blankets and emerging when she was hungry or just to look around. I was sure that she had come with us in the hope of finding Jiggs, although I hadn't mentioned him in a long while.

We meandered through the shanties, hoping to find a space for ourselves somewhere but becoming more and more disheartened. Even amongst other outcasts we were met with suspicion and threatening looks, no one was prepared to let us settle where we might encroach on their precious pitch. I think we were both beginning to wish we hadn't left the camp when our luck suddenly changed. As we approached a clutch of trees in search of shade, a woman came out of the blackened carcass of an old vehicle. It had no wheels and one side had slipped into a crack in the earth, but it was just recognisable as a burned out bus, its glassless windows now curtained with scraps of fabric and plastic and the roof covered with brushwood and stones in an attempt to keep it cool.

The woman was ashen skinned and bent over with age – she must have been fifty or more - and at first I thought she was going to shoo us away, as everyone else had. But on looking us up and down she approached the cart and began to rummage through the contents.

'Is she going to steal from us?' Surrana asked me.

'I don't think so,' I said, 'and it will hardly be difficult to stop her if she tries. Look at her, I'll be surprised if she hasn't been robbed of everything herself.'

The old woman was picking things up, sniffing and stroking them as if it would help her decide something. Finally, she lifted her head, cocked it to one side and spoke to us.

'You cumsh inshide,' she said, 'yesh, yesh, I takesh you in!' She had a strange accent and barely a tooth in her mouth, both of which made her nearly impossible to understand, but her eyes were kind and it seemed she was inviting us into her bus. Surrana looked at me and waited for me to respond; over the last few months she had learned to trust my judgement and I was proud to have become the decision maker.

'I think,' I said, 'we should go in.'

Once inside we nearly choked in the stinking air; the bus was full of debris - things the old woman must have been collecting for years to eat, wear or furnish the bus, but which were mouldy with age and saturated with rodent piss and droppings. It was so suffocatingly bad that we started to leave, but the woman took my hand and pulled me further in, jabbering and gesturing until I finally understood.

'Surrana, I think she is saying we can stay, maybe in exchange for helping her to clean the bus.'

The woman nodded and squeezed my upper arm, 'You shtrong!' she exclaimed, and I nodded. 'Yes,' I replied, 'and we will help you. What is your name? My name is Ash and this is my mother, Surrana.'

'Shushana, Shushana,' the woman repeated, taking hold of my mother's arm and stroking it admiringly, 'Tikertyboo. Tikertyboo.'

'What does she mean?' Surrana asked me, since I now appeared to be the interpreter.

'I don't know. It must be her name. Are you Tikerty?' The woman nodded vigorously and grinned. Her breath was foul but I tried not to draw back. Instead I guided her towards the front door of the bus and told her to sit down.

'Is there water nearby, Tikerty?'

'Yesh, yesh' and she pointed in the direction of the setting sun, smiling and nodding again. I looked around me and saw two metal buckets, both overflowing with rotting vegetation and crawling with ants and flies; I covered my nose and mouth and picked them up, trying not to retch.

Surrana had moved back as close to the door as she could, but the woman had reached for her and was clutching at her skirt, 'Shushana shtay! Shushana shtay!' she pleaded and my poor mother had no choice. She hunkered down next to the old woman and, as I left, Tikerty was playing happily with the string of beads around my mother's neck. The cat wisely remained outside, observing its new surroundings and hissing at anyone who approached the cart. Once the bus was finally habitable Chapstick was prepared to earn her keep, dealing efficiently with any mice or rats that dared to come back. She was as revered and spoiled in our new home as she had been at the camp, and had become quite plump by the time she died.

Wretched as our life was in the shanty settlement we were luckier than most. We cleaned up the bus as well as we could and, over several journeys, I managed to take all its contents to the nearest rubbish site, where it was instantly picked over by beggars and rats. While Surrana and Tikerty stayed in the bus, both to tidy it and to guard it against squatters and thieves, I went on foraging trips and almost always managed to bring back enough for us to make a meal or to trade in exchange for one. It was during those early forays that I really learned the art of invisibility because I had to. At the camp there had been solidarity and understanding, a shared empathy between us. In Maidentown there was a hierarchy even amongst the low castes, a savage need to pick on anyone weaker to avoid being the one at the bottom of the heap. Everyone seemed to despise or victimise someone else and, after the early days when I let my anger and defensiveness get the better of me, I became adept at sliding through crowds and seeking the shadows where I could, generally avoiding notice and confrontation. I often stopped at the shrines in town and listened to the sermons, observing the small groups of devotees that gathered there and their behaviour towards each other and the passers by who paused to ridicule them. I tried hard to emulate their tolerance and forgiveness, envying the easy affection that they shared and longing, but never quite daring, to join them. I didn't have the courage then to add to my existing problems by being despised for anything else.

Then one day, when I was bartering at one of the stalls on the main road, I saw Mamma. She was driving the wagon and, even if she'd noticed me in the shadows, she would not have been able to recognise me beneath my all garments. Nonetheless, I was surprised at how much dread she could inspire in me still; as soon as she had driven on past, I quickly finished my business and hurried back to tell Surrana.

When I told her about Mamma - warning her that we must be careful now we knew she still came here for the big market days - Surrana surprised me by saying, 'No, Ash. I shall seek her out and ask for her help. She is my half sister and she loved me once. If she knows we are here, and what conditions we live in, even she must take pity.'

I did not believe for one moment that Mamma's heart would soften and I told Surrana not to go, but she was determined. After several hours she came back, hot and flushed but seeming satisfied, 'In the end it was her pride,' she said, 'I told her how shocked all the grand and important people she trades with would be to know that her sister and her sister's child were reduced to living here. I also told her we were hungry and she has promised to bring us some provisions.'

So every few months, for five or six years after that, she would come to the shanty with food, clothing and goods for us to use or to sell. She came into the bus alone, parking the wagon nearby and staying only for as long as was absolutely necessary. Then the day Akara turned fourteen she took her to auction, sold her and paid us our last visit.

She came from a cantina, the smell of liquor on her breath, and said that Akara had gone. I had never seen the poor child, never got the chance to tell her that I loved her or to say goodbye. I hated Mamma with all my heart in that moment.

20 CHANGES

Only five more days. It seems hotter than ever in here and, after Two's escape attempt and Banjo's suicide, the Guardians are more vigilant than before. There will be no more exercise for any of us for a while, I'm sure.

There are now Guards patrolling inside as well as out, and when Eleven isn't occupying the stall next to me another Guard is; they all look so alike that I just think of them all as Elevens although I suppose that, like us, they have names. My Due Death Date is so close now that I have no expectation of adoption, only the desire to keep on scribbling and a tiny, unquenchable shred of hope, but for what I don't know. So I continue to eat without appetite and exercise without energy. I try to take care of myself: washing, bathing my eye and doing all that I can to improve my appearance, knowing that my mother raised me for a better destiny than this. Sleep is hard to come by and harder with each passing night, when I lie awake wondering what death is like and where we go from here. I hope something will benefit from the remains of my skinny little body. Perhaps they will feed me to the pigs.

The good news is that, since the rains came, there has been more food and a regular supply of reasonably fresh water. Breakfast this morning was a cooked hen's egg, two tomatoes and four large segments of orange, which were brought to me by a new Guardian whose name is Colim Sang. Gareff showed him round yesterday and was being quite deferential so I think he may be a higher rank. I don't think I like him, but I don't know why. Perhaps it is because he is dressed in black and even has thick dark netting entirely covering his face so you can't see his features at all, not even his eyes. There is also something strange and unreadable about his behaviour towards me which makes me uneasy. Nonetheless, I was careful to be polite and grateful when he brought me my food.

'Thank you, this looks very good. Please, Colim Sang, can you tell me where Adelmo is?'

'Do you mean Adelmo D'Afrar?' he said, his voice muffled behind the netting.

'Yes, of course, I'm sorry. Adelmo D'Afrar.' I was annoyed at my mistake. I realise how relaxed my behaviour has become with some of the Guardians – particularly Adelmo and Mariam – and if every move is now being watched and everything we say might be reported then they too might be at risk. They have each, in their ways, been especially kind to me and I feel I should protect them. I remembered how nervous they had both seemed on occasions recently and a sudden pang of misgiving made me question Colim Sang again, 'I wondered if Adelmo D'Afrar might have been taken ill as I believe he sometimes is. I'm only concerned in case it is something infectious,' I added by way of explanation.

'Yes, he's ill,' Colim Sang replied bluntly, 'Eat your breakfast.' And with that, he left.

Although it is only two days since I have seen Adelmo or Mariam, the simultaneous absence of my only two allies is worrying. The arrival of new Guardians and the extra Guard patrols has created a different atmosphere in The Kennels, a heightened sense of menace beyond my own fear of impending extermination. It has a familiar feel to it that I can't explain; I only know it has something to do with Malakai's death and that it is important for me to remember.

No one has taken Banjo's place in the stall to my left and they didn't bother to block the gap. I still look through it sometimes as I pace around my little prison, half expecting to see him and letting hatred of Isabella occupy my thoughts. I think of Beetle too and wonder if Mamma is taking care of him; if I somehow get out of here alive I will find him. In the meantime I must keep alert, aware as I am of the sense of increasingly imminent danger.

*****

I don't know whether Malakai's mother had ever seen a real French chateau when she created the Montagne estate, or whether much of the old continent that Malakai claimed she had travelled from even still existed at the time. But if Malakai's mother had told him she could fly I think he would have believed her. Whatever the truth, Madame de Montagne had built something spectacular. As we passed the hemp fields the dusty track became a straight, gravelled avenue, bordered by cypress trees and leading directly to a palatial building that looked as if it had been carved out of stone quarried from the honey coloured cliff behind it. There were trees and ornamental shrubs everywhere and, immediately in front of the house, a fountain teeming with little fish. As we pulled up to the main door I could see Malakai on the steps, flanked by servers awaiting my arrival with pretty paper parasols so that I did not have to walk even an inch exposed to the blazing sun.

Inside, there was a circular hall with a high, domed ceiling and marble floors; six arched doorways with studded wooden doors led off to other rooms and the walls were dotted with mirrors and paintings. A large stone staircase rose from the centre to an upper floor and the steps were decorated with blue and green mosaics. Malakai stood beside me as I gazed round in awe and delight, 'Oh, it's wonderful,' I said.

'I'm pleased you appreciate it, Akara. Now, I'm very tired so I will retire. You'll be shown your rooms and I will see you in the morning. Bonne nuit.'

I looked at him blankly.

'It means Goodnight.'

'Oh. Goodnight, Malakai,' and then, because it seemed as if I should, I thanked him. Emanuel, the young man who had handled the hawk earlier, was by Malakai's side as he left and they went into one of the ground floor rooms, shutting the door firmly behind them and leaving two servers guarding the door. *What should I do now, Mamma?* I wondered and her voice in my head was as clear as if she had been there beside me: *Start behaving like a mistress, Akara and make yourself worthy of the Patron who has just paid a great deal of money for you.*

'Would someone please show me to my quarters?' I asked as confidently as I could, and immediately someone was next to me, guiding me towards the staircase and leading me up to the next floor. To our right were several doors, all made of thick, carved wood with stained glass fanlights, and lit with wall mounted lamps in matching leaded glass on either side. The effect was like one of the gorgeous illustrations in my Rubaiyat and the thought reminded me that I had not seen Mamma's woven box since we left the litter. But as soon as the door was opened and I walked through I could see the box in front of me, lying on an ottoman at the foot of an enormous four posted bed draped in sumptuous brocades and spread with a silk quilt and velvet cushions. There was a large window, its wooden shutters thrown open but covered with a white lace blind to keep out insects and dust. The walls were covered in tapestries illustrating scenes from history or legend: men, women and children picnicking in green leafed forests or playing in flower filled meadows, and hunting parties chasing animals I didn't recognise. This opulence surrounded me every day for three years and I very soon became accustomed to it. It would have been easy to forget the harsh realities of life elsewhere if I had not occasionally caught glimpses of it when I accompanied Malakai on trips, or on my rare visits to parts of the estate where conditions were very different.

Leading off from the bedroom was a small annexe with a water closet and a washing area suffused with incense. Later, I was shown to the bath house on the ground floor where I was taken to be immersed every morning in a sunken pool filled with cool, perfumed water. If Malakai was expecting guests and my presence was required then I would be bathed as many times in a day as he considered necessary to do him credit. At night there were enormous fires lit, inside the chateau and out, and animal skins piled on the bed so that I need never feel cold. I thought of poor little Beetle in his tiny cupboard, without even human warmth to give him comfort, and I determined to make Malakai change his mind about bringing him here when he was in a more amenable mood.

I slept soundly that first night, exhausted in spite of my excitement. After I'd eaten, I was undressed and washed by two little Protégés who became my constant attendants when I was in my private quarters. I'd never seen identical siblings before and I was fascinated by them; they were so alike – both small, with neat doll like features and pale pink skin - that I never learned to tell them apart, or to work out whether they were boy, girl or neither. Their voices gave nothing away because they hardly ever spoke but they smiled, nodded and were so efficient that it was almost like having another limb, with one often starting a task and the other finishing it, or moving in unison like a mirror image of each other. It was impossible to guess their age and when I asked them one day they simply looked at each other and shook their heads; they didn't know. They were referred to as the Twins and they slept on a large cot beside my own bed, always holding hands or locked in an embrace as they slept.

When the Twins had finished washing and drying me they stepped aside and were replaced by a very lovely girl, older than me, with striking features and glorious auburn hair hanging in a loose plait down her back to her waist.

'My lord Malakai sent me,' she said, her eyes lowered respectfully and her hands folded in front of her.

'I know you!' I exclaimed, 'I've seen you somewhere before.' She didn't reply and I stood puzzling over why I might recognise her. Suddenly, it came to me, 'You were with Malakai in the cantina that day, weren't you? In Maidentown?'

'I expect so, lady Akara,' she replied quietly.

'I'm very pleased to see you again,' I said, quite forgetting how small and foolish she had made me feel when I'd smiled at her and she hadn't smiled back. Now I was just happy to see a familiar face, as if I was not so far from home after all.

'What's your name?' I asked.

'My lord Malakai calls me Dominique. It's a French name.'

'Oh. Are you French? Like Malakai's mother?'

'No,' she replied, 'It is what lord Malakai chooses to call me.' She refused to look directly at me, her eyes taking on that faraway look they'd had when I first saw her.

'What's your real name?' I said it kindly, hoping to make a friend of her, but once again she rebuffed me, 'I don't remember,' she said, though it was clearly a lie, 'May I get you ready for bed now, lady Akara?' And with that she produced a long cotton shift, cuffed with lace and decorated with satin ribbon, which she held out ready to slip over my head. I was happy for her to cover my nakedness; I felt shy and exposed in front of her condescending gaze, as if our positions should be reversed and I should be attending her. In spite of her inferior status Dominique seemed to possess the natural poise and pride that my mother had spent fourteen years trying to instil in me; I decided it would be wise to watch and learn from her.

From then on I woke every day with a determination to prove my worth. I stopped saying please and thank you to the servers and eventually began to assume my role as mistress of the estate.

*****

What happened to my documents? Why can't I remember? As another day passes with no Visitors to this end of the passage my need to piece together the last weeks of my life at Montagne becomes more urgent. Without those memories I can't finish the story I'm trying to assemble in my head and everything will be wasted.

Day thirty eight and a foul smelling wind has been swirling around us since last night; I stopped writing when Colim Sang brought my supper, not wanting to invite his curiosity, but it was too late.

'What are you writing, Ten?' his voice was muffled behind his face covering and I tried to pretend I hadn't heard him. He repeated himself, moving closer to me but keeping his face averted as if I smelled bad, which I accept I probably do.

'What is it you're writing?'

'Nothing important, Colim Sang. Just something to help take my mind off things.'

'Ah yes, your Due Death Date is soon, isn't it?'

'In four days' time,' I said, trying to slip the paper out of sight. But the Guardian was persistent, 'May I see?' and he held out his gloved hand in a way which made it impossible to refuse. I gave him the first sheet, frantically trying to remember if I had written anything which might get me into trouble. Colim Sang swept his eyes over the page before handing it back and looking meaningfully at me, 'Your calligraphy is excellent, Ten.'

'Thank you. I've been practising.' I picked up my supper bowl and began eating, 'This is very good, Colim Sang. Is it pork?'

'Yes, we slaughtered one of the pigs to celebrate the arrival of the rains. Have you eaten meat before?'

'Of course, many times,' I answered truthfully without thinking, but immediately regretting it. I hadn't meant it boastfully, but it sounded arrogant nonetheless. I had taken Adelmo's warning words to heart and I didn't want to make an enemy of this new Guardian in the way that I had Gareff.

'Where do you come from that you were lucky enough to have plenty of meat?' I couldn't tell whether he was being sarcastic or simply suspicious. I tried to be careful and vague with my reply.

'I belonged to a wealthy man a long way from here. He had a great many animals and we always ate well,' I said.

'And before then?' All the time he was speaking Colim was wandering around my stall, picking things up or straightening them in an apparently idle fashion. I watched him from where I was sitting at the end of the bed, knowing that I could do nothing to stop him if he decided to search the space thoroughly and came across the rest of my paper or the pods Mariam had given me.

'I was with my mother.'

'Ah. Where was that?'

So many questions, Colim Sang. Do I trust you or not?
I said nothing.

'Where did you live with your mother, Ten?'

If he was determined to get an answer from me I couldn't see the harm in telling him the truth. It occurred to me that, friend or foe, Colim Sang could hardly make much difference to my life now.

'We had a small croft somewhere to the north of here, I think. Not too far from a place called Maidentown. I lived there with my little brother and my mother until I was fourteen and then Mamma sold me.' The Guardian nodded thoughtfully and began to turn away. But then he seemed to change his mind and swung back suddenly in my direction; as he did so the edges at the neck of his robe parted slightly and I caught a glimpse of the medallion hanging from a chain around his neck. Its polished brightness stood out against his dark undergarment and I wondered if it was like the charm that I'd seen Mariam wearing and that she'd been praying over just before Eighteen's extermination. It stirred another memory in me too, but before I could think about it the Guardian spoke, bending down as he did so and reaching out to touch my face, 'What happened to your eye, Akara? How did you get all these injuries?'

Colim Sang's voice was soft and his touch gentle, but I flinched at the sudden gesture and, as I did so, a flood of memories came surging back.

21 LA VIE EN ROSE

The day after my arrival at Montagne I was shown around the estate, or at least part of it. Malakai owned many hundreds of acres and it was not considered necessary for me to see everything.

I was woken at eight in the morning when Dominique brought me my breakfast tray and the Twins opened the shutters to let the light stream in. They stood on either side of the window, moving in perfect symmetry like dancers, communicating in some silent, mysterious way they had. They performed the same ritual every morning and evening for three years, checking the room for poisonous insects or venomous reptiles and carefully capturing any they found. The creatures would be contained in bottles or bamboo cages and removed by servers, who then released them safely outside, unharmed. Legend had it that the Twins were immune to toxic bites and stings, and Malakai - who was neurotic about any risk to his own health or mine and also very superstitious - had paid a vast amount for them. Whether or not the story was true, they did have a remarkable way with animals and I never saw them get bitten. They accorded great respect and gentleness to everything except mosquitoes and flies; Malakai hated them and, as with anything that my Patron disliked, they were shown no mercy.

I ate breakfast in bed that morning and most days after that. Dominique would stand by quietly whilst I drank my coconut milk and picked at the berries and shelled nuts which were presented in cut glass bowls or delicately painted pottery. Once again I felt shy and self conscious in front of her, trying not to chew loudly or do anything which might appear gauche. I still don't know how she managed to make me feel so clumsy and belittled, since she hardly spoke unless required to and rarely looked directly at me.

After the Twins had taken me to the wash room to cleanse, oil and perfume me, Dominique would dress me. There was a large cupboard in my dressing room and it was filled with the most extravagant and gorgeous clothes I had ever seen, every yard of which would have probably cost more than my mother could have afforded in a year. Another cupboard housed scarves, head dresses, purses, sandals and shoes in every colour imaginable and decorated with pearls, pau shells and coloured stones. The Twins were responsible for cleaning, repairing and altering my outfits and sewing new ones from the fabrics and trimmings I purchased. When Malakai and I went to markets and auctions together we would return with new animals, ornaments or servers for the estate and a wagon full of material and trinkets for me. I became quite greedy for possessions and casual about their cost, knowing that my Patron never refused me anything; except, as it turned out, for the two things I most wanted.

My first morning Dominique advised me to wear a comfortable cotton shirt and lightweight trousers, cuffed at the ankle, and picked out a pair of soft leather boots which were laced at the sides, thick soled and had a small heel.

'Will I be riding?' I asked her a little nervously, remembering how strong and swift Malakai's horse had been and hoping that my Patron hadn't forgotten that I couldn't yet ride. Then a happy thought crossed my mind, 'Will we be on camels?'

'No, my lord Malakai has no camels.'

I was so disappointed, 'Why doesn't he?' Surely someone as rich and important as Malakai could have kept a hundred of the beasts if he'd wanted.

'He considers them to be ugly and bad tempered creatures.'

'Oh,' I replied, watching her as she knelt to lace up my boots, 'We'll be on horses, then.'

'No, not horses. You will be travelling quite a distance on your tour around the estate and my lord Malakai will not want his beloved horses tired out in the heat.'

She stood up and viewed me critically, just as Mamma had done a few days before. She was taller than me, slender but with a womanly shape, and her eyes were the colour of jade. I had never felt envious of another girl before but I was jealous of her – of her loveliness, her natural grace and her confidence. But at the same time I realised she must also envy me – or at least resent me - because, in spite of her beauty and her obvious gifts, I was Malakai's principal Protégé and she was not. Our relationship was not destined to be a good one.

'Well,' I said, with as arrogant a tone as I could manage, 'Perhaps you could tell me what mode of transport we *will* be using.'

'Bicycles,' she announced bluntly. Then she handed me a pair of chamois gloves and stepped aside to allow me to leave the room.

Xavier, Malakai's foreman, was waiting for me in the rear courtyard. He was a large, loud man with a big bellowing laugh and a bulging belly. He was standing between two three wheeled bicycles – contraptions I'd never seen before, although I'd seen two wheeled ones being sold in Maidentown. The tricycles had a single seat at the front and a double seated, semi enclosed arrangement behind, well cushioned and shaded with a canopy from which hung curtains of thick mosquito netting.

'Greetings, my lady Akara,' the booming voice echoed around the courtyard, 'Today I am going to show you some of the estate. Please feel free to ask any questions and to request a stop at any point if you need to do your toilet. You will find a hamper on the seat beside you, with water and sweetmeats; but we will pause for a meal and a rest at midday. Come,' and he gestured for me to climb onto the back seat of one of the tricycles. Dominique secured the netting firmly around me with ties and said, not very convincingly, 'I do hope you have an enjoyable day, my lady.'

We were joined by two young, muscular drivers who pedalled us out of the yard and into the blazing sun, onto a flat, paved track heading northwards. The vast, honey coloured rock that formed the backdrop to the chateau loomed in front of us, shimmering in a golden haze like a mirage. As we approached it I could see fissures in the face of the rock which glittered with thin streams of water running down them; where they pooled at the bottom there was a collection of canals, channelling the water to the chateau and the various outhouses around it.

'They are called leats,' Xavier informed me, 'The waterfalls feed into them and keep a constant supply going to the chateau; on the other side of the outcrop are more springs and they irrigate the crops in that direction. Our engineers have created a wonderful gravity fed system here and only once in the last thirty years has the water supply dried up.'

The sun was baking and it was a relief when we reached a narrow passageway that split the massive boulder formation in two. As we drove into the shade and I gazed around me I could see small trickles of water everywhere, all coming from the same mighty spring above. The rocks were dotted with scrubby trees and plants and I was delighted to see dozens of goats clambering about everywhere, the bells at their throats tinkling as they nibbled at the vegetation. Life was flourishing there and I truly believed, in that moment, that I was in the Promise Land which Mamma had always assured me did not exist.

As we emerged into the sunlight again on the other side the ground fell away quite sharply so that we were looking down into a vast canyon a hundred paces below. As far as the eye could see there was a patchwork of different crops with men, women and children weaving and working amongst them, all wearing similar, light coloured loose pants and shirts and large brimmed hats. A few of the men and women carried babies in woven baskets on their backs and one was even suckling a child at her breast as she worked.

'We call the plantation workers Coolies,' said Xavier, 'They plant, prune and harvest all the crops and tend the animals. Montagne boasts many cattle, pigs, goats, poultry, mules and buffalo; what produce we don't use ourselves we trade, and the estate is very successful as you may imagine.'

I had never seen so many apparently strong and healthy people all in one place.

'Where do they all come from, Xavier? Are there camps nearby?' I thought of the miserable shanties near Maidentown and the weak and sickly people who lived in them.

'Oh no, my lady,' Xavier said with a laugh, 'they live on the estate, in huts mostly or with the animals in barns. They are all branded, of course, so that there is no risk of them being stolen or... getting lost. Lord Malakai breeds his own Coolies here, meaning that nearly all the babies are born perfect. Or at least,' he corrected himself, 'perfectly suited to the work they will be doing.'

I thought of Beetle. 'What happens to the ones that

aren't perfectly suited?'

There was no reply.

'Xavier? What happens to the imperfect children?'

When there was still no response from the foreman I said, 'You told me I was free to ask you anything.'

'Yes I did, my lady, and so you are. But there are some questions which are best left unanswered.'

After Xavier had talked a little longer about the estate, pointing out more vegetables, grains and herbs than I had ever even heard of, we paused for a mid day meal. I was thirsty but not very hungry, although the cheese, olives, figs and bread sticks looked delicious.

I had forgotten until now just how disturbed I was that day by what Xavier had left unsaid, because I'm ashamed to admit that my misgivings about Malakai were soon conveniently put aside as I learned to enjoy all the luxury and privileges that were showered on me. My days passed in almost nothing but the pursuit of pleasurable education and entertainment: reading, learning to ride and dance and developing the skills required of a companion to someone important and influential.

I hardly saw Malakai during the first few months, except when he wanted to assess my progress and assure himself that I was being groomed to become the paragon he expected. He would summon me alone to the library, which is where he spent most of his free time, and invite me to read aloud to him which I did willingly – always choosing a book which would manage to please us both. A particular favourite was my Rubaiyat, since Malakai did not have his own copy and was impressed by mine, praising Mamma for having acquired it for me and reminding me how fortunate I was to have had such a mother. 'Between us,' he would say, 'your mother and I will have created an exceptional Protégé,' and I would smile in agreement.

Malakai tired easily and, after a few pages, he would

hold out his arm for Emanuel to support him and take him back to his room. Emanuel was rarely far away and stayed constantly alert so that the second our Patron needed him he was to hand. He was as dedicated and faithful as Malakai's giant hounds, the Great Danes that followed him almost everywhere, and became anxious if they were separated for too long. Once, when Malakai left for one of his trips and Emanuel was left gazing mournfully after him, Dominique slipped away from my side and I overheard her scolding him, 'You are a fool, Emanuel. You must know that Malakai feels no loyalty to you. As soon as you are no longer useful or pleasing to look at he will dispose of you. It hurts me to see you waste your devotion on him, brother. You should do as I do and be obedient but no more. He doesn't deserve your love.'

'You don't know him as I do,' Emanuel replied, kissing her cheek affectionately, 'And it hurts *me* that you can't. He has… secrets which explain a great deal.'

I never found out whether Dominique and Emanuel were really siblings, many of the Protégés referred to each other as 'Brother' or 'Sister', and were bound to each other in a way that I would never be with any of them. Much as I longed for friendship my unique status set me apart, and the lonelier I became the more I tried to hide it, aware that it was a sign of weakness and that Mamma would not have approved.

After our mid day meal we had a new relay of servers pedalling us back to the chateau, but we didn't return by the direct route we had taken in the morning. We turned back through the passageway but then went wide, travelling slightly west and towards a group of barns and outbuildings where Xavier pointed out the olive presses, a forge and a workshop. It seemed there was everything necessary on the estate to make it self sufficient, including plenty of labour. Everyone we passed was occupied with something, but they all paused as we passed and lowered their heads respectfully. What expressions they had on their faces it was impossible to see.

Dominique's face, however, became easy to read very quickly: she despised me and barely bothered to disguise it. As I grew in confidence and authority so she grew in her dislike of me until it became completely mutual. After a few months, when I was certain that Malakai was pleased with my progress and I'd grown used to him indulging me, I asked him to dismiss her.

'Why? Is she disobedient?'

I couldn't lie. 'No.'

'Then what? Is she inefficient?'

'No. But...'

'It seems you have no good reason, Akara, to have her dismissed. She is very pleasing to the eye and I want your chief attendant to reflect your own status. She will stay.'

If he wasn't going to let me have my way over Dominique then he could hardly deny me my next request. I had deliberately waited to broach the subject of Beetle again and had prepared myself to deal with his expected objection to the boy's appearance, 'Please, Malakai, may we send for my little brother? If it offends you to look at him then I will keep him out of sight but let me have him near me, please.'

'I do not change my mind over such matters, Akara. Even knowing that he was somewhere under my roof would be unbearable to me. Unless you want him to live away from the chateau with the Coolies then I suggest you accept my answer. Now, you have exhausted me with your unnecessary demands. Je ne suis pas content.' He gestured for Emanuel who swiftly came to his side and assisted him. I couldn't help thinking that Malakai was exaggerating his frailty as he hobbled to the door; how could a short conversation be so tiring? I was angry with Malakai, but also a little alarmed – it was the first time my Patron had expressed displeasure with me since my arrival. I had become over confident about our relationship – perhaps in the way that Banjo had with Isabella – and my Patron had reminded me of that. I felt chastened and frustrated and I took it out on Dominique. If I couldn't get rid of her then I would at least demonstrate what power I had at every opportunity. I began to speak to her in an increasingly superior manner and eventually it became my normal behaviour with everybody.

Perhaps, if they had been a little more understanding of a fourteen year old girl feeling forsaken and alone, then I would have been grateful for their kindness and tried harder to be treated as one of them; as it was, I came to believe that I was simply fulfilling my mother and Malakai's expectations of me.

'People,' Malakai informed me when I was questioning him after my first tour of the estate, 'like to know their place. It gives them security. The caste system works, Akara.'

'But, who decides the castes, Malakai, and which people go into which one?'

'It is always the powerful who decide things.'

'And what makes someone powerful to begin with?'

'Wealth. Fertility. And beauty such as yours, my little Protégé, has enormous power if used correctly and accompanied by provenance. One day you may even become a Patron yourself and you will see how well the system works for you.'

'Malakai,' I said, thinking of poor Ash and how badly he had been treated, 'why is it so bad to have something that isn't even contagious? If it's just a disease that isn't catching, why are we so afraid of it?'

'Any perceived weakness is abhorrent, Akara; humans needs to be resilient and productive or another catastrophic event will wipe us out. That is why perfection such as yours is so prized,' said Malakai, sounding so like my mother that

I almost laughed. 'Alors, enough questions, Akara. It must be time for your dance lesson.'

Although I had a formal tutor, it was Emanuel who taught me how to dance in the wild, free way that made me feel especially alive. It came about by accident, as a result of my proving my dominance over Dominique after I had been at Montagne for nearly a year. Malakai had gone away for several days, without me or Emanuel, but accompanied by Xavier and a number of servers along with carts and wagons loaded with produce from the estate.

I had plenty to occupy me and I especially loved spending time alone in the library. Although there was always a perceptible relaxation in the atmosphere at Montagne when Malakai was absent, the household still adhered to all its rules and routines and I'm sure I was suspected of informing him if ever it didn't. I thought that, if I shut myself away, I would neither be aware of any transgressions nor tempted to report them. And I was also keen to spend as little time with Dominique as possible. Since she was forbidden access to the sacred library I was safe there; only three servers were allowed in to keep the room clean. I was intrigued by them because they were all so old and, by Malakai's standards, not prepossessing; not one of them was under forty years of age, judging by the condition of their skin, and they can't have had more than thirty strands of grey hair on their heads between them. They were neat and clean of course, dressed in identical grey cotton trousers and Nehru collared shirts, with matching kid gloves to protect the books as they swept and dusted. I asked Xavier about them. Malakai's foreman had become my unofficial instructor, if not my friend, and if I had questions it was Xavier I would ask in Malakai's absence. I understood that he simply wouldn't answer me if he considered it better not to, but generally he would tell me anything I wanted to know.

'Ah yes, the Greys!' Xavier exclaimed with a smile, 'They are unics that belonged to my lord Malakai's mother and because they'd been favourites of hers he kept them on when she passed. They know how and where he likes things kept and he trusts them. In all the years they've been here they have not progressed beyond a few words of the French language he has tried to teach them and they come out with some amusing things sometimes.'

'Really?' I said, 'I don't think I've ever heard them speak.'

'Not to you, perhaps,' Xavier replied and left it for me to interpret his response.

So, at least when I was present, the Greys dusted and swept in reverential silence, handling the books as little as possible and with great care. If they came across an open manuscript I would sometimes see their lips moving as they studied it, practising pronunciation of unfamiliar words to pass on to the others, often incorrectly according to Xavier.

'Silver plate is a favourite,' he told me, 'it was many days before we worked out what they were trying to say,' and he laughed his deep, rumbling belly laugh which I loved to hear because laughter was something I so rarely heard, except when Malakai held one of his infrequent but extravagant feasts. On those occasions his guests, who often travelled many miles to attend, would set up tented camps on the estate and stay for several days. It was for their benefit that I was taught to dance, in one of the slow and seductive styles that Malakai chose in order to show me off. I knew how much it pleased him to have me admired and coveted and he enjoyed teasing his visitors when they asked what price he would consider selling me for.

'Ah, my Akara is a jewel,' he would say, 'and if I ever choose to let her go from my collection I'm afraid it will be for more than you could ever afford.'

Far from being insulted, this only seemed to ignite their

desire to possess me and I lived in dread of the day when Malakai might relent and sell me. With Malakai I felt safe, if not loved in the way I longed to be, and I was beginning to understand that there were worse fates than being kept as a pet. I had never been invited into Malakai's bedroom in more than eleven months of living under his roof and I was almost certain that he must be impotent. He gave no indication that he required anything other than a pretty and docile ornament and I was very content to be exactly that.

Dominique also attracted a great deal of lustful attention but, unfortunately, Malakai could not be persuaded to sell her either.

So the night I learned the thrill of dancing for my own delight and no one else's was, as I said, just after Malakai had left for some days to conduct business. I had retired at the usual time but couldn't sleep; there had been a particularly stifling sirocco blowing south across us that day and the evening hadn't cooled as quickly as it normally did. I lay uncomfortably on top of my bed, telling the Twins to fan harder to cool me down until their arms became so tired I eventually allowed them to stop. They soon managed to fall asleep, snoring gently in each other's arms, but even when the night chill finally descended I lay awake and unsettled. I thought I could hear music coming from somewhere but knew I must be wrong; with Malakai gone the chateau normally descended into near silence at night, as if the household was grateful for the rest. Or perhaps it was fearful that any noise might reach him and risk encouraging his early return.

After hours of sleeplessness I left the bed and went to the front window, opening the shutters quietly so I didn't disturb the Twins, and gazing out at the ornamental fountain and the glinting shapes of the fish moving slowly around it. I was still certain I could hear music and, wondering why I hadn't done so before when Malakai was absent, decided to explore and investigate. After all, I wasn't a prisoner in my room, I was the chatelaine and free to go where I wished.

I wrapped a long velvet robe around myself, tying it at the waist and raising the soft mohair collar to warm my neck. It's hard to believe now that I had such things available to me, things I took for granted until I no longer had them. I don't recall precisely but I expect I slipped on a pair of sheepskin moccasins before picking up a lantern from the carved wooden chest at my bedside and softly opening the door. There was no one about and I waited a moment to be sure that Dominique had not heard me and come out of her room, which was just across the landing from my quarters. Dust from the sirocco had settled on the glass domed ceiling above me so there was no light from there, even if the sky itself was clear, and I walked carefully with the lantern to the top of the staircase, listening for the music and trying to determine its direction. I was convinced it came from Malakai's rooms below, although that should have been impossible, so I began to descend the stairs but lost my footing and dropped the lantern, which clattered noisily down all the way to the bottom. I rushed to pick it up, relieved that it didn't appear to have cracked the marble floor but thinking I should go back to my room before I did some real damage. As I bent down for the lantern the door to Malakai's room opened and Dominique appeared.

I don't think either of us knew what to say at first, she looked guilty and I felt it, but by the time I'd risen to my feet I had recovered some composure. Closing the door firmly behind her, Dominique stepped towards me, smiling uncharacteristically and preparing to steer me back to the stairs, 'Are you unwell, my lady? May I help you back to your room?'

'No, I'm not unwell. What were you doing in our Patron's room, Dominique?'

The girl also seemed to have recovered herself, replying without hesitation, 'Oh, I heard some noise and thought perhaps lord Malakai had left his gramophone instrument running by mistake.'

'If he has then it should be stopped, but it is not your business to deal with it. You should have reported it to me. I will see to it; please step aside, Dominique.'

'Oh there's no need, my lady,' the girl replied, blocking the door, 'I will take you safely back to your room and then I can attend to the instrument. Our Patron would be most unhappy that you've been disturbed at all.'

She said it with such assuredness that I almost allowed myself to be led away without protest, but I suddenly realised that if Dominique won this battle then I would probably end up losing the entire war and I couldn't let that happen.

'Stand aside, Dominique, I will deal with the gramophone.'

When she still didn't move I took a step closer to the door and said, in the low threatening voice I had often heard Mamma use, 'You are right that Malakai would not want me disturbed and he would certainly be unhappy if he thought I'd been defied. Get out of my way.' And with that I pushed past her and opened the door.

22 REVELATIONS

I wrote for as long as I could yesterday, trying to record scraps of memories as they came rushing back like a tsunami. My eyes hurt, my wrists ached and I became stiff from sitting but still I wrote. Apart from the Guardians carrying out their usual routines The Kennels have been horribly quiet; there have been no Visitors at all for two days now, Banjo's stall remains empty and the Guards who occupy Eleven, on and off, are just an occasional, anonymous presence. Even when they're not there an atmosphere of foreboding seems to hang over the place; or perhaps that's just how I'm feeling because I only have two days left now. It feels as if my guts are permanently tied in knots and my heart sometimes threatens to burst out of my chest. Last night, when I'd finally put down my pencil and attempted to sleep I was so anxious that I decided to take one of Mariam's pods to see if that would help. When I was sure there were no Guards or Guardians nearby I retrieved the package from its hiding place, unwrapped it carefully and discovered that the pods were covered in mildew.

Should I try one anyway? I couldn't risk it. Although Malakai regularly smoked or ingested many strange things, including fungi and mildews, they were specially grown for him in the plant room and Emanuel knew how to prepare them safely. I was never told the secret of their benefits or allowed to try them myself. 'You do not need them, Akara,' Malakai insisted, 'and I want you kept pure, inside and out.'

'Why do *you* need them, Malakai?' I asked, but he wouldn't give me a direct answer and his eyes, as always, gave nothing away. 'Ce n'est pas important. Come, read to me now and choose something that is not too douloureux.'

I became used to the smell of Malakai's hookahs and pungent cigarettes everywhere. Sometimes, if we were travelling in the litter or were otherwise at close quarters, I would find the smoke making me sleepy and Malakai would stop for a while. But I always suspected that he saved the strongest preparations for use in his private quarters or when he was alone on trips.

*****

So, when I opened the door to Malakai's room after pushing past Dominique that night, I was not surprised to find it still shrouded in a sweet smelling fog, although he had left the chateau hours earlier. The room was dark with only a few candles casting a soft glow here and there, giving a flickering impression of sumptuous fabrics and heavy, ornate furniture. The floor was covered in soft piled rugs, woven in shades of gold and red to match the bed coverings and the plush curtain drapes which were drawn across the windows. Just visible at the far end of the room was a table with a gramophone on it and a figure standing next to it, winding the handle.

At first I thought it must be Malakai; that he had returned early and unexpectedly. But as my eyes became accustomed to the dim light I saw that it was Emanuel, naked except for a cloth around his loins, and holding a loosely rolled cigarette in his left hand as he wound the gramophone with his right. Dominique had followed me in and closed the door behind us, causing Emanuel to turn and smile, expecting to see her alone, of course.

'My lady Akara!' he exclaimed, surprised but not alarmed, although he had been caught out in the most punishable behaviour, 'Please come in and join me,' and he held out both arms to welcome me, shedding cigarette ash as he did so.

'What are you doing, Emanuel? How dare you behave like this while our Patron is away! What are you doing?' I couldn't help but repeat myself, I had no idea what else to say or how to deal with the situation. As I waited for an answer, Emanuel turned back to the gramophone and very gently lowered the needle onto the revolving record beneath it. I was familiar with most of Malakai's musical tastes, which tended towards the mournful except when we were hosting a feast and musicians were brought in to accompany the drunken antics of our guests. I often passed Malakai's rooms to hear some sad orchestral piece coming from them and I was seldom tempted to linger because they made me want to cry.

The music Emanuel was playing was lively and joyful, like the gipsy tunes they played in Maidentown which I had always been thrilled to hear. Emanuel began swaying to the melody and then turned to dance towards me, graceful in spite of his obvious intoxication. He had a smooth, slender body with neither hair nor nipples on his chest, and his bare feet were small like a woman's. Apart from the loin cloth he wore nothing but ear rings and an eight figure identification number tattooed on the inside of his left wrist. I could see drops of sweat dripping down his cheeks, running unchecked onto his lips, until he got closer and I realised they were tears.

'My lady Akara,' said Dominique as she drew to my side and I prepared to do battle with her once again, 'please don't misunderstand. Emanuel has reason to behave in this manner and doesn't deserve to be punished.'

'What reason?' I couldn't take my eyes off the slim, supple figure as he twirled and gyrated around the room, the candlelight catching his glistening eyes as they wept. She hesitated before replying, 'He is always like this when lord Malakai is away; he can't bear to be left behind.'

'Are you telling me it's devotion that causes this madness? That's ridiculous.'

'My lady, it's the truth. Emanuel has been with lord Malakai since he was a child. He's grown up looking after his Patron with such care and love that his heart gets broken when lord Malakai goes without him.'

'I don't believe you,' I said, although I was almost convinced.

'He doesn't do any harm. Lord Malakai allows him a supply of tobacco and medicaments, so he's not stealing anything. He does no damage, everything is carefully replaced and tidied and it doesn't happen every night.'

My own body was being drawn to the rhythm of the music and, when Emanuel approached me again with outstretched arms, I let myself be led into the centre of the room and danced with him. It was a reckless thing to do in front of Dominique, but there was a silly, vain part of me that wanted to show off in front of her. I'd never known such exhilarating freedom and sensual pleasure and we must have flung ourselves around the room with utter abandon for several hours until, at last, we were exhausted and Emanuel curled up like a baby on a thick sheepskin rug in front of the dying fire. Dominique, who had stood for the entire time just watching from the shadows, gently placed a woollen blanket over Emanuel who grabbed her wrist and mumbled, 'Thank you, 'Nique. Don't tell him. Please don't tell him how I cry for him,' and then fell asleep. 'Don't worry, brother,' Dominique assured him, then I heard her whisper to herself, 'Not that he would care.'

When she'd closed the gramophone and returned all the

records to the cabinet they'd come from, Dominique stood facing me and waited for me to speak.

We both knew that the night's events would now remain our secret; I was not going to admit my part in any wild behaviour to Malakai and it was true, no harm appeared to have been done. It meant, of course, that I could not really prevent anything similar from occurring in the future, although I never dared join in again but only ever danced alone to the memory of the music in my head.

Our shared secret should have created a bond between us but it didn't. Dominique remained as cold towards me as ever and Emanuel, when we encountered each other the following day, appeared to remember nothing about it at all.

*****

It's late in the afternoon and the natural light will be fading soon on this, my fortieth day. I'm still reeling from the shock of earlier events and it will be a struggle to keep calm enough to commit them to paper.

I had been writing all morning, recalling the night I danced with Emanuel and almost ready to face the next part of my story, when Colim Sang came with my mid day meal. I was very relieved to see that Mariam was with him although I didn't dare say so; as she hovered at the other Guardian's shoulder she smiled and nodded at me sympathetically. I know she will be truly sorry to see me die and it doesn't matter how I say it now, two days cannot be turned into anything more than 48 hours, not even in French.

When I'd finished my meal of lentils in a thick tomato and alium sauce it lay heavily on my stomach. 'It is important that you eat,' Colim Sang had said, 'you must keep your strength up.' *Why?* I wondered. *Do I need to be strong just to get to the end of the passage to die? What is the point in wasting a meal on the condemned? Perhaps they really are fattening me up to serve to the pigs.*

As I sat on my bed considering whether I might have the courage to do as Banjo had done, Colim Sang returned to collect the plate. He came alone and lingered for a while by the door, looking up and down the passage way and peering into stall Eleven as if to be sure it was unoccupied. Then he came and sat next to me on the bed.

'Thank you for my meal, Colim Sang,' I said nervously, handing him the plate and hoping it would encourage him to leave. But he sat in silence for several minutes, looking at me and breathing heavily through his mask of black netting. I stiffened and tried to prepare myself for a fight, but I knew there was no way I could defend myself against him in a locked stall with no one either able or willing to help. Assaults by Guardians or Guards are known to be very rare as so few of them have either the desire or the ability. But such attacks do happen and, though I may not be the prize I once was, my womanhood is still obvious under the fading bruises and my face not as horrifying when I have my patch on, as I do today.

'Akara…' Colim began in a voice thick with some emotion.

Discourage intimacy, I thought to myself, *and maybe he'll go away.*

'Don't call me that. My name is Ten,' I said, surprising myself. I've spent nearly six weeks refusing to be known by a number and suddenly I was embracing it.

'No, it isn't,' the Guardian contradicted, 'I know who you really are, and you know me.'

I stared at him blankly, 'What?'

He took my hand in his and faced me full on, though still I could not make out any features behind the mask. I could hear Gareff and Ridrick heading up the corridor with fresh water and soap to hand out and I knew that if I screamed it wouldn't take them long to reach us. I wrenched my hand from his and started to rise just as he lifted his mask, showing a face as pale as milk with curls of white blonde hair falling over his forehead. My hands went to my mouth to silence the gasp of shock.

It is ten years since I last saw him and we have both changed. He must now be twenty three years old, a fully grown man who is tall and deep voiced. Where I remember him as completely bald he now has hair. But there was no mistaking that extraordinary complexion and those stunningly blue eyes. The voices were getting closer, I had a million questions to ask but I couldn't speak. I sat, shaking my head in disbelief.

He looked anxiously towards the corridor and hurriedly removed the chain from around his neck, pressing it into my hand before fumbling to replace his mask.

'Akara,' he whispered, 'I dare not talk to you now. We are both in grave danger and there is more going on than I can explain to you here. I will try to return to you tonight. Till then, don't despair, and keep faith.' He stood up just as Gareff arrived at the stall, his eyes looking from one to the other of us suspiciously as he placed the jug of water on the stool and passed me a slab of oatmeal and poppy seeds encased in musty smelling oil. I still couldn't speak, not trusting my voice, and I know the hand that took the soap was shaking; but I had enough presence of mind to keep the chain safely hidden behind my back until they'd both gone.

I waited a long while before I felt it was safe to even move. I'd been clenching my hand so tightly that, when I unfolded it, there was a deep imprint left on my palm from Colim Sang's chain. The pendant, now that I could see it close to, was simply a shiny piece of cheap metal: flattened and crudely fashioned into the shape of the sun. An elusive memory finally forced its way through and I recognised the old bottle top I had found on one of our last adventures, the one he had promised to turn into a piece of jewellery for me just before he disappeared.

23 PROPHECIES

I don't know what Ash is doing here. I don't even know if I really believe it is Ash, now that he's left my stall. I believed him when he was standing next to me, showing me the pendant round his neck. But it's a bottle top, anyone can find a bottle top. I am so confused, afraid to be hopeful and afraid not to be, since the next sunrise but one brings my last day. Nonetheless, I know it's important to keep the medallion safely out of sight so I press it into the soft slab of greasy soap and mould it in my hands until it's almost completely hidden. Then I put it under my pillow.

The Kennels are oddly quiet, the heat suffocating. It is too hot to move around so there is nothing left for me to do but write, and writing means remembering. It is time now for me to face the horrors of my last days with Malakai but I wonder where to begin.

*****

For three years I was secure, safe and spoilt at Montagne, enjoying all the benefits of Malakai's Patronage. I had no obligations except to please him and be a credit to the household when we had guests. In spite of all

I learned about my Patron's likes and dislikes in that time, he remained a mystery to me as a person. He was private and secretive and only Emanuel was ever seen going in or out of his room, except when Malakai was absent and the Greys went in to clean it.

After the night in Malakai's room when Emanuel and I danced so wildly together I had expected, or at least hoped, that Emanuel and I had formed some sort of bond. But Dominique was right, he appeared to remember nothing about his intoxicated behaviour and my participation in the joyous romp and it was never discussed; he remained respectful and polite towards me, but otherwise oblivious to everything except the needs of his beloved lord and master. Dominique, however, became an increasingly painful thorn in my side and my dislike and resentment of her grew. This did not concern Malakai; as long as she remained pleasing to look at and obedient he was satisfied and made his irritation very clear if I even hinted at my frustration with her. Since she was not required to accompany me everywhere, as long as someone did, I took every opportunity to get away from her, preferring to spend time with Xavier if I wasn't in the library with Malakai or alone.

Even in three years I did not manage to see the entire estate, partly because it was so vast and much of it consisted of field upon field of crops which held no particular interest for me, but also because there were areas I was not permitted to see. I was not told directly that anywhere was forbidden, but discouraged so firmly that it was not worth attempting. Without Xavier's assistance, for example, I could not get down into the canyon to see the farms and animals that the Coolies were tending. Nor was I ever invited into any of the servers' huts around the chateau itself. I soon lost the desire to see inside any of them anyway because Xavier made it clear that they were merely simple dwellings and, 'Not worth your attention,' as he put it, with a beaming smile. There was too much richness and delight to be had elsewhere anyway: I could wander for hours in the lush gardens, the orchid house or the stables and cool off in my own private pool surrounded by palms and banana plants, orange trees and vines heavy with grapes. It was very easy to forget what punishing work was being done in the crippling heat by those whose job it was to quench my thirst and feed my hunger. I never had to pluck a fruit or peel it and I suppose I became very lazy and demanding, with Dominique's silent air of contempt only serving to make me worse. I would order her about and expect her to do the most ridiculous tasks: fetching my shoes when they were practically at my feet already, or shifting a particular log on the fire at night because its position didn't please me.

I had no reason to think that my life would change soon. The anxiety of my early days, when I thought Malakai would mate with me or even hire me out to breed from, soon faded. Although I knew that one day he might sell me on, before I became too old to reliably bear children and my value diminished, I imagined I would have equally as comfortable life with a new Patron and I was very happy at the thought of having children. But I had as many as fifteen childbearing years ahead of me, possibly more if I proved to be as fertile as Mamma, and I was still young enough to view that time as being far in the future. Besides, if I had questions about the future I was, at long last, going to have the opportunity to put them to Celeste.

Malakai's astrologer had a late, but significant, part in my story and one which I did not recognise at the time. Along with a large estate and its sumptuous contents, Heloise Montagne had bequeathed another legacy to her son in the form of an old retainer called Celeste. The story was that Celeste had come from France with Heloise to escape an epidemic and was over one hundred years old, a claim which added to her notoriety but probably held little truth. She lived in a small, brick hut several hundred paces away from the chateau and contained within a small, walled garden which she chose to share with a motley and noisy collection of poultry and wildfowl. I was surprised that Malakai was prepared to tolerate them so close to our accommodation but he seemed happy to indulge her. The old woman never emerged from the hut and relied on servers to deliver her food, fresh water and whatever else she might need.

Celeste was Malakai's oracle, just as she had been his mother's, and he depended upon her prophecies to advise him when to travel, when to harvest, when to make his biggest trades and when to make his most expensive purchases, including Protégés. Malakai informed me that Celeste had foreseen the coming of a 'bright and exceptional star' not long before he acquired me, which was how he had been certain that I was worth the unheard of price he had paid at the auction.

He would visit her at least once every week even when, as was increasingly the case, he was too exhausted to walk there and required the use of a litter. Sometimes I would go with him as far as the edge of the garden but no further. He would command the litter to stop and then, no matter how tired he was, would pick his way carefully across the garden alone, lifting the hem of his robes and doing his best to avoid the poultry shit. It proved Celeste's influence over him that Malakai was prepared to sully himself in order to visit her, unaccompanied even by Emanuel. Whatever she said to him was for his ears alone.

Her gifts did seem remarkable. Often Malakai would return to me with detailed information and predictions, particularly about the management of the estate; 'Celeste tells me that such and such a crop is ready to pick,' he would say, or 'Celeste has warned me that several of the cattle are sick and need to be culled.' And he would faithfully pass on this news to Xavier with appropriate instructions. It seemed curious, I thought, that I would sometimes see Xavier slipping quietly away from the rear of Celeste's hut just as Malakai had arrived at it. However, the estate was thriving and it was no business of mine to interfere.

On the first day of May this year 2092, I had my seventeenth birthday and Malakai had planned a feast, with music and entertainment to rival that of even the previous two years. I had new clothes, of course, and the expectation of more jewellery as well as a pure bred Arabian stallion already waiting for me in the stables. I wanted desperately to break and school it myself, but Malakai wouldn't hear of it and, as usual, reminded me of the unnecessary risks. With every month, it seemed, my Patron became more concerned about my safety and my health.

'You have exceeded even my expectations, Akara. I don't think I have ever seen greater beauty or purity in a human being and you become more precious to me every day.'

'Thank you, Malakai. I'm happy that I please you,' I replied, although only his words expressed his pleasure; there was no evidence in his hooded eyes, or his behaviour, that indicated affection or delight. He rarely touched me and never attempted closeness.

'Today, my jewel, I want you to visit Celeste; it is time that you had the opportunity to consult and learn from her.'

'Certainly, Malakai, I would be very happy to.'

In truth, I was fascinated to hear what Celeste would have to say about me, and more than a little curious to finally meet her. Malakai instructed Dominique to dress me in something appropriate for my visit, which she did with a bad grace, choosing my least becoming outfit and lacing up my boots just a little too tightly. I wondered whether, as it was my birthday, I might broach the subject of her dismissal once again later and even considered pretending that Celeste had suggested it.

Malakai came out with me to the litter, insisting that it was too hot to walk although I would have preferred to.

'Are you coming with me then, Malakai?' I asked.

'No. I need to rest before this evening, but I shall be eager to hear what Celeste has had to say when you return. Alors, take me back inside, Emanuel. A bientot, Akara.' And with that he shuffled off, leaning on faithful Emanuel's arm and waving me away.

It took only minutes to reach the walled garden and I remember how the air was particularly thick with the perfume of flowers because Malakai had brought more in for the occasion. There were torches everywhere, waiting to be lit as soon as dusk arrived, and the sound of instruments being tuned in the tent where the banquet was to be held. It did seem as if it ought to feel like a very special day, but somehow it didn't. The extravagance and ceremony were no longer novel and I suddenly had a melancholy vision of an endlessly unsatisfying future, surrounded by wealth but forever lonely.

I stepped out of the litter at the edge of the garden and took the last thirty or so paces alone. I didn't pick my way delicately, as Malakai did, because I was thinking that I would enjoy seeing Dominique's hands getting covered in chicken shit when she removed my boots later. Her nose would wrinkle with distaste and those long, graceful fingers would need to be scrubbed for a long time before I would allow her to touch me or the magnificent costume I planned to wear that evening.

I reached the door of the brick hut and took hold of the long cord hanging beside it, ringing the bell as I had seen Malakai do. A small, fragile voice came from the darkness within, 'Come, Akara d'Fiuri. Sit down and let us look at you.'

I stepped into the cool gloom of the hut, which was decorated with swathes of multi coloured fabrics and cluttered with artefacts: crystals, icons and wooden totems competing for space on little stools and tables, and pages of illuminated text and hieroglyphs all over the walls. At the back of the hut was a small wooden door and a glassless window; on the floor by the window was a tripod with a large brass telescope, facing heavenwards. To my left was a large silk screen and, to my right, a simple wooden bench with a single candle fluttering in the wall sconce above it.

'Sit, child, sit,' repeated the voice from behind the screen.

I settled myself on the bench and wondered what to do next.

'Greetings, Celeste,' I ventured at last.

'Welcome, Akara d'Fiuri, native of Taurus. We celebrate your birthday today with you and wish you continued health and future happiness. Do you have questions for us?'

Oh yes, Celeste - but I don't believe you could answer any of them. Malakai may be convinced by you but I am not. It all seemed ridiculous to me: the carefully constructed atmosphere of mystery and the way she talked. I wanted to laugh but dared not risk offending her for fear of angering Malakai if she told him. While I was trying to compose myself she spoke again, 'We see you have your mother's sceptical nature, child, but you must learn to open your mind and your heart,'

The mention of Mamma sobered me immediately, though at the time I didn't think to wonder how she knew anything about my mother's nature.

'Forgive me. I have many questions, Celeste, but I don't know how to ask them.'

The pleasant coolness in the room was turning to a chill that made me shiver and I turned to the doorway behind me to see the colours of the setting sun burnish the sky. When I turned back towards the screen I could hear Celeste moving, as if ready to leave, and I thought of Malakai's reaction if I returned to him with nothing to report. I got up from the bench, ready with an apology, but Celeste spoke first, 'Sit, Akara d'Fiuri. Impatience will not serve you well, and the runes will speak in their own time.'

I sat down and there was a clatter as Celeste tipped the rune stones out and scattered them on the floor. Two or three of them rolled beyond the screen and I could make out the symbols on them, although they meant nothing to me. She used a long, wooden rake to gather in the pebbles, so I could still see nothing of Celeste herself, other than a dark sleeve peeping out as she shuffled them around. It was mesmerising to watch and I was becoming drowsy, my thoughts wandering back to Mamma and her cynical dismissal of the mystics and diviners who plied their trade in Maidentown: *Charlatans, Akara. Avoid them.*

As if she could read my mind, Celeste's voice crackled from behind the screen, 'Your mother,' she said sharply, 'was both less, and more, than you are aware of. You must learn to find your own truths.' She continued playing with the stones, tutting and muttering to herself as if irritated with the outcome. At last she sighed, as if resigned, and I settled myself comfortably, anticipating predictions of great wealth, many children and perhaps a warning to beware of dark and mysterious strangers.

The voice was so hushed and faint that I had to lean forward and put my ear next to the screen to hear it, 'The runes will not tell us what lies ahead and nor will the stars, it seems you will choose your own path, however ill advised. Again and again I am seeing Uruz, Thurisaz and Dagaz - the signs of the bull, the thorn and illumination. There is great danger and immense heartache to be overcome, and I warn you that arrogance and vanity are not the vessels with which to navigate them. Take heed of that, Akara d'Fiuri, because all your questions have but one answer.'

I heard the scrape of a chair and the rustle of fabric behind the screen and knew my audience was coming to an end. I was disappointed, I had hoped for something more theatrical and dramatic than this.

'Thank you, Celeste,' I said, as humbly as I could, 'I would be very grateful to hear it.'

'Don't insult us with insincerity, child. One day you may truly be open to great knowledge and acceptance, but today we fear for you and your false pride. Here, Akara d'Fiuri, native of Taurus and daughter of the sun, is your answer.'

I held my breath, half believing for a fleeting moment that I was about to learn a great truth about my life.

'You shall see that which you have not yet seen.'

I let out my breath. Was that it? Was that the great pronouncement I had walked through chicken shit to hear? The woman spoke in nothing but riddles! But it was not for me to question Malakai's need to believe in her; I would report back to him and be sure to sound suitably impressed; after three years I knew well enough how to tell him what I knew he wanted to hear.

I could think of nothing better to do at that moment than to repeat my thank you, with as much sincerity as I could muster. Celeste did not reply. As I stood, I noticed one of the runes still lying on the floor a foot or so in front of me and I bent to pick it up. I turned with it in my hand just as a small figure was scrambling down from a stool behind the screen. We both froze, and I found myself looking down into the hooded face of a tiny woman – no more than thirty inches tall and so lined and shrivelled that her eyes were nothing more than creases in the folds of skin. I don't believe she could actually see me, but she knew I was there and, after a moment's pause, she held out a child like hand and I placed the rune gently on her open palm. She ran her fingertips over it and a grim expression briefly crossed her face before she said, 'It is the final omen.' As she closed her hand over the stone I just had time to see the symbol etched on its surface; it was a simple X, which meant nothing to me at all at the time.

Back in the litter I was aware of the increased activity
going on around me: servers hurrying here and there with
trays and decorations, lighting the torches and setting up
couches and divans around a large, low table in the tent.
Some of them stopped to look at me and others had paused
in their work to whisper and giggle amongst themselves,
infected by the festive atmosphere and doubtless expecting
to benefit from left over wine and food later. I still felt
strangely detached from it all, failing to muster the
excitement I knew I should be feeling at the efforts being
made in my honour. If I had only had someone to share it
with – Ash or Beetle, or a friend on the estate – it could
have been magical watching it together. There was to be
entertainment brought in from far and wide: fireworks,
jugglers, magicians and gymnasts – and more food and
drink than we could even have dreamed of when we were
living on Mamma's croft. The music would be livelier than
Malakai's usual sombre choices, and this year I might even
be allowed to move freely to it instead of performing one of
my tutor's boring choreographed dances.

It was my birthday and I decided to try very hard to
enjoy it. But in spite of myself I felt a chill in my heart at
Celeste's ominous words; they had not been full of the
approbation and flattery that I had expected and I cursed
her for succeeding in spoiling my special day.

Back in my room, after I had bathed and been dressed, I
admired myself in the long, gilt mirror. Dominique stood
behind me and I glanced at her reflection, catching the look
of contempt before she had a chance to hide it. If I had not
been so angry with her, so resentful of her unjustified
dislike of me, I would have thanked her at that moment. In
spite of her animosity she had made me look spectacular
and I was overwhelmed by the result. I saw in the mirror

the woman that I knew Mamma had wanted me to become: proud, graceful, perfectly groomed and prepared for a dazzling future. At last my stomach fluttered with excitement and I could hardly wait to be paraded in front of our guests for everyone to admire and for Malakai to flaunt with pride.

And if we had been friends I would have told Dominique how very pretty she looked, because she did. Her clothes were not as fine as mine but they fitted her well and the colours suited her, having been designed to complement my own. I wore a low necked gold bodice and matching, raw silk trousers, belted with a wide bandeau studded with jewels. Over this I wore a rich coat of claret velvet and trimmed with Mongolian fur. My ears, neck and wrists were bare, ready to receive the jewellery Malakai had promised me, and I had just a single gold chain with tiny charms dangling from it around one ankle. My mind flew back to the day of my ear piercing in Mamma's house and the cheap, tawdry bits of metal the woman had tried to persuade her to buy. What a long way I had come since then and what, I wondered, would Mamma think of me if she could see me now.

I had expected to be given my birthday gifts at the feast so that Malakai could display his wealth and generosity in public, but I had been sent word that Malakai wished to see me in his rooms and I took this as a sign that he considered this a particularly momentous occasion and perhaps a significant point in our relationship. Dominique accompanied me down the stairs and as far as the door to Malakai's room where I held up my hand and told her to leave me.

'I will let you know when I need you again, Dominique.'

'Yes, my lady Akara,' she replied and I felt a particular tension between us, as if we both knew that the balance of power would have shifted by the time I emerged from

Malakai's room.

24 FRIEND OR FOE

My thoughts were interrupted by the return of Ash bringing my supper. He lifted the netting from his face, as if to remind and reassure me that it was indeed him, and I could no longer have any doubts. I wanted to throw myself at him, to hug and hold him and cry with relief but we both knew that now, more than ever, we needed to be careful. One of the Guards had taken up residence in Eleven, relieving her boredom in between patrols by spitting into a small metal bowl which she kept shifting noisily around the room to test her accuracy.

'We'll talk more later, I hope,' Ash whispered, 'I'm on duty all night and eventually that idiot next door will sleep, but I must tell you something important now, Akara and I expect that you will be shocked by it.' Then he took my hand in his and, very quickly and quietly, told me his story.

When he had finished, wary of staying longer and arousing suspicion, he left me with my supper and, brushing my cheek with his lips, urged me to stay strong and believe that he loved me and would do all that he could to save me.

I sat for a long time afterwards unable to understand or accept what he had told me.

My mind is in chaos with Ash's revelations and I have no appetite to eat. So the man I have loved as a brother is no longer that, but what? A cousin? And my mother has a low caste sister who betrayed her with the man she loved. What else about my life is a lie? Beneath the turmoil of these emotions is also the ever present and increasing dread of tomorrow, my last full day before my Due Death Date. How can Ash save me? It seems impossible.

25 TRAVELLERS

It must be ten or eleven years since we have seen each other, when she was still a child of seven and I had barely reached my thirteenth year. I admit I had despaired of ever seeing her again and it has taken a lot to convince me that the thin, scarred, half blind creature they call Ten is indeed Akara. She is very much changed from the girl I remember.

The Guard, I am certain, is only pretending to be asleep – snoring so obligingly loudly that it is almost laughable. Akara sits beside me with enough light from the passageway torches for us to see the fear in each other's faces. We have so much to tell each other but we know it is too dangerous to talk and my heart aches with love for this girl, who will surely die if I cannot find a way to prevent it.

Mamma's last visit to us in the shanties was on the day Akara was sold. She said she no longer cared if people found out about us, she had made enough money from Akara's sale to survive without depending on breeding any more. Besides, after what she considered her failure with Beetle, it would have been too big a risk to take. Of course, the truth was that she was too old by then anyway.

'Here,' she said, thrusting a purse of coins into my

mother's hand, 'and you may have these books since Akara no longer needs them. Sell them if you want.'

Surrana took the small pile of books and tears welled up in her eyes, 'I remember this one, Fiuri. And this! We found them together, didn't we? Thank you, sister. I shall never sell them.'

'I don't know where they came from,' Mamma said dismissively, her voice brittle, 'but selling them might spare your son from the fight pits.'

'Ash will not be fighting,' Surrana said.

'Well, he will need to do something I suppose, since you are past having any value yourself. He must be nearly twenty,' she continued, 'and looks strong enough. He'd make a decent price as a server to someone who could overlook his abominations.'

An old and primitive anger rose up in me, at her callousness and at the knowledge she had sold my childhood companion – whom she knew I had loved - without letting us ever see each other one last time.

'We don't need your help today or ever again, Mamma,' I said, holding back the curtain and leaving her in no doubt that she should go. With one final look of scorn at us all, Fiuri d'Ursoola left without another word.

Surrana, Tikerty and I continued to live in the bus, surviving from day to day on what we could find, barter and earn. We talked constantly of building a better life elsewhere, but leaving Maidentown was too dangerous to attempt without a plan. There were always rumours of other places where the climate was kinder and there was food and fresh water in abundance, but no one seemed quite sure where they were; some said north, some said east and some said you had to travel to the deserts in the south before crossing an ocean to get to them. Very few were prepared to take the risk, and those that did never returned of course. Then one day a small group of *exhausted travellers arrived from the west, looking for shelter and desperate for food. Amongst them was a man and his daughter, whom he had pulled for miles on a roughly constructed stretcher. The girl was in terrible pain and Surrana gave her the last of the opium lettuce which we had been saving to sell. We brought the two of them into the bus and, after some cornmeal and drink and a long sleep, the man told us their story. His name, Colim Sang, is the name I borrowed for the purposes of applying to be a Guardian at the Adoption Centre.*

Colim and the woman he was bonded to were servers to a merchant family who traded silks and spices between settlements in the far west. They had successfully borne a single healthy child, a daughter whom they called Oriana and whom they cherished. When she was almost nineteen, Oriana had her first bleed and showed every promise that she would therefore be fertile, like her mother. Several of the merchant family members tried to claim her for themselves then, either to mate with or to sell on, and a fierce argument broke out between them. They were vile and brutal people and Colim was determined not to let them have his beloved daughter. One night the family escaped from the camp and began to flee on foot towards The Borderlands, which they had heard would offer them opportunities for concealment and work.

But they knew they would be pursued by their masters and, when it was clear that heatstroke and exhaustion were defeating them, Colim helped his daughter and her mother up into the branches of a giant tree; then he covered the family's tracks as best he could and began to walk in the opposite direction to divert their pursuers. When the merchants found him they kicked and beat him, but he did not betray his family and eventually the thugs gave up, assuming that the girl and her mother were already dead and leaving Colim to share their fate. Colim crawled back to where he had left his family and helped the woman down safely, but Oriana tumbled from the tree and broke both legs in the fall.

Oriana's mother helped Colim to construct a stretcher from some filthy plastic sheeting they'd found and the two straightest branches they could break off the tree. She eased their daughter's pain as best she could with sativa leaf pulp and covered her with her own rags to help protect her from the sun, but just as they finally reached a watering hole she herself collapsed and died. Colim and Oriana stayed for two days, mourning her and waiting till the last wild creatures had devoured her body and only the ants and vultures remained.

'We were grateful,' Colim said, 'that she left this life in a better way than if she had been caught and returned to our Patrons. And her death served to help us survive, which is what she would have wished. When a hungry pangolin came to gobble up the ants and termites, I killed and roasted it. Once we'd eaten the flesh I used its bones to make splints for Oriana's broken legs, made some repairs to the stretcher and we began our journey again.'

It took them four or five more days to reach the far outskirts of Maidentown, where they joined another group of travellers looking for refuge. I asked Colim if they intended to stay in the town, warning him that, whatever they had been told, it did not assure them much safety as runaways, 'If you are branded, the Registrar will soon hear about it and check the records. I'm afraid you haven't travelled so far that they can't track down your Patrons and inform them.'

'Then we will carry on,' said Oriana, speaking for the first time. Her voice was tight with pain but she sounded very determined.

'You're not well enough,' I argued, 'You must stay here at least until you are stronger and not crippled.'

'I don't know how long that will take and I'm not

prepared to be a burden on you when you clearly have so little yourselves. We will carry on,' she insisted.

'How will you travel? Your father can't carry on pulling a stretcher, he's weak and tired.' I admired her spirit but I was right about her father, he was in no condition to continue and nor was she.

Eventually both Oriana and her father agreed to stay with us whilst they recovered. They contributed what they could in return for our hospitality, both being proud and Oriana proving to have the stubbornness of one of Mamma's mules. She and Tikerty would sit and make things out of the scraps that Surrana and I collected on our foraging trips, and Colim fixed two rusty bicycle wheels to an old car seat to create a mobile chair for Oriana to use whilst her legs mended.

Somehow the weeks passed and turned into months. Oriana became stronger and managed very well, though she was frustrated by her dependence on us and the time it was taking for her bones to heal and her skin to recover from the blistering sunburn she'd suffered. When she needed to go outside I would carry her out of the bus and then Surrana would push her in the chair to the latrines area and help her do her toilet. Oriana found this ritual so humiliating that she began to refuse food and drink in order to avoid it; only Tikerty's constant nagging eventually wore down her resistance – perhaps Oriana could no longer bear Tikerty's appalling breath in her face. Aside from that, the two became deeply attached to each other and their affectionate bickering soon became an amusing entertainment for the rest of us as they worked; if one suggested blue beads for the necklace they were making then the other would insist on green, and if Oriana picked black thread to stitch a garment then Tikerty would argue for using white.

When we started to talk once again about leaving Maidentown it was somehow understood, without the need for discussion, that we would be going together. We began to make serious plans, and to start asking questions in earnest of those who might be best placed to know the answers: market traders, pedlars and travellers who had actually seen some of the lands beyond The Borderlands.

'Don't go west,' one merchant said, 'the region has been laid waste by locusts. We'll be lucky if they don't head this way next.'

'There is no free land in the north,' another warned us, 'it's all divided up into estates already and they don't take kindly to newcomers. But if you you go east you'll end up in one of their Detention Compounds for sure. The Governors are merciless there, and more likely to kill you than leave you to compete with their precious animals for food.'

However wild and far fetched some of the stories, it was clear that we would be as undesirable and unwelcome elsewhere as we were in Maidentown. Most of us were virtually worthless: Surrana and I because of our low caste appearance and Colim because of his age. More than one of the traders expressed an interest in Oriana, assuming that she would regain full use of her legs, but she made it very clear that she did not intend to ever be owned again. By anyone. 'If I choose to be bonded with someone one day that will be a different matter,' she said, and I sensed Surrana looking at me meaningfully, though I refused to catch her eye.

But, with nothing to lose, we were determined to move on and all finally agreed that the most promising reports were of the southern regions. Beyond the Mammoth river and the desert, it was said, was a vast expanse of water with a thousand paradise islands, all lush with vegetation and teeming with animal life. It sounded like a fairy tale but we were eager for something to believe in and a purpose beyond just surviving. We began to pack up our few belongings and prepared to leave. Whenever one of us had doubts Colim, whose wisdom and humanity I will forever aspire to, would say, 'Of course we are afraid, but we already live our lives in fear. At least the journey will be made in hope. And if no Promise Lands exist then we must create our own.'

However, the day before we originally intended to leave Maidentown I encountered my old friend Adelmo in the market square and all our plans were scattered to the wind when I saw Akara's face on a poster.

Adelmo had been coming to Maidentown for a number of years, arriving every two weeks or so with his wonderful drawings which I would sometimes pause to admire. To begin with we would just nod in recognition of each other but seldom speak beyond a brief greeting. Then, when Colim and Oriana arrived, I began regularly checking the posters around the town to see if they were being hunted and Adelmo noticed my increased interest. One day, just as he'd finished replacing one of the old posters with a new one, he asked if I was looking for someone in particular.

I wanted to trust him; there was something about this man with the long, sad face and the solemn voice that I had liked from the very beginning. But I knew nothing about him, where he was from or what official role he had, if any, and suspicion of strangers had become a habit. I answered him with cautious questions of my own and that's how I learned, for the first time, about the Adoption Centres in the Eastern region and the wretched souls kept there until they were claimed or destroyed.

As time went on, Adelmo and I grew to trust each other and become firmer friends with every meeting. A day came when we sat outside one of the cantinas with a jug of wine he had paid for and I knew it was time to be completely honest with him. I let him see my entire face so that he could know the full extent of my afflictions and pull away if he wished. He seemed neither shocked nor disgusted but took my hand and said, 'I've learned not to judge, my *friend. I only care about what's in here,' and he pointed to my heart. I would have embraced him then, but he had already attracted disapproving looks and whisperings by sharing wine with me and I had no wish to make things worse for him. He confided that he was becoming increasingly nervous about his position at the Adoption Centre, sensing that rules were tightening and his Guardianship was at risk if he was suspected of leniency; he was concerned about reports of excessive socialising with the lowest castes getting back to his superiors.*

'When I first started at The Kennels,' he confided, 'it was in the belief that we were helping the needy to a better life through adoption, or easing their suffering in a humane and painless way if there was no other hope for them. But something troubling is happening and it makes me very uneasy.'

The first hint of a disturbing change had come when he was told to stop posting his drawings. Where once he had been encouraged to find lost family or new Patrons for the inmates, and had full permission to travel once a week to Maidentown to do so, suddenly it was forbidden. There was no reason given. Adelmo, still anxious to do what he could for as many as possible, began feigning illness in order to get away, but it was becoming very difficult. He could no longer draw every new arrival but had to consider who might best stand a chance of being reclaimed or adopted and then pretend to the other Guardians that he was merely practising his drawing skills. In spite of Akara's injuries she managed to convince Adelmo that she was worth his efforts and her sheer determination to prove her identity gave him some valuable information to work with.

'It is hard to stop her from talking to be honest, Ashley - though sometimes she does herself no favours by it I'm afraid and has not endeared herself to everyone.'

'Tell me what you know, Adelmo, so that I can be certain it is her before you put yourself in any more

danger.'

What he told me of his conversations with her was almost enough to convince me, although she sounded very different from the child I remembered. Of course, she had grown up and, according to her own account, had become the celebrated Protégé Mamma wanted her to be, until something terrible happened and brought her to the Centre with what Adelmo described as horrific injuries.

'Please find out what you can, Adelmo,' I urged him as we parted, 'and I pray the Divinity will keep you safe.'

'And you, my friend. Oh, and if you find any paper to give me when next I see you then I will pass it on to her. She practises her writing and draws quite beautiful designs, which I like to encourage; she has little else to occupy her, poor child.'

'Then give her this,' I said, tearing a small corner off one of the old posters, 'but don't say it's from me, we mustn't raise false hopes,' and I wrote the only three words I could think of to encourage her, which were: KEEP WRITING TEN.

When Surrana and I returned to the bus I was full of excitement at the thought of having found Akara, but concerned at the effect it would have on our plans to journey south. I had no idea when Adelmo might return, if at all, and what we would do then if he did. I was determined that the others should not be delayed by me choosing to stay behind but they all insisted they should remain with me, at least until Adelmo had been able to come back with more news.

'Don't be stupid,' Oriana said, with the fierce, belligerent expression on her face that she always wore when trying to hide her feelings, 'you're certain to need our help when you finally come up with a rescue plan, so let's not waste time arguing about it. If I can trouble you to carry me out to my chair now I'm going to begin by doing

something useful and I suggest you do the same.'

When she came back two hours later I realised that she was no longer wearing the little gold earrings which had belonged to her mother and were the only things of personal value she had. Before I could speak, she handed me an oilskin package containing forty three krona. 'Don't!' she commanded when I started to thank her, and she spent the rest of the day tucked away in a corner, sewing furiously and speaking to no one.

We spent the next few days gathering up everything we thought worth carrying with us, and selling everything else. Every afternoon I would go to the market square to trade and then to revisit Akara's poster, wondering once again how she had ended up where she was. Had she escaped from somewhere? Was someone looking for her? The only thing I knew for sure was that she was due for extermination in less than three weeks and I had no idea how to prevent that from happening. I took to visiting the shrines of the Divinity too and offering up prayers under my breath from a safe distance, assuring myself that it was not cowardice but caution which governed my discretion.

To my surprise and relief Adelmo returned within a week, but at great risk to himself. He had travelled through the night to reach us, in order to return to the Centre in time for his next shift, and had managed to find the burned out bus without having to ask too many questions. Strangers always attracted attention and that was the last thing Adelmo wanted. He called quietly to me from outside and, as soon as I recognised his voice, I hurried to invite him in. Surrana went out to revive the brazier fire and heat some coffee, sweetened with the honey and nutmeg which were our next day's rations but which we gladly gave to our visitor, and Tikerty tethered Adelmo's mule safely where we could keep a close eye on it. When she'd given it water and the nose bag of oatmeal that Adelmo had brought with him she joined us inside and we all gathered round to listen to what he had to tell us.

'I am certain, my friend, that we have found your Akara but, apart from that, the news is not good I'm afraid. Something is happening in the eastern region but I am not sure what, or who, is behind it. It seems that the collection wagons are no longer bringing people to the Centre but taking them elsewhere – if, indeed, they are collecting them at all. There are more Guards than inmates occupying the stalls now and hardly any Visitors any more. The chances of Akara being adopted are almost non existent; our only hope is to rescue her.'

'How, Adelmo? Tell me what I must do and I will do it.'

'I have a plan of sorts,' said Adelmo, looking at each one of us in turn, 'but I have to warn you that it will almost certainly fail.'.

26 'THAT WHICH YOU HAVE NOT YET SEEN'

The smell of vomit hit my nostrils as soon as I entered Malakai's room; no amount of incense could disguise it. My Patron lay naked on the bed in a tangle of saturated sheets, whilst Emanuel knelt beside him, dabbing him with dry cloths and crying uncontrollably.

I stood in shock for several moments, my hand to my mouth and unable to comprehend what I was seeing, until Emanuel looked up at me with swollen eyes and pleaded with me to help.

'What can I do?' I asked, backing away, 'What's wrong with him?'

On hearing my voice Malakai turned towards me and beckoned me closer. In spite of my disgust I could not disobey. The room was almost as dark as the last time I had been in there and far colder; there was no fire lit and only four or five lanterns to see by. Even so, as I drew nearer to Malakai I could finally see what had been covered and hidden from me for so long.

Malakai's thin, feeble body was grey and mottled and covered in sores and scabs, some half healed and others open and weeping or bleeding. His face was a skull, the skin stretched like thin paper across it and the hollows of his eyes as dark as the night outside. Floating through the open windows came the faint sound of the music tuning up for the party, but what I was most aware of was Malakai's tortured breathing and the harsh, croaking cough which interrupted it every few seconds.

'Sit, Akara,' Malakai whispered in between coughs, patting the bed beside him. I was already so close that I could smell his rancid breath and the sour sweat pouring off him, but I did as he asked.

'Send...send...' Malakai began, but was overcome with another fit of coughing. I looked at Emanuel and said, 'What is he trying to say?'

The poor boy could hardly speak, he was so distraught, but eventually he managed to control himself.

'He wants you to send for your brother.'

'My brother?'

'He tells me your brother is a physician and can help him. I've done everything I can but he's too sick now, he needs more. Please my lady Akara, please help him.'

So Malakai was finally prepared to have Beetle under his roof and my first reaction was one of joy that I would see my little brother again. But then an awful realisation struck me: I did not know how to send for him. I had no idea what directions to give, no real sense of the distance between here and Mamma's home because I had always assumed that, when Malakai finally agreed to fetch Beetle, he would arrange it as he had done everything else. I tried to stop myself panicking and to give myself time to think.

'Yes, of course we must do that, Emanuel. I'm sure my brother can help, but he will need to know what medicines and treatments to bring with him so you must tell me exactly what is wrong with lord Malakai.'

'I don't know! I don't know! He has been in poor health all his life, but today he suddenly became much worse and I...I'm afraid he has been poisoned.'

'Poisoned? How?'

'I don't know!' he repeated, 'Maybe something in the fruit he had this morning. He kept being sick after he'd eaten it and now his guts are empty but he has fever and coughing.'

'What about all the sores, Emanuel?'

'My lady, he has had canker and ulcers for many years. I tend to them and make him comfortable with the drugs I can procure but I'm afraid. He has never been like this, please help.'

I too was afraid. I looked down at the man writhing and retching in agony next to me and felt both revolted and completely helpless.

'I don't know what to do, Emanuel,' I confessed, 'My brother would come and may be able to cure him but I don't know how to find him. Should I send for Xavier? He will know what to do, I'm sure.'

'No, don't send for anyone,' said Emanuel and he leaned close to me and lowered his voice, 'No one must know how sick my lord Malakai is. We must pretend that all is well for as long as possible.'

At that moment there was a knock on the door. Emanuel and I exchanged a look and I nodded my understanding. As the boy tried to quieten Malakai I went slowly to the door, my heart beating fast and my head full of nothing but panic. I looked back to check on Malakai and Emanuel one last time before opening the door as wide as I dared without allowing a full view of the room to whoever stood outside. It was Dominique.

As soon as I opened the door the girl's nose wrinkled in disgust at the smell and I tried frantically to think of some explanation for it. I adopted my most imperious manner.

'What is it, Dominique? I am trying to help my lord Malakai choose his costume for the evening and it doesn't help us to be disturbed.'

'I'm sorry lady Akara but your guests are arriving and

lord Malakai always likes to greet them himself, as you know.' She tried to peer past me but I blocked her and had a sudden inspiration. I lowered my voice as if inviting her into my confidence.

'Dominique, I'm afraid Emanuel became a little over excited. He and our Patron indulged in rather too much wine to celebrate my birthday and Emanuel has been...unwell. Unfortunately both Malakai's costume and the boy's have been spoiled so they both need to bathe and dress again.'

'You must allow me to help, my lady, and to send the Greys in to collect the soiled clothes. That is not something you should be doing,' and she took a step towards me.

'No.' I said, closing the door a little, 'Lord Malakai forbids it. Emanuel and I can manage and the less fuss there is made of the incident the less trouble Emanuel will be in.'

The thought of Emanuel being punished seemed enough to make her reconsider. She hesitated and I took the opportunity to make a final attempt to get rid of her, 'As for our guests, Malakai has asked that you yourself should greet them and act as hostess in my absence. He holds you in very high esteem, Dominique and I must say you look very beautiful this evening. Please do the necessary honours for us until we can join you.'

I really left her with no choice. Not for a moment did I expect her to to fall for my flattery, but she dared not defy Malakai's command. I waited for her to submit and watched her as she walked away; then I summoned one of the servers nearby and instructed them to bring jugs of fresh water and some towels and to leave them outside the door for Emanuel to collect. Since this was the usual custom it roused no particular suspicion and it would not have surprised the household that on the night of my birthday I was being allowed the privilege at last of entering my Patron's rooms.

I went back to the bedside, where Malakai appeared to

be less feverish and sleeping peacefully. Emanuel looked up at me and said, 'I've given him some opium tea but it will only help the pain and suppress the cough. We must fetch your brother, my lady, to make him better.'

'But, Emanuel, how can we do that without telling someone where to go to find him? We must speak to Xavier and take his advice.'

'No! I will go. I have loved lord Malakai like a son loves a father and I will find a way to get to your brother. If I head towards Maidentown I will soon meet someone who knows of your mother and can direct me. Fiuri d'Ursoola is an important person, if your brother is still with her then I will find him and bring him back. I have gold and krona ready, your mother will not refuse.'

'But what about me, Emanuel? You can't leave me alone with him. I don't know what to do or how to look after him. We must tell someone.'

But Emanuel stood up and shook his head, 'It's too dangerous. If the household knows lord Malaki is ill there are some amongst them who will take advantage of it. You must believe me, my lady, and do everything you can to pretend that all is normal.'

'How will we explain my staying in his room? What will they think?'

Emanuel placed a hand against Malakai's forehead and asked me to do the same. I was reluctant but Emanuel insisted, reminding me that I would need to be able to do a great deal more than that while he was away. Malakai's skin was clammy and unpleasant to touch and he was beginning to shiver. We covered him with the lightest of the blankets and Emanuel closed the windows and lit the fire. Then he sat back on his heels, took some deep breaths to calm himself and began to give me instructions:

'Give him some water as often as he asks for it but only offer the tea when you think the pain is too much for him to bear. I've made a very strong infusion which should last until I return with your brother, but you must be careful; too much and he will become unconscious.'

He stood up and went to the wash room, returning with towels, soap and a jar of ointment. 'You will need to use this on the boils and lesions, my lady, to stop him from going mad with the itching.' When I refused to take it, repulsed at the idea of touching Malakai's skin and afraid of infecting myself, Emanuel was firm with me, 'You have to do everything you can to stop him from crying out. Once the others know how ill he is, both you and he will be in danger. You have to believe me, my lady; I promise you that whatever his affliction is it cannot be caught from touching him; I've been tending to lord Malakai for ten years and not been affected. There are more towels and cloths in the wash room and I will put dressings on the worst of the open sores before I go. I will also instruct the servers to bring regular meals and refreshments to leave outside the door but not to disturb you under any circumstances.'

'How will you explain it, Emanuel?' Although our Patron's habits were often secretive and unpredictable I could not see what reason could be given for my staying in Malakai's room, possibly for days, and especially on the night of my own birthday celebrations.

'I will think of something, lady Akara,' Emanuel replied, carefully removing the soiled bed linen and replacing it with fresh, clean cotton sheets and pillows, gently rolling his master first to one side then the other with an efficiency that proved long practise. I stood by, feeling useless and scared. Emanuel bundled up the laundry and tossed it all onto the fire, gazing thoughtfully into the flames until at last he turned to me and said, 'I have an idea.'

27 THE PLAN

Adelmo's idea was to engineer Akara's escape from within by my replacing him as a Guardian.

'Do you mean for me to pretend I am you?' I asked, incredulous.

'No, that could not possibly work. But I have sown the seeds for you to take my place because I'm unwell. I've told the others that I have a friend who has recently come up from the southern region in order to become bonded to my sister. Since I'm in poor health and you are seeking work you have offered to take my place, temporarily at least. They believe you worked at one of the Detention Compounds so they will expect you to be more than qualified to carry out a Guardian's duties and maintain the discipline and vigilance required.'

'And your sister,' I said, 'What does she think of the idea of being bonded to a Ghost?'

'Well,' Adelmo replied with a rare smile, 'If I had a sister she would be very fortunate to have you.'

We spent the next few hours plotting, discussing, arguing a little and finally agreeing on a plan that we were all reasonably happy with. Adelmo emphasised the risks so *that we could be in no doubt as to the danger we would be in, but no one was prepared to let me do it alone. At first Adelmo suggested that Oriana at least should be kept well out of harm's way – either by remaining in Maidentown or waiting at some point further south for the rest of us to join her, if and when we could. Oriana swiftly rejected the idea of course in her usual contemptuous way, 'I'm not helpless. My legs are stronger now and I can walk at least part of the way. If I have to be pushed in my chair then I'll be able to carry things on my lap.'*

So it was settled. Adelmo was to return to the centre and prepare the way for me; we would follow shortly afterwards and work out more details of the plan as we travelled. After he had embraced each of us in turn, my friend stepped out into the freezing night air and I watched him lead the mule carefully through the maze of tents, the smoke from the camp fires forming its own kind of embrace around him as he disappeared.

28 DECEPTION

When I woke I was alone and I remembered that Ash had left in haste with Ridrick. Although I understood it would have been dangerous for him to stay with me any longer I felt, not for the first time in my life, utterly abandoned. All I could do was to wait, and to try - as Ash had instructed - to have faith. But I had nothing and no one to believe in except for him although he, like Mariam, seemed confident that we were governed by the great Divinity that powered the sun. Mamma would not have agreed; and it seemed to me that even blind Celeste, with her star signs and runes, was as likely to be right as people who worshipped at shrines and sacrificed precious food to some unseen god. It didn't stop me praying though; if any gods were listening I didn't want to miss the chance of being heard.

The sundial showed me that the day was already well advanced; the usual time for breakfast had passed and I was hungry. I could hear voices further down the passageway but there were no Guardians washing down the gullies or passing out food, only a Guard in stall Eleven, perched on the edge of his bed and picking his feet. The air is so humid it's like inhaling warm water and my hands are sweating so much that I couldn't grip a pencil even if I felt like it.

The two Guardians who eventually appeared with some food were not Ash and Mariam, as I had hoped, but Gareff and Ridrick-Oola. I would have been grateful for the sight even of Adelmo, who might have offered me a little kindness knowing my Due Death Date is tomorrow, but I could expect no such compassion from Gareff.

'Well, well,' he said, in his usual sarcastic tone, 'so our Queen Bee is still here. What a pity no one has realised what a gem we have in our midst. Sadly there will be no Visitors today, Ten, as we are closing the Centre down but,' and he leaned closer to hand me a bowl of thin soup, 'try not to worry about tomorrow; I'm told it will be very quick.' He stood up, a broad smile on his ugly face, while Ridrick hovered behind him, breathing heavily and bathed in her own sweat.

'The Centre is closing?' I looked from one Guardian to the other and they both nodded.

'It is. The new Eastern Region Governor is making a great many changes and no longer sees a need for Adoption Centres. There will be a new...' Gareff paused thoughtfully, searching for the words, 'system in place. However, Ten, it won't affect you, other than meaning that you will probably be our last ever inmate. Under the current regime anyway.'

'What an honour that will be, Gareff,' I said, matching his sarcasm.

'Be careful, Ten,' Gareff replied in a softly threatening voice, 'You still have twenty four hours to get through and I can make them very uncomfortable for you. You may have fooled Adelmo and Mariam into feeling sorry for you but they're no longer here and I can assure you that there are far worse things to suffer than the mercy of a quick death.'

*****

When Emanuel told me his idea I could only hope that the others would believe him, because I had nothing better to offer.

'I shall say that our lord Malakai has chosen this night to consummate his patronage of you because Celeste has advised it. When did your last bleed finish?'

'About ten days ago,' I replied.

'Does Dominique know that?'

'Of course.'

'That is good. If Celeste has decreed that your stars are most propitiously aligned for fertility at present then no one will question you remaining in this room for the few days it will take me to fetch your brother.'

'But how will you explain your absence, Emanuel?' I asked. However much I longed to see Beetle I was afraid to be left alone, nursing a sick man who could no longer protect me and surrounded by people who Emanuel had implied might be hostile.

'I will pretend I'm going to the procuress in Maidentown for drugs to enhance lord Malakai's virility. It is no secret that our Patron has not been inclined to mate before and that he might therefore need some assistance, given his age. Please don't worry, my lady Akara, I will give very strict instructions that you are not to be disturbed. Dominique will be very happy to be hosting the party and she will acquit herself more than adequately.'

I had no doubt at all that Dominique would be delighted to take my place and I grudgingly admitted that she would make a gracious and personable hostess. Emanuel finished doing what he could to make Malakai comfortable, gathered up a few necessary items for his journey and prepared to go.

'Take whatever you need, Emanuel,' I urged, 'whichever of the horses will carry you most swiftly and whatever you think you need to offer my mother in return for my brother. And please come back soon.'

'I will, my lady. And I ask that you take care of our master. Even if you do not love him as I do, that is because you do not see him as I do and perhaps, in caring for him, you will begin to understand a little.' And with that he knelt by the bed, pressed his lips to Malakai's hand and began to weep again. Malakai's eyes slowly opened and it seemed it took all his energy just to focus on Emanuel's face and whisper, 'Hurry back, my little unic.'

'I will, my lord,' Emanuel promised, wiping the tears from his face and rising to his feet as if suddenly strengthened by sheer determination. It was humbling to witness the power of such genuine devotion and loyalty and I wanted to assure Emanuel that I would do all I could for his beloved master.

Even so, as we parted at the door it was all I could do not to beg the boy to stay, but to pretend as much confidence and optimism as I wished I felt.

'May the stars grant you luck, Emanuel and a successful journey. Embrace my brother for me and come back safely with him.'

When, with great caution, we opened the door, the sounds of music and singing left us in no doubt that the festivities were continuing very well without us. I watched Emanuel summon one of the servers to him and engage in a short conversation. The server listened attentively then nodded and glanced in my direction before positioning two men to stand guard outside Malakai's room; I saw the sly looks they exchanged and wondered how convinced they were by our story.

Emanuel played his part well by announcing, but not too loudly, that he would be making haste to return from Maidentown as soon as he had purchased the required items from Carolan d'Savoy's premises.

'I wish you and Lord Malakai joy, lady Akara, and hope the stars will bless your union. I will speak to Dominique as

I leave and remind her of all your instructions.'

I simply nodded, afraid that if I spoke my voice would betray me. I turned back into the room and closed the door firmly behind me, leaning against it feeling weak with fear and wishing that I had just one ounce of Emanuel's courage. I made a solemn oath to myself that when he returned – whether with or without my brother – he would be handsomely rewarded for his service. But, whatever happened to Malakai's brave and most trusted Protégé, he didn't return to the Montagne Estate and I never saw him again.

For three days and nights I stayed alone with Malakai and the dogs, in a room that was a furnace by day and would have been as cold as the mouth of hell at night if I had not kept the fire constantly lit. I dared not let the torches or the fire die out in case I couldn't relight them, and Belle and Beau found the day time heat so uncomfortable that they took refuge in the washroom, lying restlessly on the marble tiles and panting. At nightfall, they came into the bedroom and curled up on the sheepskin rugs by their master's bed, much like the Twins did in their cot by my bedside. Malaki himself sweated and shivered in turns, regardless of the temperature in the room, and I spent almost every waking minute trying to cool him down or warm him up. I collected the trays that were left regularly outside the door, but Malakai would not eat and would only drink little sips of water when I insisted. Otherwise he only wanted opiate tea, or to suck on the herbal hookahs Emanuel had prepared for him and which seemed to soothe him briefly. I dared not leave him except to use the water closet; the minute he sensed my absence he would begin to moan and whimper. On the first evening the noise from the fireworks at my party muffled the sound, and I peeped through the curtains to watch for a while. It already seemed unbelievable that all those magnificent celebrations were taking place in my honour whilst I sat in a fetid room in all my finery and nursed a dying man. When the fireworks ended and the noise from the party eventually died down at dawn, I became afraid that the servers would hear Malakai calling out when the pain became too much, so I wound up the soundbox and played records to muffle the sounds. The melancholy tunes that were my Patron's favourites made me miserable but appeared to comfort him and seemed more appropriate than the gay and energetic gypsy music that Emanuel and I had danced to so long ago.

To begin with I had to close my eyes when applying ointment to Malakai's sores and cleaning the boils which constantly erupted with disgusting yellow pus, but after a day or so I became used to the sight and the smell of his rotting skin. He was being eaten alive by whatever ailed him and I soon knew in my heart that even Beetle would not be able to save him. Alongside pity for my Patron was my growing anxiety about what would happen when he died. I expected to inherit his estate but was certain, based on Emanuel's warnings, that my authority would be challenged - not least by Dominique. I was only just seventeen and would be needing the support and experience of people I was no longer certain I could count on. Emanuel would be devastated by Malakai's death and might not even recover from it and Dominique was never going to be easy to command. My best hope was Xavier and I decided that he would be the first I would call upon as soon as I had to.

As the fourth day dawned I was exhausted after another night of nursing and worrying. I lit more incense, fed the fire with the last of the wood, and returned to my chair at the bedside. Malakai was the colour of yellowed parchment, the bed was soaked with his urine and his mouth was bubbling with bloody phlegm. I put a damp flannel on his forehead and offered him what comfort I could.

'When Beetle comes, Malakai, he will make you better and you will be so glad you sent for him. We can build him a comfortable little house on the estate and you can consult him as you do Celeste, without ever having to look at him. I will be so happy to have my brother nearby and I will work very hard at my French so that you will be proud of me.'

I had a sudden, inspired thought and placed my mouth close to his ear, 'Malakai, mon petit; maman est la.'

Malakai's eyes fluttered open and he struggled to speak.

'Hush, mon tres cher, tout est bien,' I soothed, stroking his forehead with genuine tenderness.

'Maman?' he mouthed, his clouded eyes staring at some far distant place.

'Oui, Malakai, maman est la,' and I took his hand in mine. It was cold and surprisingly dry and weighed no more than a feather, but the fingers curled round mine and there was the faintest smile on his lips. It was true that I could not love my Patron as Emanuel did, but at last I believed I understood him a little. His disdain for all that was ugly was really an expression of self disgust after all; he could not abide imperfection in others because he could not bear to be reminded of his own. Perhaps I was deluded by my pity for him, but I felt sure I could have come to care for him if he had only shared the truth with me as he had with Emanuel. All I could do now was offer him some solace by making him believe his mother was close. I should not have received such comfort from having my own mother nearby, though still I wished she was.

Hours must have passed while I remained perched on the bed as Malakai's breathing became shallower and his fingers slowly released their grip on mine. Just as the last rattle rose in his throat the door opened and Xavier walked in.

I had looked up hoping to see Emanuel but almost as glad to see Malakai's foreman; now someone else could take responsibility for a while so that I could get some rest and gather my thoughts. The one thing I would do immediately would be to send out a search party for Emanuel.

'Xavier, I'm so relieved to see you. Lord Malakai is dead and Emanuel is missing, I need you to organise things for me.'

To my surprise Xavier burst into loud and prolonged laughter, his chins and his belly wobbling in unison as he rocked back and forth.

I was disconcerted by his extraordinary behaviour, 'Xavier, I think you misunderstand me, our Patron is dead.' When the man continued to laugh I stood up and tried to conduct myself with a confidence I certainly didn't feel.

'Stop it, Xavier. Stop it.'

'I'm sorry, *lady* Akara,' Xavier replied with mocking emphasis, 'but this is very amusing. For three days we've been listening to what we thought were cries of ecstasy, although it was hard to believe that the little runt could *find* his cock, let alone use it. Now I see that Dominique was right; she said that if our Patron was capable of fukking he would have done so with her, and long before now.'

'And I knew that Emanuel must be lying,' Dominique continued, appearing at Xavier's shoulder, 'about going to Maidentown for aphrodisiacs, because he would never have left his master's side for so long on an errand that a server could undertake.'

Suddenly the room was full of people, all covering their mouths and noses with disgust at the smell but crowding round to look at Malakai's body.

'Take it away and burn it,' Xavier commanded,

Four or five servers moved towards the bed and began wrapping Malakai up in the sheets he was lying on. I tried to stop them, shielding the body and pleading with Xavier.

'No, this is wrong. He must be given a traditional sky burial, next to his mother's shrine.'

'I wouldn't feed that putrid corpse to my worst enemy, never mind an animal. Burn him and let his ashes scatter wherever the wind takes them. Take it!' He turned to Dominique, 'Send for someone to clear up this shit.'

'How dare you, Xavier,' I said, 'This is my estate now, I give the orders.' But I said it without conviction; I already knew that my power had died along with Malakai. All I could hope to control was my own rising fear as Xavier burst into laughter again.

'What shall we do with this foolish girl, Dominique?'

'Sell her,' Dominique replied immediately, 'We'll take her to market and put her up for auction.'

'An excellent idea. Where did Malaki keep all his papers, do you know?'

'Yes, they're in the merchant's chest by that window. It's locked and there is a secret to its opening but I know what that is, Emanuel told me.'

'He must have been drunk then,' I exclaimed, 'Emanuel would never have betrayed Malakai's confidence otherwise. Now those papers belong to me anyway - you all belong to me.' It was a stupid thing to say from such a weak position and I immediately regretted it. 'I mean that I will be pleased to give you all your freedom if you just give me my own documents and let me go.'

Dominique shot me a scornful look and walked to the fireplace. Her fingers searched amongst the tiles decorating the wall above the mantel and removed one that was loose; sitting on a small ledge behind it was a key which she held up with a triumphant smile. She went to the chest, put the key in the lock and released the lid, exposing what appeared to be a complex marquetry puzzle beneath. As she concentrated on moving the wooden pieces back and forth Xavier watched intently, nodding as each one successfully clicked into place. I knew that once they gained possession of my registration documents I was as good as lost because, without a tattoo, I had no way of proving that the papers were mine and they could do what they liked with me.

I can't be sure what happened next. Perhaps I tripped or simply fainted; I was weak with hunger, exhaustion and even something like grief, or at least a sense of loss. Malaki, my provider and protector, had gone, leaving me friendless and vulnerable. He had been generous and not unkind, had spoiled and indulged me in almost every way possible, and had never harmed me physically; I was overwhelmed by the horror of the last few days, and the new threat of what might lie ahead. Perhaps someone struck me as I tried to prevent Dominique from stealing my papers, but that would have been unwise since I was of most value to them if I remained unmarked. As it was, I only remember lying half conscious on the floor, my head feeling as if it had been split in two and the sweet metallic taste of blood in my mouth.

Someone picked me up and carried me to the bed, now stripped of its linen but still rank with the stench of Malakai's sickness. Through a bloody mist I could see his body being dragged roughly along the floor in its makeshift shroud because no one wanted to touch it, and it left a trail of foul smelling fluid in its wake.

'Give her some water,' I heard Xavier say and I think it was Dominique who held a cup to my lips, but I couldn't drink; my mouth was so swollen my lips wouldn't open and the water just dribbled down my chin. I remember worrying that my beautiful clothes would be spoiled, until I realised that all I was wearing was my silk underclothes. My bodice and trousers had been removed and my exquisite velvet coat was no longer on the chair where I had placed it that morning. The room was being ransacked.

People were shouting and calling out to each other in the hall, Malakai's dogs were barking and my head was spinning with pain and confusion. I drifted in and out of consciousness, with no sense of time except an awareness that night had fallen. Xavier was issuing orders, calling for torches and fires to be lit and for someone to, 'Put some ointment or something on the girl's face, we'll never sell her looking like that.'

'Is it worth even trying now?' Dominique asked.

'Just take her with you and see; that eye looks pretty bad where it caught the corner of

the chest but the rest of her looks sound. If no one wants her or she becomes too much of a nuisance then abandon her. Take the Greys and sell them too, if you can. I suggest you leave as soon as the provisions and documents you need have been loaded.'

'You talk as if you are not coming with us, Xavier.'

'No, I'm staying here. The estate still needs to be managed and the household controlled and I'm best placed to do that. Do you hear them out there? If I don't restore order quickly there will be damage done.'

'But that's not what we agreed,' I could hear the suspicion in Dominique's voice and the soothing tones in Xavier's as he tried to placate her, 'Dominique, you need only be gone for a few days and when you return we will be bonded and can govern Montagne together as it should be governed.'

If the argument continued I wasn't aware of it. I came to lying on the hard wooden boards of a cart, with the sun rising ahead of us as we bounced along a rough, stony track. Next to me were the Greys, huddled together in spite of the mounting heat. As I think about it now I suppose they must have been at least as frightened as I was, they had probably never left the estate before and would not have expected to outlive Malakai and be sold on. But at least they had each other. They paid no attention to me as we continued to rumble along, my head exploding with every bump and rattle. I couldn't see who was driving the cart, but trotting along beside us was Dominique, riding Malakai's favourite Arabian stallion and wearing one of my prettiest outfits and what looked like my newest pair of leather boots.

I drifted away again, too weak to ask for food or water, and woke to another sunrise and a raging thirst. The cart had stopped and we were under the merciful shade of some trees, with the horses and mules tethered and feeding from nose bags. There were five or six servers milling about, chattering and chewing on meat from the spit roasting on the nearby fire, and I could hear Dominique's voice above the rest. I managed to raise myself up on one elbow and tried to get someone's attention, 'I need water. Someone bring me water.' It was Dominique who came over to me eventually; she peered into my face, cupping my chin just as my mother used to do in order to turn my head this way and that.

'You are a sorry mess, mistress,' she said, her voice full of malice, 'I don't think there is anyone who would pay good money for you now,' and she turned to speak to one of the men, 'Get her out and leave her under that tree. She can take her chances with the wild animals.' The man climbed up into the cart, grabbed my arm and began to pull me out. I protested and struggled but I had too little strength and no one tried to help me. My hands and knees scraped across the splintered wood as the man yanked me forward and I lost my balance completely, toppling out of the cart and hitting my head again as I fell.

How long it was before the collectors from The Kennels came across me I don't know, but I remember them lifting me onto the wagon and the smell of ammonia salts under my nose bringing me round. At first I thought it must be night – the sky was so dark and the landscape bleached of all colour except for a carpet of grey. The ammonia burned my throat and nostrils and made me cough but there was something else too: all around me the air was thick with ash. Everyone was struggling to breathe, choking on the black dust from a volcanic storm which must have been raging for days and was finally settling. Horrible as it was, I am sure that storm saved my life; it had kept the animals away and the dust cloud had blocked the blistering sun and saved me from roasting alive.

Should I have been grateful to my rescuers? Without them I would certainly have remained where I was, bleeding and starving to death. But as they loaded me onto the cart there was only bitterness in my heart and the conviction that I had one person to blame most for my ruination; the same person who had stolen my clothes, my documents and my rightful inheritance. Perhaps what had kept me alive until then was sheer hatred of Dominique, unaware as I was that one can have more than one mortal enemy in this life.

29 RETURN TO FIURI

At the very last moment, just as we were packing our final personal belongings, Surrana told me she would not be coming with us.

'What? Why?' I asked her, astounded by this late announcement.

'Because I must see my sister one last time and try to be reconciled with her. And there is Beetle to consider, how could I face Akara without being able to tell her that he is alive and well? And if he is sick, or even dead, then she must know the truth..'

I couldn't find the words to ask all the questions I had in my head. Surrana took my hands in hers and looked into my eyes with a steady and reassuring gaze, 'I will join you I promise, my son. When I first got you back ten years ago I said I would never leave you again and I meant it. This parting is just for a few days because I could not live with myself if I didn't go. My hope is that I will bring Beetle back with me and we can be a proper family in our new home. I need you to tell me you understand and that you have faith we will see each other again very soon. Please, Ash. For my sake and for Akara's you have to let me do this one last thing.'

How could I refuse her? How could I have faced Akara knowing I had denied her the opportunity to see her little brother again, or at least know how he fared? When I told the others of Surrana's intentions no one attempted to dissuade her; instead we all helped to fill a sturdy pack with food, water bottles and other necessities, including her documents in case she should need them. As we were securing the bundle onto her back she said, ' Now I have a surprise for you ...'

Surrana led us outside, where Colim was waiting with a harness in his hand attached to a small, sturdy donkey. Behind the donkey was a two seater trap filled with old cushions and blankets and Colim beckoned to Oriana to climb up and make herself comfortable.

'Where did you get this?' I asked, amazed.

'Oh, we had a few things between us still to trade,' Colim replied, 'including Oriana's chair and some items of Surrana's which she was willing to part with.'

I looked at my mother and waited for her to say something. After a moment's hesitation she said, 'It seems that certain things are much in demand these days amongst those who can afford them; they may despise our blue veined skin but they covet our pubic hair if we have it, whatever the colour. I sold my golden muff to the wigmaker for a very good sum and just think, when it grows back I can sell it again. Now, get on your way. I will follow you and find you as soon as I have made peace with my sister, and if all goes well I will have Beetle with me.'

Surrrana did not come back with Beetle. She did join us safely after just a few days but she was alone, although able to tell us that Beetle was well and had made the choice himself to stay with Mamma.

When Surrana had reached our old home she was shocked to find Mamma very sick and almost unrecognisable. Beetle was looking after her with his potions and tinctures but she was plagued by the recurrence of her old allergies and raddled with the liquor and drugs she consumed to ease the torture of them. Whilst she hardly greeted her sister with joy, she didn't turn her away and was eager to hear news of Akara when Surrana told her that she was on her way to see her.

Surrana had intended to tell Mamma that Akara was in an Adoption Centre and that, if she had any conscience at all, she would hurry to claim her daughter before it was too late. But it soon became apparent that Mamma had long since spent all the money from Akara's sale and would not have been able to pay the fee even if she had wanted to. Besides, Mamma talked so proudly of Akara and what she had achieved that Surrana could not bring herself to contradict her when she said, 'I knew I had done the right thing by her, selling her to Malakai. I could have let the bidding continue, you know, and that whoremistress Carolan might still have won her, but I wanted better for my daughter. Such a jewel deserved to be cherished.'

'Yes,' agreed Surrana.

'As it was,' Mamma continued, 'I achieved a great price for her and we have managed well on it until now, have we not, Beetle?'

Our little brother was also changed, as one would expect. He was still small for his age but muscular and strong in spite of his size. His limp did not seem to hamper him much and he was caring for Mamma, and the few animals they had left, all by himself. The house was bare of any luxuries as far as Surrana could see and she guessed that most things of any worth had been sold to provide what comfort Beetle could procure for Mamma who lay on a low, thick mattress with soft cotton cushions and blankets to relieve the maddening irritation of her skin. When Surrana took the opportunity to follow Beetle into the larder for a private conversation he immediately questioned her about his sister.

'Is Akara truly well and happy, Surrana?'

'She misses you, Beetle,' my mother answered truthfully, 'I've come to take you back with me so that we can go to her together. I have some money to give to your mother.'

'Oh no, I can't leave her, she needs me. I am happy knowing that Akara is well and that she hasn't forgotten me, but my place is here with Mamma. You can tell Akara that our mother treats me better now and that I am safe. Tell me where you are going and one day, perhaps when I'm no longer needed here, I can join you.'

'Of course she has never forgotten you, Beetle. She would have sent for you long before now if she could, I'm sure.'

'That makes me very happy. Please embrace her for me and tell her I love her.'

Then Mamma called out for him and, once again, Surrana had no heart to disabuse him of his belief that his sister was still living in comfort with her illustrious Patron. She gave Mamma all the money she had on her, for which she received no thanks I'm afraid, and left her to her bottles and noxious smelling pipes. Beetle came out to embrace her and repeat his message to Akara, before returning inside to tend to Mamma.

Surrana made good progress and reached us within days, largely thanks to the kindness of other travellers who let her ride in their trailer with the sheep they had collected from Maidentown market. We had set up a little camp near the Adoption Centre which was easy for her to find and our relief at seeing her was only matched by our disappointment that she did not have Beetle with her. We had tried to put our time to good use by making plans, but concern about my mother had been preoccupying all our minds until she returned to us. By then Adelmo had managed to visit us on several occasions, each time with more disturbing news about the changes at the Centre and the urgency of Akara's situation. He had, as agreed, set the scene for my arrival as a replacement Guardian and arranged for me to be accommodated in the main palace building with his non existent sister, to whom I was now supposed to be bonded. This begged a rather perplexing question. It was obvious that there was only one person suited to playing the part of Adelmo's sibling but I hardly dared ask her, knowing that I could expect a sharp and cutting response. However, Oriana turned to me and spoke first, 'I told you I would prove useful at some point. I'm willing to pose as your mate, if you can bear to pretend attachment to a near cripple.'

'Don't call yourself that, Oriana. I... I... would feel privileged. I mean, I would be very grateful, happy even...' I was completely tongue tied and embarrassed by my clumsiness. We were only pretending, after all.

'And I would be humbled and honoured, Ash, if I were to be bonded to you,' Oriana replied, with a mockingly exaggerated bow. Her eyes were sparkling with mischief and I had never seen her look so animated before. We smiled at each other and I looked round at the others, who were all unusually silent but obviously amused. 'What is it?' I asked Surrana, but it was Colim who answered, 'Do you not think it would be a very good idea to conduct an official bonding ceremony? Just to save you both the effort of pretence.'

It seemed that everyone had realised the depth of our affection for each other except for us. Or perhaps just me. Surrana, who loved Oriana like a daughter, was delighted, as was Tikerty who leapt about like a child shouting out 'Yesh! Yesh!' until she was dizzy. We had a short and solemn ceremony where Oriana and I said a few words to each other and our four witnesses proclaimed testimony. Adelmo used the cord from his keffiyeh to bind our wrists and pronounce us bonded for life.

I suddenly felt very shy and unsure and it was Oriana who put her mouth to mine for a kiss. I wish Akara, and indeed Beetle, could have been there to feel the love that seemed to embrace us all. We never knew such tenderness and affection with Mamma and it is only when you experience it that you realise what a gift it is. My heart was so full I almost wept.

There was no time for celebration though; Adelmo was urging us to go with him to The Kennels and begin to put our plans in place. Oriana and I said farewell to Surrana, Colim and Tikerty and left them, challenging their anxious faces with our falsely brave ones as we hurried towards the Centre.

30 MASQUERADE

Adelmo had warned me about Gareff. When we arrived at the old palace building it was he who greeted us and he did not attempt to hide his initial animosity. I had taken great care to clothe myself in black, both to hide my complexion and to convey what I hoped was an intimidating air, in keeping with what he'd been told of my background. Oriana was dressed in the best garments she and the other women possessed so that she would look convincing as the bonded companion to a Detention Compound Administrator. If our plan was to succeed we needed to convince Gareff and the others of my superior experience and status. After so many years of trying to be inconspicuous and unthreatening the masquerade did not come easily to me.

'So, Colim Sang,' Gareff began, 'you are Adelmo d'Afrar's oldest friend, we understand. And this must be his sister, to whom you are recently bonded. Allow me to offer my congratulations.' He presented himself to Oriana with a slight bow, raising himself slowly to look her up and down as he did so. She held herself steady and with admirably proud bearing, but I knew she wasn't strong enough to remain standing straight for long; if Gareff realised she

was in less than perfect health then we would be exposed: an Administrator would never condescend to be bonded with an undesirable or a low caste.

'Thank you,' I replied curtly, 'But we have come a long way so some refreshments would be appreciated before we continue with the pleasantries.'

'Of course. Come this way and Ridrick-Oola will show you the room we have prepared for you. I don't know how the facilities here will compare with what you are used to, Colim Sang, but we do our best with what we have. All the Guardians are housed in this main building, along with some watchmen for our security; the other Guards occupy the stables or vacant stalls in the old kennels whilst we prepare for the new arrangements. I imagine you will know all about the proposed changes, since Adelmo informs me you are in the confidence of our new regional Governor.'

Fukk, I thought. It was an inspired idea for Adelmo to have come up with in order to impress Gareff, but unfortunate that he'd not mentioned it to me; I was caught off guard, particularly as I didn't even know who the new Governor was. Gareff waited for my reply.

'Of course I do, Gareff,' I said, reinforcing my superiority by not using his full name, 'but the Governor instructed me to look to you, as senior Guardian here, to appraise me of the details as you understand them. It is important that you yourself are clear as to the process.' I was having to think fast, keeping vague but sounding authoritative, whilst increasingly aware of Oriana's tightening grip on my arm as she leaned on me for support. Adelmo had been right about Gareff though, feeding his vanity was the key to his heart; we both knew that he was no more senior than half a dozen other Guardians here – including Adelmo – but he responded to the implication that he was favoured.

'Certainly, Colim Sang. Now we have reached your room perhaps you would like to rest before joining me for a

tour of the centre? This is Ridrick-Oola, one of our longest serving and most valued Guardians.' Standing by the open door was a woman whose smell was so overwhelming that it was impossible to remain near her for long. I ushered Oriana inside, thanked Ridrick and turned to Gareff, 'Wait here for me and I'll join you shortly. Oriana Sang will remain in our room and acquaint herself with the accommodation while you and I visit the Centre,' and I closed the door behind me before Gareff could argue.

This palace, although faded and crumbling, is dazzling beyond anything I've ever ever seen. Our room was vast and well furnished, with elaborate carvings on the walls and ceiling and an adjoining annexe consisting of a china water closet and a sunken bath, chipped and grimy but still unimaginably luxurious to someone who has lived in a rusty old bus and washed in slimy waterholes and muddy creeks. There was food and drink set out for us on a brass tray which had been left in the cool of a little stone alcove and, after I'd been refreshed by several cups of fresh orange juice, I left Oriana to enjoy the feast. She settled herself on the bed with a plate of fruit, cheeses and smoked meats and an expression of such contentment that I almost wished we could stay here, just so she would be forever happy. But I was also desperate to begin my mission – of seeing Akara, confirming that she was indeed my cousin, and engineering her escape. I dreamed of us all being far away, safe and beginning our new lives together; I was full of hope and self belief on the strength of my successful role play so far and I assured Oriana that she could relax and enjoy the comforts of our surroundings whilst I was gone.

The contrast between the accommodation in the palace and the conditions in which I found Akara nearly broke my both my heart and my resolve. As Gareff led me out of the main building and across the courtyard, the baked earth hot beneath our feet, he announced proudly that blocks one to five were already empty of inmates, all of whom had been successfully disposed of, 'It means we will be able to start work on the Governor's plans as soon as we get the instructions. We have just a few left in occupation in Block Six, including some we are waiting for decisions on.' He looked at me, expecting some response, but all I could do was nod as if I understood. 'Here,' he continued as we entered the block itself and began to walk down the corridor, 'are the kitchens on your left - which I myself oversee; the infirmary, showers and laundry on your right and a provisions room next to the kitchens. You will see the livestock, vegetable gardens and the bee hives once we go out at the far end of the corridor but first I will show you the stalls.'

Just before we turned right to go down another corridor I glanced at the large metal door to my left which he had not identified. 'We'll save that for the end, shall we?' Gareff said, smiling broadly before drawing his scarf across his nose and mouth to offer some protection against the stench which greeted us as we turned into the rows of stalls. The smell of piss, shit and the Divinity knows what else, hit my nostrils from the steaming gullies running down either side. There was no roof to the passageway and the blazing sun was at its height, cooking us mercilessly as we made our way past each miserable cell, few of which had anything more than tattered plastic and metal sheeting above them to shield the inmates from the elements. Sweating and uncomfortable as I was I had to take my time, checking each stall to see if Akara was there and feigning my approval at the terrible conditions. Although Adelmo had told me she was in the tenth stall I couldn't be sure that Akara hadn't been moved and I had to approach my encounter with her as innocently as I could.

As we passed fifteen and fourteen to my left, and eight and nine to the right, my heart was thudding in my chest and my mouth was dry. Was I about to see her at last and *what should I expect? Adelmo's drawings had, I thought, prepared me for her injuries but still, I confess, it was both a shock and a disappointment when we stopped at the tenth stall and I saw her for the first time.*

She was sitting on her bed, writing. When she looked up I nearly gasped at the sight of her poor face and she was so changed that I felt sure we had come all this way for nothing. The sorry creature before me could not be my Akara. I needed a moment to collect myself and Gareff obliged me by talking, as usual. He does love the sound of his own voice. It was apparent that he had a particular dislike of the girl and was almost gleeful as he paused in front of her to say, 'This is Ten. She has only five days left now before her Due Death Date and very little hope, I'm afraid, of being claimed or adopted in spite of her many, obvious gifts,' He sniggered and then lowered his voice very slightly, as if to be discreet, but ensuring he was clearly audible, 'She has delusions, poor child; sits scribbling away and pretending she had an education and a high caste background but she has no documents and who, looking at her, would believe she was ever someone's Protégé? Frankly, Colim Sang, extermination will be a blessing for her if that's what the Governor decides. Now, moving on: stalls eleven and twelve are only occupied by Guards currently so let me take you outside and show you the gardens and the bee hives, of which I am particularly proud.'

As Gareff turned and began to waddle down the passageway I looked into the girl's face and saw nothing in her haunted expression that might convince me she was once the sweet, innocent girl of our childhood. It was not until the following day that I knew I had indeed found my Akara.

Gareff carried on talking as I followed him down the passage, boastfully claiming responsibility for reducing the inmates' rations and other such 'improvements'. 'I've long suspected,' he said importantly, 'that things would have to change and we would need a far more rigorous system for weeding out the weak and feeble. When I heard that the new Governor was of the same mind I was most pleased and I expect the Project to be a great success.' Then, as we reached the big metal door at the end of the passage he said, 'The Extermination Chamber is not in use at present, shall we take a look inside now?'.

31 MEMENTO QUI SIS

It was a relief to be outside, in spite of the ferocious heat. Had we stayed inside that chamber for a moment longer I would certainly have become faint and collapsed. As it was, I had to struggle to control the vomit rising in my throat and prevent my legs from folding beneath me. I turned immediately to the font and helped myself to a cup of warm water, trusting that Gareff could not see my hand trembling.

'Are you quite well, Colim Sang?' Gareff enquired.

'Perfectly. I perhaps should have had something to eat before we began our tour but I confess I was very eager to see the Centre and I'm most impressed by what you have shown me so far.'

'That is very gratifying, Colim Sang and I hope you will be equally struck by the efficiency of our husbandry.' He chattered on as we walked through the kitchen garden, passing the poultry house, the goat shed and the pigsties. I made noises of approval but could hardly take it all in, though I could see now why Gareff was so proud: the Guardians have achieved wonders with the land here, persuading things to grow and livestock to breed successfully. The recent rains had saturated the ground,

filled the old ponds and fountains and irrigated the crops; everything was flourishing. There had been no need to reduce the inmates' rations at all.

'As you can see,' Gareff continued, 'We are well prepared as far as provisions are concerned. How soon do you think the Governor will need to have the accommodation blocks ready?'

'How much do you need to do to them?' I countered, hoping his reply would give me a clue as to their future use.

'Well, we have repairs to make, as you saw, as well as improvements to the sanitation and so forth. As you know, the Governor has stipulated that hygiene standards must be of the highest, in order to keep the subjects' condition stable before they are moved on. But I'm afraid we cannot do much without the generator we've been promised and at present we have Guards and servers idling about just awaiting instructions. I had expected that you would be issuing those, Colim Sang, but perhaps not. May I ask when you last had a conversation with the Governor?'

'I spoke to him just before I left the Eastern Detention Compound,' I said, as confidently as I could and deciding to embellish, 'And he was still in discussions with the engineers.' I was floundering, my mind desperately trying to grasp what the implications of Gareff's words might be. A generator? Sanitary conditions? A terrible sense of dread spread through me.

'Ah, I see. Yes, of course, Colim Sang. I must try not to be impatient, must I not? Would you excuse me now, I have a great deal still to do and Nineteen's Due Death Date is tomorrow, so I must supervise the preparations in the Extermination Chamber. I confess it's one of the tasks I enjoy most.'

I returned to Oriana that first night, sickened and disturbed by what I had heard and seen, but still ignorant of just how much danger we were in. I shared my doubts that the pathetic occupant of stall ten was who she claimed to be, but we both agreed that I must persevere. We talked, kissed and explored each other's nakedness but, at the very moment it had waited twenty three years for, my dick failed me. Oriana was as soft, desirable and eager a woman as I had imagined so many times in my dreams, but I was tortured by dark thoughts that kept me limp. Whatever the truth about her identity, the girl who claimed to be Akara would die in that terrible place, and the knowledge of it would haunt me forever unless I could save her.

Eventually, with Oriana's sweet words soothing me, I managed to sleep. The next morning, in a change of strategy, she gave me a stern lecture and I promised to try and present myself with assurance and authority.

I began by insisting upon visiting the stalls alone, telling Gareff that I wished to evaluate them for myself without his influence, helpful though it was. He agreed, bowed obsequiously, and left me. There was watery broth being offered for the inmates' breakfast, but I took tomatoes, an egg and an orange from our room to give to Ten, marvelling at how well it is possible to live if you have the means.

Our plan had been for me to establish myself as an authority within the Centre, to familiarise myself with the Extermination Chamber and ensure that I was there and in control on Akara's Due Death Date. It sounds impossibly simple and unrealistic now, reliant on my being able to deceive all the Guardians and somehow get Akara out of the chamber alive to where Surrana and Colim would be waiting for her. How they were going to get inside the Centre grounds unchallenged was something they were going to have to work out for themselves. How Oriana and I were also going to escape and join them was another puzzle. Adelmo had done his best to help and had warned us it would not be easy, but even he had not been aware of all the dangers and could not have foreseen the one mistake on my part that would ruin everything.

In between my visits to Akara I tried to familiarise myself with as much of the Centre as I thought was important. As far as I could see there were only three possible ways of escape from block six once we had got Akara out of her stall. One route was via the door to the courtyard, which always had at least a dozen Guards milling about just waiting for some sort of trouble to occupy them. The second possible exit was through the arch to the smallholding and the cattle shelters, both of which were guarded even more securely by Guards with dogs. Even if we got that far, I had no idea how big an area the smallholding covered and what then lay beyond it and I dared not ask too many questions for fear of rousing suspicion. The third way was from the rear door of the Extermination Chamber, which led out to a walled yard with an enormous refuse incinerator and side gates into the pig and goat enclosures. But of course, in order to leave by the rear door you first had to enter it by the front one.

The more Oriana and I discussed it, the more convinced we became that we must appear to let things take their course until the very last minute, trusting that Surrana and Colim would be in position outside as arranged. Oriana and I had been able to explore outside a little, on the pretext of taking some exercise and without, we thought, attracting much attention. Although tiring for Oriana it was good for her legs, which were becoming stronger by the day. Once beyond the Centre, Adelmo had managed to find us on two occasions and was able to carry messages back and forth between us and the others. We insisted that Adelmo himself could not be present for the actual escape, if he were discovered to be involved we felt certain there would be very bad consequences for him. The more we heard about the new Governor's intentions the more menacing they sounded.

Gareff sought me out at every opportunity, anxious to make himself invaluable it seemed and keeping me informed of every new development. 'It is just as well,' he confided, 'that Adelmo is not here. As his friend you must be aware that he sometimes has too soft a heart. You and I understand, of course, that what lies ahead is all for the greater good, but I'm afraid Adelmo might not have the stomach for it. Several of the old Guardians have, in fact, been removed recently for that very reason. Isolde, Lamar and Mariam are all considered unsuitable for the task ahead and will be found other positions elsewhere. There is also, of course, the question of Adelmo's poor health, which does seem to be a recurring problem.'

'Which duties, particularly, do you think Adelmo d'Afrar would find distasteful?' I asked, although I was almost afraid to know the answer.

'Oh, I'm quite sure he would have acquitted himself more than adequately with regard to collection and maintenance of the specimen groups, but I suspect the selection process would have proved hard for him; Adelmo could never help but have favourites. In fact, he became a little too attached to some of the current inmates, I'm afraid.'

I fancied that Gareff looked at me a little slyly then and it worried me.

'Tell me, Gareff, you mentioned that some of the current inmates were awaiting decisions. Does this mean a potential delay to any of their exterminations?' I made it sound as if this was a source of irritation to me and was gratified when it drew more information, including the new Governor's name.

'Ah yes, Colim Sang. We have two internees with imminent Due Death Dates – Ten and Seven – who may be worth retaining as specimens. Both are physically inadequate but might be considered suitable owing to their other attributes. As you're aware, Governor Chen is as

interested in intellect and ability as in physique.'

'Yes, indeed. He might well be keen to reserve them, as you say. Are the inmates themselves aware of this?' I tried to select my words carefully, concentrating on the possibilities opened up by what he was saying, rather than the disturbing implications. Might there be another way of saving Akara's life if her extermination could be postponed or even cancelled? And, if so, at what cost to her? Whatever Governor Chen wanted specimens for I could not imagine that it was anything good.

'Oh no,' Gareff replied with a nasty laugh, 'We've found it is much easier to control them with the threat of imminent death. Ten in particular is an arrogant individual whom I, for one, would be happy to see the back of.'

At that point, to my relief, Gareff had been called away to attend to something in the kitchens. I hurried back to the palace to find Oriana and tell her what I'd learned. We both felt I'd done well to find out as much as I had, although it was unsettling and really took us no nearer to a real plan.

Late on Akara's last night but one I was able to visit her alone, having told Gareff that I would carry out assessments of the two inmates whose decisions were still pending. I visited Seven first, quietly observing the young boy sitting inside who was of dark complexion and apparently in good health. There was no evidence of white disease, or any other affliction, that I could see and I wondered how and why he had ended up here.

'What's your name, boy?' I asked, expecting him to stand respectfully for a Guardian and come to the door. He did not respond. I asked again, louder, but still he did not reply. I looked then at the board hanging by the stall and read that he was an itinerant scribesman of uncertain age and that he was deaf. When I shook the metal door vigorously it eventually attracted his attention and he

leaped to his feet. Then I was at a loss; he may be able to read lips and possibly to speak, after a fashion, but in order to find that out I would need to remove my dark net mask and risk being seen, not only by him but by any one of the real Guardians who might suddenly appear. His eyes were on my covered face, searching for something to respond to, but all I could do was speak louder, 'Can you hear at all? Where are you from? Where were you educated to become a scribe?' The poor boy just shook his head, holding his hands up to his ears and waiting for me to understand. 'Have you anything to write on?' I mimed but he shook his head again and showed me empty hands. His stall, as I looked around it, was virtually bare except for a miserable little bed and a slop bucket which was full to overflowing. I was glad he couldn't see the tears in my eyes as I turned away from him.

I tried to compose myself before I reached Akara's stall; I knew she needed to see me being strong and confident. I unlocked the padlock and considered the possibility of not relocking it when I left so that she could choose her own opportunity to escape, but I would make that decision when the time came. For now, I must give every impression of rigorously following the rules.

I sat down next to Akara on the bed and had to remind her of caution when she said excitedly, 'I'm so very happy that you are my cousin, Ash!' She lowered her voice obediently and clutched my hand, 'I want to know everything. Everything about your life since I last saw you. Where have you been and what have you been doing? You look so handsome and grown up now,' then her face fell. 'You must be very shocked to see me looking this way. I'm so sorry, Ash,' and she began to cry. I wiped the tears from her cheeks and shook my head, 'You have nothing to apologise for, dear Akara. And don't distress yourself, scars will make no difference to my love for you.' She began to speak again but I raised a finger to my mouth,

'There will be time enough for talking when we are safely away from this dreadful place, but the Guardians could check on us at any time and the other stalls will soon be occupied by Guards again when they have finished their shifts.'

I had brought fruit for Akara to eat and we drank the stale water that remained in the jug from earlier. It had not been replenished and I was tempted to call for someone to refill it but it seemed wiser not to draw any more attention to ourselves than necessary. After a while my cousin rested her head on my shoulder and I did not have the heart to push her away. I put my arm around her and comforted her as best I could, soothing her in the way I imagined Oriana might have done, until at last her head dropped into my lap and she fell asleep.

I kept my ears strained for the sound of anyone approaching, every sinew of my body alert to danger, but we stayed like that for what must have been hours. The atmosphere became increasingly gloomy and heavy, with a familiar smell in the air that usually presaged some severe weather. Eventually I had to ease the cramp in my hand, removing my gloves to massage my stiff fingers as I watched a parade of fire ants wrestling with a plum stone we'd dropped on the floor; if they didn't succeed in removing it then I must remember to do so myself, I thought. Without disturbing Akara, I was just reaching down to pick up the glove I'd dropped when a pungent new odour reached my nose and I looked up; there, standing by the door, was Ridrick-Oola, smiling and sweating profusely as usual.

I was quick to hide my hands and to alert Akara to the Guardian's presence with a nudge. 'Yes, Ridrick, what is it?' I said, hoping to convey impatience rather than alarm whilst I fumbled to put the gloves back on under the folds of my robe.

'I've brought Ten some milk and honey, Colim Sang.

And you've been so busy you must be tired. Gareff invites you to take some refreshment with him; he's in the kitchens.'

'That's very kind, Ridrick-Oola, but...' I was about to say that I had not quite finished my subject assessments for the Governor, but I realised that – having already taken several hours – it would seem improbable so instead I agreed, 'You're quite right, we've done enough.' Akara was sitting upright beside me, tense and silent. 'That's enough for now, Ten,' I said, 'I will be reporting back to the Governor and may have news for you later today.' A flicker of anxiety crossed Akara's face, but she nodded to show that she understood I intended to return to her soon. We had not discussed any plans I might have for engineering her escape, and my thoughts of perhaps leaving the door unlocked for her were out of the question now Ridrick had appeared. I could only pray that I might have something encouraging to tell her when I came back.

Ridrick, wheezing and puffing by the door, took a step forward. I rose to my feet and snatched some paper from the bed saying, 'I'll pass your plea on to the Governor, Ten,' I said, 'but I make no promises.'

Although I longed then to embrace my cousin and urge her to be brave, I left her without another word or a backward glance, pausing only for Ridrick to step aside so I could pass. As I started to walk down the corridor I heard the Guardian say, 'Drink this. I've been told you must be given nourishment after all, just in case the Governor chooses you,' before banging the door, snapping the padlock shut and following me down the passageway.

I instructed Ridrick, as firmly as I could, to tell Gareff I would join him shortly; when she started to protest that Gareff wanted me immediately, I called out, 'He can wait,' and I hurried instead towards the palace. As I crossed the courtyard I heard what might have been distant thunder, or perhaps the sound of the earth cracking and crumbling somewhere nearby, and the sky was still dark and gloomy although it was close to dawn.

When I reached our room Oriana was lying awake on the bed and she immediately jumped up and ran to me. I explained what had happened in the hours since I'd left her, too tired by then to hide my anxiety and pretend that all was well.

'It doesn't sound good, Ash,' she agreed, 'If Ridrick saw your hands she will certainly tell Gareff that you can't possibly be the rank you're pretending to be.'

'I know,' I said, 'it was stupid of me.'

'Well, yes,' she said, with her usual bluntness, 'but you're tired and you've been so brave I'm still proud of you. What's that in your hand?'

'It's just some papers I picked up so I could pretend to Ridrick that Akara had been taking half the night to write a plea of mercy from the Governor to spare her.'

'What's written on them?' said Oriana, unfolding the crumpled sheets. We smoothed them out on the table and they were covered in Akara's intricate designs. There were poems she'd illustrated, and little drawings of people and animals, all done with remarkable detail. When we turned over one of the pages there was a decorated heart entwined with the names 'Akara and Ashley'. I looked at Oriana and she smiled, kissed me tenderly on the mouth and said, 'You'd better go and rescue her, my love.'

I told Oriana to stay safely in our room, and made my way back to block six. The sky was no lighter and the rumbling seemed louder and closer. When I reached the kitchens Gareff was supervising the skinning of a dozen or so rabbits. The ovens were all lit and the heat was intense.

'Ah, Colim Sang,' he exclaimed as he saw me, 'how very good of you to join me.' I thought there was an unpleasant edge to his voice but it could have been my imagination. He kept me waiting for several minutes whilst he fussed around *the kitchen, issuing orders, tasting bits of this and that and enjoying himself. 'Let us go somewhere more comfortable, shall we?' he said at last, leading me out into the passageway and back towards the courtyard, where it was only a little cooler. The sky was dark with purple clouds and the early morning air already stuffy and hard to breathe. Gareff gestured towards one of the stone benches and we both sat down; he summoned one of the Guards and dispatched him to bring fresh water saying, 'Our esteemed visitor looks uncomfortably hot, we can't have him passing out on us.' I was sweltering - overcome with nerves and exhaustion and longing to loosen my headgear and take off those fukking gloves but completely trapped.*

'Drink! Drink!' Gareff commanded, seeming amiable at first but with increasing insistence and menace in his voice. I had no choice. I averted my face and lifted the netting carefully, sipping what I could without tilting the cup too much and exposing my skin. I tried to take control of the situation again by challenging him, though my voice sounded shaky and unconvincing, 'So, Gareff, skinning rabbits I see. What great occasion merits the killing of so many of our valuable animals?'

The Guardian presented me with an exaggerated look of surprise, 'But surely,' he said, 'You must know that Governor Chen is making an inspection soon and we'll be expected to provide a feast?'

'Well of course,' I said with my heart sinking to the pit of my stomach, 'I was simply not aware of the exact time of his arrival since I've not seen him recently, as you know.'

'No indeed; it certainly must be quite some time since you've seen the Governor,' said Gareff with slow deliberation and a strange expression on his face, 'I believe, Colim Sang, that she will be here before the end of tomorrow.

32 NESSUN DORMA

I couldn't sleep. I sat alone on my very last night, wondering what had happened to Ash and why he had deserted me. I was too afraid to be hungry, which was just as well since I had not been fed, or even visited, since Gareff brought me breakfast.

My stall stank and the flies were worse than ever, but more interested in the contents of my slop bucket than in me which was a blessing. Looking up at the patches of sky I could see through the tattered roof I realised why it was still so hot and sticky, in spite of the lateness of the hour: there was a warm wind pushing huge, dark clouds with alarming speed through the humid air. Perhaps there will be a storm tomorrow, I thought. Perhaps I will drown before they have a chance to exterminate me.

My final day and Ash has not appeared. It is well past dawn, but I only know that because the torches have been extinguished; the sky is very dark and threatening and there is a sulphurous smell in the air. Why hasn't Ash come to me and told me his plan for my escape? My head is full of doubts and contradictions: time drags but goes too quickly; I trust Ash but have misgivings too; I am torn between hope and despair.

I look in the mirror and I'm no longer horrified by the image I see there; it is a face I could live with now. I recall Ash's words to me when I was reluctant to let him see me without my eye patch; he said, 'A tree is no less beautiful just because it has lost its leaves, Akara. You may not be the perfect princess Mamma wanted you to be, but you are young and strong and you have learned lessons here that have brought you some wisdom, I think.' After he'd said that I felt better about myself and even dreamed that someone might yet want me as I am. Banjo would never have been mine, no matter what I looked like, but Ash and I have always loved each other . Now he's not my brother perhaps he could learn to love me in a new and different way. We could find Beetle and be like a proper family together, somewhere safe far away from here. If I tell myself that all that could be possible then I can be brave for a little longer.

Now I know for sure that I will not see Ash again. Gareff left me a short while ago, just before mid day, having arrived with as much self importance and dignity as he could manage in the midst of the wild cyclone raging around us. This time there is no refreshing rain, but a hot, sulphurous wind depositing clouds of yellow soot and making the atmosphere increasingly oppressive. Every now and then the earth trembles.

At first, Gareff tried to make his grand announcement from the doorway, but I couldn't hear him over the noise of the storm and the rattling metal doors, so he had to come inside. He lifted his voice against the wind ,'Well, well. So it seems there are people of influence who are interested in our Queen Bee's fate.'

He was trying to study my expression but I said nothing, not knowing which way this was going to go.

'You have had,' he continued, 'a stay of execution, as it

were. Right at the eleventh hour.'

My heart leaped. *Ash,* I thought, *Ash has managed to convince them to release me.* The relief was overwhelming.

'You don't seem surprised, Ten. Don't you want to know who's magnanimity has saved you?'

I grinned at him then, triumphant that somehow my clever cousin had defeated him.

'Oh dear,' Gareff said, taking a step closer to me, 'I do so hope I haven't misled you in any way. You didn't think that ridiculous imposter calling himself Colim Sang could be responsible for your reprieve surely?'

I felt as if the blood had frozen in my veins.

'No, unfortunately your inept rescuer is facing his own particular demise. You, however, have attracted the attention of our new Governor and have been selected for quite another purpose than extermination. Isn't that good news, Ten? You always believed you were special and so you are!'

The ground shivered again, so violently that we both had to steady ourselves. Gareff was suddenly in a hurry to go, 'Well, I have a great deal to organise before the Governor arrives and we've had notice that it will be within the hour. I'll leave you to contemplate your good fortune, Ten, and to consider what interesting plans our new Governor has in store for you.'

I had no words. All I could think of was what might be happening to Ash, but I didn't dare to ask.

Pausing dramatically by the door, Gareff pretended an afterthought: 'Oh, I wonder if you would care to know who the new Governor is? You are already acquainted, I believe, through Banjo Safarr – the unfortunate boy who hanged himself, if you remember. Our new Governor is none other than the lady Isabella Chen. Such a magnificent woman, and so full of marvellous ideas for...future improvements.'

And with that he left, banging the door shut behind him

and bustling off down the passage just as the next tremor shook the building.

33 BEHIND THE STEEL DOOR

Oriana and I were taken to to the Extermination Chamber and shackled to the wall. We had some freedom of movement, enough to sit or lie down, and were left with bread and some water. We were glad to have each other but frantic knowing that Akara – if she was even still alive - would be alone and must by now believe that I had abandoned her.

I had realised my terrible mistake the instant Gareff took such pains to stress that the new Governor was a woman. I've since cast my mind back to wonder if I had missed a vital clue in all our conversations over the last few days, but Gareff had been very careful throughout to remain unspecific. He had been waiting to catch me out all along.

We had sat on the courtyard bench in silence for some time, both aware that my exposure as an impostor was complete and that any argument on my part would be pointless. There was almost a strange sense of relief, now that we were both stripped of pretence, and when Gareff stood up and said, 'Shall we go?' it didn't require the Guards standing nearby to assist me. I rose and followed him inside and we went directly into the chamber, where I was stripped of everything except my undergarment. Even that was a blessing, as the chamber was sweltering in the heat from the incinerator and there was very little ventilation. Under Gareff's supervision one of the Guards examined me thoroughly for identifying brands or tattoos before attaching a narrow metal cuff to my right ankle, along with one to my right hand, and connecting both to one of a number of iron rings on the wall.

'What of Oriana?' I asked Gareff, more afraid for her than for myself.

'She won't be harmed for the time being. I'll have her brought here and Governor Chen will decide on both your futures when she arrives. I must ask,' he added as he was about to leave, 'who are you really? And just why are you here?'

There seemed no reason not to tell him now. 'I'm Ashley d'Surrana,' I said, publicly acknowledging my real mother's name for the first time.

'And your purpose? I know it must have something to do with Adelmo and that girl in Ten. What is it?'

I turned my head to the wall and refused to answer. Moments later Gareff was back beside me, his head close to mine and his breath against my cheek, 'I'm only curious; it's of no importance to me and the Governor will find out soon enough if she cares to know. She may even choose to keep you for a while. Let me tell you what will await you then, you filthy aberration. You'll be kept here in one of the new holding pens whilst they decide what to do with you. If you're lucky, you will be exterminated and used for animal feed. If you're less fortunate, however, you'll be selected and taken to the island along with the other specimens; and I can assure you that, from what I've been told, the rest of your miserable life will not be pleasant.'

Before he could continue, the building was shaken by a series of rumblings – longer and louder than any we'd had before – and the trembling walls and ceiling sent a shower of dust and masonry on top of us. Gareff, brushing the debris from his robes and trying to maintain his composure although he was clearly unnerved, called to two of the Guards to fetch Oriana and then set up guard outside the chamber. As he prepared to leave he said, 'We'll be certain to find Adelmo and send him your greetings, Ashley d'Surrana. And you'll doubtless see Ten tomorrow if we bring her down for extermination. I'm sure you would be interested to see how the process works, and I would certainly enjoy showing you. Disappointingly it seems more likely that she will be taken to the island, but I daresay I will get as much satisfaction from observing her participation in the research. And one day soon, scabs such as you and your kind will have no place at all in our new society. Only absolute perfection will be tolerated.' And with that he waddled out, still brushing dust from his shoulders.

'What possible use could such a society have for you then, you stinking Pissbag!' I called after him, my anger finally getting the better of me, as it used to in the old days.

Oriana was scared but unharmed when they brought her to the chamber. She too was stripped of most of her clothes and left with just a shift to cover her. She was shackled, like me, and sank immediately to the floor, her legs weak with fear and the exhaustion of a long, sleepless night. We could just reach to touch hands and take comfort from looking into each other's eyes, full of the reassurance of our love. I confessed the fatal mistake which had exposed us and she raised her eyes heavenwards and said, 'Ah well, I expect your first mistake would have been enough to condemn us anyway.'

I squeezed her hand. I did not tell her what Gareff had told me about the holding pens and the possible future which awaited us, but asked instead about Akara's drawings, concerned that their proof of her connection with me would incriminate her even more. Oriana assured me they were safe: wrapped in a silk scarf and placed carefully on top of the tallest wardrobe in our room, well hidden.

I was congratulating her on her quick thinking when the earth shook again.

We did our best to keep each other's spirits up through that long, terrifying day and the night that followed. By the next afternoon the storm was still raging ferociously outside, we had eaten all the bread and drunk most of the water and no one had been back to replenish either. Torches that had been lit had been allowed to go out, and even through the thick metal doors we could hear the squeals and screams of frightened animals and the shouts and cries of men and women as they rushed about inside and out in panic.

'What do you think will have happened to the others?' Oriana asked me and I tried to reassure her, 'Colim and Adelmo will have got them all to safety, I'm sure. They will have had plenty of time after yesterday's warning tremors and Tikerty is gifted at reading the weather.'

'But they won't have wanted to leave us behind, will they? I'm afraid they will have stayed.'

I couldn't argue with her, I could only hope that Adelmo had found them shelter somewhere, although I had never known quakes as violent as this before. The cracks in the chamber continued to widen and spread, weakening the stone enough that we were able to pull away from the wall and scramble underneath the huge wooden bench that ran along the wall on the other side, just as most of the ceiling collapsed. The incinerator disintegrated and was smashed beneath the rubble, along with most of the other equipment and tools. The noise was ferocious. We clung to each other as the table shook above us, see-sawing up and down with every ripple of the earth and threatening to break, but it stayed solid and protected us until the earth had stopped moving and the world finally became still.

I suppose we were there for some hours, waiting until we were sure it would be safe to clamber out from under the table. I scrabbled about in the rubble by the incinerator and found a small cleaver which I used to hack away away at the padlocks on our cuffs and release us. Apart from cuts and bruises we were miraculously unharmed, but disoriented and shocked as we stumbled about in the ruins. The sky was returning to its familiar, shimmering yellow haze as the clouds of smoke and ash began to clear, but the sun was setting and we were going to need light.

In spite of our exhaustion, and the pain in Oriana's legs, we spent that entire night climbing over masonry and crushed bodies in our search for Akara. We found candles and flints and we soaked rags in oil from the olive presses to make torches, trying to get our bearings in the chaos around us. After the initial silence the night had begun to come to life. There were people still alive: two Guardians I recognised but whose names I didn't know, and quite a few Guards who were looting the dead and dying or rounding up the surviving animals and making off with them.

We heard someone groaning as we approached what we guessed was the remains of the infirmary. Trapped under the weight of two dead bodies we discovered Gareff, his legs and one arm crushed and mangled and having lost a lot of blood from a deep gash in his side.

'I can't leave him,' Oriana said, stooping to investigate the wound and shaking her head when she saw how severe it was, 'You go on and look for Akara; I will be quite alright, he's in no fit state to hurt me now, Ash – he's dying.'

So I continued, constantly tripping over rubble and losing my way, until I found myself by the palace itself, remarkably intact apart from a fracture in its front wall. Guardians and Guards had evacuated and scattered; the building was deserted, serene amongst the devastation of its surroundings. I thought of Akara's drawings; it suddenly seemed very important to save them and I almost ran up the stairs to our quarters where, just as she had said, Oriana had placed the pages on top of an armoire, wrapped in silk.

When I returned to Oriana she was sitting beside Gareff's body, dazed and too tired to move. She'd covered the guardian's face with a small cloth, but every other inch of him was crawling with flies. I carried her back to our bed in the palace and we both slept for a long time. At first light of the next day I left Oriana to rest and resumed my search of what was left of the kennels, listening for the slightest sound, looking for the tiniest clue and at last I found something. I could have overlooked it, or dismissed it as just another piece of debris, but it was glinting in the sunlight, just as it had been on the day we first found it. I wiped away most of the grit and earth and put the chain around my neck, convinced that finding our old bottle top again was a sign. I began to scrape and scrabble at the stones and bricks around me, heaving aside the sheets of plastic and the rusty metal bars until I reached the bare earth. There was no body, and no other sign of Akara herself but a few torn sheets of paper, fluttering in the breeze that was bringing the first hint of cool, fresh air from the north. I gathered the pages up, clutching them to my chest as if they were Akara herself.

Squinting into the sun I scanned as far as I could see, searching vainly for something amongst the wreckage all around me. If Akara had survived, she could be anywhere; but I had found her once and I could find her again. I turned and began to make my way back to the palace, marvelling again at how calm and undisturbed it was amidst the ruins of the other buildings. A tiny emerald lizard, perched on what was left of the kennels' old sun dial, cocked its head to look at me as I passed but didn't pause in its curious little dance, raising each leg in turn from the scorching stone to stop its feet from burning. It was so comical that I smiled, in spite of myself.

Oriana was waiting anxiously for me when I returned, scolding me for leaving her behind even as she embraced me. I showed her what I'd found and told her that, with no sign of a body, I was still hopeful that somewhere, somehow, Akara was alive.

34 QUO VADIS?

The last tatty pieces of my roof have blown away; if I look up, my one useful eye gets clouded by grit and dust and I have only dirty water to clean it with. So I keep my head down and continue writing while I can, constantly blowing away debris from my paper and struggling to see words through the smudges.

'Dearest, beloved cousin,' is all I have put so far. I don't know what else to say.

I no longer think the world may fall in on top of me; it is more likely that the earth will yawn and swallow me up. The wind has dropped now and there is an eerie silence in between each colossal rumble. It's as if the land is holding its breath, just as I am, waiting for the next growl and the shifting ground that comes with it. This is a quake like no other I have experienced – louder, more violent, more terrifying. I have called out for help but no one comes. I even called for Ash by name, hoping that he was somewhere nearby and would reach me somehow, or at least hear me and answer.

There is a lot of shouting and screaming outside, but suddenly one voice rising above it all: a deep, throaty voice that stops my breath.

'Steady the horses, you simpletons!'

It's her.

'Round up what animals you can and get them to safety. You there! Take me to block six; I want the deaf boy and the girl in Ten got out before the whole place collapses.'

So she has come, and all I can do is wait. I imagine her in the courtyard, stepping down from a fancy carriage as the horses whinny and snort in fear and their hooves clatter on the shifting stone. I imagine her striding into The Kennels, resplendent in spectacular clothes, with her hair elaborately dressed and her bracelets jangling as she approaches my stall. I imagine her reaching the door and her cruel and seductive voice commanding me to come out.

I dare not imagine beyond that. I reach under my pillow for the pendant, still encased in its lump of soap, but it slips from my hand just as another tremor shakes the building and the ground begins to split beneath me. I scramble to rescue it before it disappears but it's gone, I can't see it anywhere and now I can hear her voice again.

'Take him out. Be careful! I don't want either of them harmed in any way before we get to the island.'

She's coming for me next, I know it.

My heart is thumping, with fear and with fury. I struggle to keep calm, I don't want her to see how afraid I am; I want my contempt to be what she sees. I look towards the doorway and prepare myself.

And then I notice. It takes me several seconds to acknowledge what I've seen because it seems too unlikely, too miraculous, too full of promise and false hope.

What I notice, just as another quake shakes the entire world, is that there is no padlock and that Gareff Orman – that paragon of duty and efficiency - has forgotten something.

He has forgotten, in his cowardly haste to run away, to lock my door.

THE END.

ABOUT THE AUTHOR

Colleen MacMahon is an English actress, artist and award winning author of short stories. She has narrated audiobooks, designed book covers, written plays for theatre groups and taught and mentored children, young adults and so-called grown ups. My Name Is Ten is her debut novel and she is currently working on its sequel.

Printed in Great Britain
by Amazon